Perverting The Course Of Justice

by Tom J Sandy

Perverting The Course Of Justice
by Tom J Sandy

ISBN 0-9546897-5-5
Published 2005 by Eye 5

Published 2005 by Eye 5.
Text © Tom J Sandy. For reproduction permission, please contact Eye 5.
Design and type-setting by Eye 5.

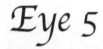

15 Spruce Avenue
Great Dunmow
Essex CM6 1YY
United Kingdom

www.eye5.org.uk

For all honest police officers and journalists
wherever they pound their beat

✝

News is anything that makes a reader say, 'Gee Whiz!'
American editor Arthur MacEwen

CHAPTER ONE

TERRY JAMES hated sitting at his desk at the best of times. The last decade had made him more desperate to escape the smokeless zone and chase stories out on the beat.

Unless he was writing up a story, the Evening Gazette's Crime Reporter could barely stand 20 minutes in the office before he needed to dash to the sanctuary of the smoking zone in the basement.

There, he could cough and splutter with fellow addicts for ten minutes without getting too much flak from his news editor.

It was a grey, windowless room; 15 square yards at most, with chairs dotted by the walls. There were three ashtrays for the smokers among the office block's 875 workers. At its peak, there could be 25 smokers flicking their ash into those ashtrays. Eleven in the morning was the busiest time; standing room only, especially in winter when few could be bothered to haul on their coats and step outdoors to enjoy some fresh air with their nicotine fix.

By the time the day-workers left for home the ashtrays would be overflowing. The smokers didn't seem to care. The cleaner wondered if they acted that way at their homes.

It was 10.30 on a sunny, June Friday. The weekend was about six hours away. James planned to escape the London smoke for two nights in Brighton with his partner of four years. His more immediate concern was whether to go for a ciggie now or hang on for his fellow addict who was putting the finishing touches to a dreary article on yet another London housing crisis. Craig Butler's piece was not scheduled to be published until Monday, but he wanted it out of the way before lunch. James had been in the office early and had filed two stories for that evening's edition. He was clear of crime duties until Monday morning and, not wanting to be considered among the Press prima donnas, was available to help the news editor fill any untidy holes.

He took a packet of Bensons from his shirt pocket, placed one cigarette between his lips and wafted another teasingly under Butler's nose. "If you go any bloody slower this is gonna go off."

"Cut the cracks and I'll be finished quicker. Gimme two minutes."

James turned away from Butler's computer and started typing away at his own. The reporters worked side by side in the cramped office with less than three feet between them. Accountants had persuaded the management to make better use of the office space they rented in Docklands. So, one floor was sub-let, and the Gazette staff arrived one Monday morning to the shock of their new working arrangement.

"This sandwich may be dolphin-friendly but this bastard management isn't journalist-friendly," read a message one of James's colleagues had pasted on the bulletin board – complete with said wrapper from tuna sandwich. Yet another reason for the crime ace's disdain for too much desk time. He finished typing and turned his computer screen to face Butler. The massive headline made Butler crack up:

Cig goes stale waiting for
aged hack to write story

"Bugger off and smoke yerself to death. I'll be right down in a couple of ticks. Almost there."

James was about to heed his pal's advice when his phone rang. He was still listening intently when Butler finished typing. Butler reciprocated the jibe and waved a cigarette in James's face. His colleague failed to acknowledge their customary joke.

He noticed James was stooped over the phone, was doing little talking and was tapping his pen against his notepad rather than taking any notes. Butler had to enjoy his smoke alone. It wasn't the same without his sidekick along to gossip and flame colleagues. James was not at his desk when Butler spluttered back onto the Gazette floor.

"He's been in with the Ed. For five minutes now," said Chrissie Harrison. "Must be a very philosophical discussion."

Butler shouted across to Phil Calvin, the Gazette's news editor who sat at a table directly behind him: "What's going on, Phil? Not like our Terry to skip a smoke break."

"Not a bloody clue, matey. Am I his keeper? Just saw him get up and make a dash for the Ed.'s room. Do we smell a scoop?"

"I can smell his bloody smoke," snapped Harrison, jabbing a finger in the direction of Butler and giving him her evil eye. "I am so glad I don't have to do your washing; hate to live with an ashtray."

"The feeling's mutual you happy old cow."

No-one had overheard James's phone conversation. Afterwards, he had gone immediately to Editor Andrew Harvey's office and entered without even bothering to knock.

"Just had a call from a contact, boss. A big one – Henry Headleigh's involved in some kiddie ring. Thought I should come and see you first."

"Involved? Involved? Of course, he's bloody involved; he's in charge of it. What are you trying to tell me, young man?"

Harvey was a craggy Scot who had joined so many of his race in acquiring a seat of considerable power at the high table of British journalism. The 47-year-old had quit his job as news editor at a national broadsheet paper to assume editorship of the Gazette three years ago.

His hard-nose for news rather than the waffly, ubiquitous women's features had sparked a steady rise in the Gazette's circulation and earned Harvey a very lucrative annual bonus.

The accountants regretted the proprietor's decision to heavily weigh Harvey's salary on bonuses. Thankfully, former porn king Bryan Richardson did occasionally ignore the moneymen. He was happy to hand over a 78-85k annual bonus to Harvey, especially as advertising revenue grew in line with circulation.

The Gazette regularly scooped the nationals on the big London stories, even those papers with more money to chuck around than commonsense. Naturally, Harvey was canny enough to know his many affluent readers wanted to know what to wear at their smart Chelsea eateries (why didn't his reporters call them restaurants these days?), and what was hot and what was not (in the pop charts, at the cinema, in holiday destinations, in clothes, in table chat).

Those issues bored Harvey rigid but he was decent enough to let his middle-ranking executives have their way. Most of the time. But give him a good old-fashioned hard news story and Harvey was like a dog gnawing on a bone; he would refuse to let go until he was satisfied he had ripped away all the flesh. In truth, Harvey would gnaw away at a story more than any sensible dog would at a bone.

"Pray enlighten me. Is this some new involvement I am not aware of? Are you going to tell me our police hero is one of the sickos?"

Harvey turned away from his computer screen and gave James his undivided attention.

"That's exactly it, boss. Just had a call from a source. He told me Headleigh has been seeing some paedos across the water in Kent, and it wasn't undercover work either. He gave me three dates when Headleigh attended private functions at the house of one of this group."

"Hang on a minute, Terry. You're telling me Detective Superintendent Henry Headleigh is indulging in the sick fantasies of this group? You're telling me Henry Headleigh is a bloody paedophile?"

"Hard to believe, I know. But, yes, it seems Headleigh has a liking for young East European girls. The Kent group has first bite at them it appears, before they are shipped off to the big cities. Of course, they're all illegals. They arrive through Dover, Folkestone and the Channel Tunnel. One of the group also has some private landing spot by Whitstable, I am told."

"Bloody hell! And you're certain this is kosher?"

"Absolutely, boss. Comes from a solid contact. I've used him before and he's never let me down. He gave me the gangland murder stuff last year. He kept me one step ahead of the herd, remember? And he tipped

PERVERTING THE COURSE OF JUSTICE

me off about the drugs killings – Harry Nickels and his mob in Basildon."

Harvey certainly did remember several of the many Terry James exclusives. He shouted through to his secretary in the annexe: "Give Arthur Jacobs a buzz, Irene. Tell him to make himself available down here in ten minutes."

He turned back to face James. "OK, Terry. Run the facts by me. Slowly."

"Well my source tells me Kent police have been keeping an eye on Headleigh for some time. They have kept it within their own paedo unit but I am told it's going to break this weekend. A raid is planned on the ring-leader's home in Chatham.

"They have seen Headleigh visit this guy's house on three occasions. He's also been spotted at parties held at two other houses in the Maidstone area. Seems he is at least discreet enough to operate outside his own patch.

"They've also found a credit card used to access sick websites. It belongs to Headleigh and they believe he uses his personal computer to access them, and not one of Essex Police's. That figures as the cops are under instructions to use only special police cards for investigating this kind of thing; to protect themselves mainly. He's known to have been in email contact with two of the group."

"Christ! This is hard to believe – Mr Squeaky Clean, Scourge of the Essex Mafia. Kids of his own, hasn't he?"

"Yes, three grown-up now."

"Happily married?"

"Never been married, Arthur, so I'm hardly qualified to comment on what 'happily married' actually means. Wife is a pillar of society from what I do know. Maybe he is just bored with her and seeks his entertainment away from home. It must get to you, doing the kind of work our Henry does."

"Yes, I can only imagine. Sick bastards. I've known many a bent copper in my day, helped nail a couple in Scotland once. But I've never come across one into kiddie porn. Sick, sick bastards."

Harvey had long since been happily married. Divorced almost eight years, he kept in regular touch with his two children even though both had surprisingly returned to Scotland to study and work. The editor of the Evening Gazette had never remarried, preferring to spend his few free hours away from newspaper duties to augment his jazz collection.

"Right, so if we want to beat the so-called big boys we have to run with this story now. That what you're telling me?"

"Yes, boss. My contact expects it to break over the weekend and the shit to fly all over Henry Headleigh. He did say there may be a few other big names involved but had no details."

"Before we get carried away with this. I know tempus bloody fugit and all that but is there any way you can make a couple of check calls now? I respect your source but I would be happier with further corroboration. You can use that desk there. Arthur will be here any minute. Suppose I'd better warn our beloved leader. Get cracking and let's see."

James settled himself at a desk in the corner of Harvey's spacious office. The accountants hadn't managed to cramp the editor's style and space. He flicked through his tattered notebook and picked up a phone. Harvey's secretary patched the editor through to the chairman. Harvey rarely discussed the content of his paper with the owner, but he was smart enough to know when Bryan Richardson needed informing.

Richardson, for his part, knew well to keep his distance. He would drop the occasional hint if he wanted a story publishing to help his other business ventures along the way; or if a friendly face needed a helping hand.

Richardson was more than happy to grease a few palms. And Harvey felt it came with the territory, just as long as Richardson didn't overstep the mark, all would be hunky dory.

"Bryan, Andrew here. Just though you should know we're working on a big exclusive – a bent cop. May make the later editions. I'm going to run it by Arthur Jacobs, of course."

"Fine, fine, Andrew. Do I know this bent bugger?"

"Don't think so. Henry Headleigh, Essex copper in charge of their child porn unit. Seems he's been dabbling with kids himself."

"Ugh. Never heard of him. Nail the fuckin' sicko, Andrew. Why can't we hang this scum? Even a bloody liberal like you won't argue the toss with me on that one, will you? No, fuckin' hanging's too good for them.

"Right, lunch beckons. Thanks for the call, Andrew. I trust your judgment implicitly as ever. Hang 'em high, hang 'em high. Hang 'em by the balls. But only after a damned good flogging, eh? I won't be back this afternoon. Good luck and have a nice weekend."

The chirpy Cockney was out for lunch within ten minutes. Seconds after Harvey had put down the phone, Arthur Jacobs appeared. He was immaculately dressed as usual, and sporting a pin-striped suit. All the lawyer's suits were pin-striped; brown was today's chosen colour. The lawyer had a folder under his arm. The contents of Jacobs's folder remained a mystery to all who dealt with him, but it never left his side.

"So then, Andrew. I do hope this won't take long. You know how I protect my Friday lunchtime above all others."

Yes, Harvey could see that the portly lawyer enjoyed his lunches. Jacobs would not be seen dead, either, at the office canteen.

"We shall try not to delay you too long. Doing the work you're paid to do can be a dreadful interference I know."

Jacobs managed to smile at the editor's feeble attempt at an upper-class accent.

"I am all legal eyes and ears. At your disposal for the benefit of our great London readership."

Harvey pointed in the direction of James. "Of course, you know our Terry here."

Indeed, he did. James kept Jacobs's legal department busier than any other Gazette journalist.

"Aha! So it is the great Terry James keeping me from Alfredo's delicious canard provencal. Found Lord Lucan hiding in the top flat at Number Ten, have we, Terry?"

"That was last week's story. Don't you ever read our own paper?"

"Cut the crap, you two. Any joy, Terry?"

"Sorry boss, the only copper I could trust with this in Kent is unavailable."

"Maybe someone could start by telling me what this is all about," said Jacobs.

Harvey let his crime reporter provide the lawyer with the facts.

"That's all we know," Harvey said to the room rather than either of the two men, in particular. "Get writing it Terry. I'll just alert the backbench then Arthur can give us all the benefit of his wisdom and expensive education. Stay in here for now. You can use that computer."

"Already on the job, Andrew."

James continued writing as the editor and the lawyer discussed the legalities of the story. Jacobs leaned back in the executive leather armchair as if in deep reflection. "Well, you don't need me to tell you it all hinges on whether or not the story is true. Damned good story if it is."

That was a rare utterance from the legal eagle. He seldom commented on the vast array of stories he was called upon to flick his blue Parker pen over.

"Yes, exactly," said Harvey. "Probably a worse crime than rape or murder in the eyes of our readers. And certainly in the eyes of our leader. I just want your advice on how far we should go with it. You almost there, Terry?"

"Sure boss. Want a look?"

"No, just print out two copies."

"Coming now. Excuse the literals. I haven't run a spell-check on it yet."

While the story was printing, Jacobs turned to James and said: "I assume it is futile of me to ask the source of this story?"

"Yes. Andrew knows the score. All I can say is this contact has always proved reliable. Remember the drug shootings in Essex last year?"

"How could I ever forget? I didn't sleep for weeks," replied Jacobs with a faint smile.

"Well this contact gave me the details on the gang leader who took the hostages."

James watched as the two men stared intently at the print-outs: 350 words from London's finest crime reporter. The editor had finished reading the story in a matter of seconds. The lawyer was much slower and making notes in the margin. He seemed to be making a lot of notes. Harvey would think an experienced lawyer like Jacobs would be aware of deadlines by now. Still, he knew better than to interrupt the vital cogs in his brain. He had to give Jacobs credit for sparing his paper from several potential defamation actions.

"Fascinating," said Jacobs to announce he had finished his perusal. "Absolutely fascinating. Caught with his hands in his own dirty till, so to speak."

Jacobs turned his chair around and laid his paper on the table so that all three men could examine his scribblings.

"As I have said, it basically hinges on truth, or, more accurately, what we can prove is true. All I can suggest are amendments in mitigation. I know you will accuse me of watering down the impact. But let's see.

"Here," Jacobs pointed at a paragraph he had underlined. "Do we know that our chap actually had sex with these underage girls? Is there any evidence? Photographs? Videos? You know what these horrible perverts are like. Or did your source just tell you he was at the parties?"

Harvey looked at his reporter. "Good point. Well, Terry?"

James thought for a few seconds before replying: "He never said, boss. Sorry. As far as I know, they are just aware that Headleigh was at the parties. I guess they are hoping to uncover evidence – photos and stuff – during the raids."

"Raids? What raids?" asked Jacobs.

"This weekend. The Kent police are planning to grab these bastards," said the editor. "Don't worry, Arthur, I have been wondering about whether we would be jeopardising any police action."

"I deliberately avoided mentioning the raids for the same reason, boss."

"Yes, gentlemen. We most definitely don't want to do anything silly like that. So let's scrub that paragraph shall we?"

Jacobs marked the offending words for deletion. "Best to simply say

Headleigh has been spotted attending these gatherings – do you have to call them parties? What actual evidence are you aware of, Terry?"

"Well I know for certain that the Kent boys have Headleigh's credit card records which prove he has been accessing child porn sites in his leisure hours. That is a crime in itself. But again, I don't want to mention that in the story for obvious reasons. He would probably have the expert knowledge to wipe his computer clean. Plus it could give the source away."

"What about the towns you mentioned? Are we happy naming those? Wouldn't that alert the people about to be raided?"

"Fair point. I could just make it 'the Kent area'?"

The men discussed a few more legal markings and then Harvey told James to write a finished article.

"Keep it tight, lad. I don't want to turn it from page one. That would hold up production."

It was approaching mid-day and the first edition had already gone to press. He had warned the backbench to prepare for a new front page. Not that any of them were allowed out for lunch during publication time, anyway.

"Overall Arthur, what do you think?"

"Well the risk is entirely yours, old boy. But if you have faith in Terry – and that I know you do – I can't see anything to worry about. I would be happier with official confirmation, naturally.

"Just be careful, very careful, about printing anything which the police could throw back at the paper. We don't want them claiming our story prevented them arresting a gang or busting open an international operation.

"And, of course, make sure our enthusiastic friend sticks to reporting the evidence he knows is definitely available."

"Thanks, Arthur. Sorry to delay your lunch but just hang around to check the finished piece."

"No problems, Andrew. Nothing quite like a juicy story as an appetiser." He winked at the editor, but still stole a quick glance at the wall clock. James had made the legal alterations and kept his story brief. He wasn't happy at the loss of impact – he had wanted as many facts in there as possible. His editor and the lawyer were satisfied, though.

Harvey walked briskly through his door and bellowed at the back-bench. "OK folks. New front page. Conor, tell distribution that second edition must not go until this is ready OK?"

Harvey went into a huddle with his chief sub-editor and the chief design artist. The three experienced hacks had the page ready within 20 minutes. Arthur Jacobs nodded his approval and informed all he could be contacted at Alfredo's if his expertise was further required that splendid day.

Two hours later, Harvey sat in his office staring at the second edition's front page. He was satisfied. A dirty copper's a damned better read than that parking crap. Even for those who didn't enjoy the luxury of their own parking space in the cramped capital.

Yes, bloody fine crime reporter is Terry James.

"Good job, Terry. Let the shit hit the fan and let the big boys chase our tails once again."

"Thanks, Andrew. Just going downstairs for a smoke now. Be back in ten minutes if anyone asks."

"Best to put in a call to the police later. Not that I expect any reaction for now. Just to clear ourselves, give them a buzz and ask for a comment when the paper's been on the streets for a couple of hours."

"Sure, boss."

James collared Craig Butler and they escaped to the smoking lounge. James had a copy of the second edition with him and proudly paraded it before his friend.

TOP COP LINKED IN CHILD PORN PROBE

THE OFFICER in charge of Essex police force's anti-paedophile unit is being investigated over his links with child pornography peddlers.

The Gazette can today reveal that Detective Superintendent Henry Headleigh has been spotted meeting members of a ring of paedophiles in the Kent area.

He has attended functions, during which some gang members engaged in underage sex with illegal immigrants.

Gangs

The children – mainly from Eastern European countries and the Balkan states – are smuggled into Britain and expected to put themselves at the mercy of the paedophiles to pay for their passage.

They are then sold to other gangs around Britain. Many are believed to end up in London where paedophiles pay up to £500 for a night with the girls and boys. Some of the children are as young as ten.

Most of them have been sent to Britain with their parents' blessing to seek a brighter future.

The involvement of Det Supt Headleigh with these criminal gangs will come as a shock to Essex Police.

He was appointed to head their new child porn unit ten months ago following the discovery of a large network of paedophiles operating out of Southend.

The 51-year-old was previously in charge of the drug squad at Chelmsford. He helped crack a £10m heroin racket two years ago when his team raided a warehouse on Canvey Island.

He is married and has three grown-up children.

EXCLUSIVE by Crime Reporter TERRY JAMES

CHAPTER TWO

HENRY HEADLEIGH was born into a police family. The Headleighs of Clacton had provided many a fine servant for Essex Constabulary. The county boasted one of Britain's earliest police forces, dating back to Lord John Russell's 1839 County Police Act, which recognised the need for more organised policing in the wake of the Chartist disturbances.

Coppers in Victorian days worked hard and long hours, earning between 18s and £1 for a seven-day week. By the time Henry Headleigh followed in the footsteps of four generations of officers, a constable's salary had increased 400-fold. Not that he was destined to spend a great deal of time among the lowly ranks.

A degree in sociology from the University of East Anglia had helped mould Headleigh into a man born to lead. He was convinced of that, and soon convinced his superiors.

Within five years of joining the police, Headleigh had left behind him the quiet seaside backwater of Clacton and had risen to the rank of inspector at the force's Chelmsford headquarters.

Unlike his Victorian predecessors, Headleigh had masses of resources at his disposal; not just in terms of manpower, but also a formidable array of high technology equipment which seemed to become more advanced by the month.

The student in Headleigh ensured he kept abreast of all the latest gadgetry. The wife he acquired after just six months in Chelmsford proved a godsend to a ladder-climber like him. Jane Dunston was a superintendent's daughter and a qualified chemist. When domesticity and motherhood took a firm grip on Jane and she dropped out of academe, Headleigh turned to their children for his educational needs. Like many police officers, he spent less time than a normal father would have liked with their twin daughters and elder son. His career came first. He soon turned to detection at HQ and scored some notable successes under the wing of the redoubtable Chief Inspector Isaac Walters.

His first murder case was a messy affair, but Headleigh was impressed watching Walters finally break a husband who confessed to killing his wife over a minor housekeeping disagreement.

Headleigh earned plaudits in high places from Walters on a later murder investigation, tracing the killer of a prostitute thanks to some dogged forensic chasing. A chief inspectorship followed, as did further successes. Headleigh put behind bars a wicked assortment of thieves, armed robbers, rapists, drug-peddlers and murderers.

By the age of 44 he was a superintendent. For a week after his promotion, he would stare admiringly in the full-length bedroom mirror at his 6ft 3in frame. He weighed in at dead-on 14st. He drank sparingly, smoking being his one professed vice – though never more than a dozen a day, even when handling mentally-sapping cases. His dark brown hair showed not a trace of grey. Not bad for a man his age. He made a promise to stay in shape until the day dawned when he would sport Chief Constable stripes.

Despite more glory heaped on his shoulders, further promotion had eluded Headleigh. He had played a key role in bringing to a successful conclusion a hijack at Stansted Airport; he had continued to bring to justice some of the county's worst villains; he headed a team that made a handful of significant drug busts; he spearheaded the war on Internet crime. It was the latter which prompted his appointment as head of the Child Protection Unit's special section devoted to catching paedophiles.

It wasn't the most glamourous of roles for a promotion-seeker, but it had gained widespread coverage owing to a number of sordid high-profile cases, particularly in the south of England.

Chief Constable James McNish wanted a high-ranking officer to take charge in the wake of bad publicity for the county's public servants. Two foster homes had been shut down in a child abuse scandal. Police investigations into the deaths of three children in care had uncovered a network of paedophiles running Internet sites and Europewide child exchanges. Some were based in Essex, yet none of the culprits was ever caught.

The final straw for McNish had been a web site set up by some sixth formers at an expensive Essex public school. For an 'exercise' they created a site featuring photographs of first form pupils in the showers. Four pupils from respectable families were expelled. The Chief Constable's son was due to enter the sixth form the following year.

Headleigh assumed his new command with a zeal which surprised colleagues past and present. He started by launching a media offensive, graduating from local radio and TV news programmes to the national arena when he spoke on platforms up and down the land.

He increased contacts with the Internet Watch Foundation and managed to close down a number of sites worldwide, a significant achievement, he claimed, considering the difficulty in police operating outside their boundaries.

Success on the home front thwarted him, however. Several parents were jailed for abusing their children, greater restrictions on homes proved beneficial, yet the paedophile gangs eluded Headleigh's team. At least the police had forced them deeper underground.

Headleigh was in a briefing room with five other senior officers at HQ when an ashen-faced sergeant burst in brandishing a copy of the Evening Gazette. "Sorry to interrupt, but I thought you should see this," he said, placing down the paper and stepping sheepishly a few feet away from the table. He obediently placed his hands behind his back and stood as if to attention.

Chief Superintendent Mary Edwardes turned the paper around so she could read it. The contents made her stand back in shock. It took her a few seconds to recover.

"Henry! What the bloody hell is all this about?"

She flicked the paper around so that her colleagues could see the front page and the banner headline. An unearthly silence, then an almighty roar from Headleigh as his impressive frame rose from the table.

"Is this supposed to be some kind of joke!" he thundered, slamming the palm of his hand on the table. No-one spoke. "Well?" he added, even louder.

The hapless sergeant was first to break the silence. "I don't think so, sir. There are billboards around town. One of the specials brought that copy in."

The sergeant made a hasty exit, trying to close the door as gently as possible behind him. He left behind him a visibly rattled Det Supt Headleigh. His face was turning purple, his mouth fixed in a crazed snarl, his hands were shaking. He banged the table once more.

"I don't bloody believe it. Who the fuck is responsible for this...this...utter, total garbage? They can't print shit like this!"

His colleagues were looking down. The only one sufficiently composed to open her mouth was Chief Supt Edwardes. "Please try and calm down, Henry. Have you any idea what this is about? ARE you being investigated?"

"Of course, I'm not being fucking investigated!" There was a fury in his eyes as he bellowed at Edwardes.

"Sit down and calm down! I know this has come as a shock to you but I will not tolerate you speaking to me like that. Not now, not ever. Just remember where you are and who you are talking to."

Headleigh looked away from his superior and muttered an apology as he slowly sank into his chair. "Yes, ma'am. Sorry, ma'am. Please forgive me, I just don't have a clue what this is about."

The meeting's agenda was rapidly forgotten as four men sat stone-faced around the oval table in the plush senior officer's meeting room. The yellow walls were adorned with paraphernalia celebrating the good and the great of Essex Constabulary. The four men seemed frightened to look at Headleigh or Chief Superintendent Edwardes; senior policemen in fear of being questioned or asked to voice an opinion.

Chief Supt Edwardes remained standing and looked down on Headleigh with a mixture of maternal concern and official gravity.

"I think we had better have a few words in private, Henry. Would the rest of you please excuse us. Inspector Grant, maybe you could make a few enquiries. And perhaps one of you could arrange for some coffee to be sent in. Oh, and rustle up a few more copies of this." She waved the paper above the table as her colleagues got up and trooped out.

Grant was alone in conveying his sympathy to Headleigh. He placed his hand on the fallen giant's shoulder and muttered: "Really sorry, Henry. Maybe have a chat later?"

When the men had left, Edwardes spoke once more to the bowed figure. "Let's wait for the coffee, Henry. I'll open a window; you may smoke if you wish."

Chief Supt Edwardes was a teetotal, non-smoking career officer; a devout Christian with three children a few years younger than Headleigh's own. He was grateful for her offer, muttered a thank you and slowly took out a packet of Dunhills from his briefcase. His actions seemed to have slowed to a crawl and he had difficulty lighting the cigarette.

The unfortunate sergeant again had the task of delivery boy. He settled the coffee tray on the table and left without uttering a word. Edwardes poured two cups and sat herself closer to Headleigh, but opposite him rather than by his side.

"Well, Henry, this is a bolt from the blue. Is there anything you can tell me?"

"Sorry for my outburst earlier, ma'am, but this is so shocking. I have no idea what this guy is going on about. None at all."

"This reporter, you mean? This..." she turned to the paper, "this Terry James?"

"Never met him, ma'am. I know the name, of course. He's covered a few of our cases in the past, but nothing in my new role. Not to my knowledge, anyway. Why he should print such nonsense is beyond me." Headleigh looked at Edwardes with reddened eyes before returning his gaze downwards.

"What about Kent, Henry? He talks about Kent and some meetings there. Have you been over the water recently?"

"You have to believe me, ma'am. I haven't a bloody clue what this is all about."

Edwardes nodded and asked again, more softly this time: "Kent, Henry? Have you been to Kent at all in the past few months? Liaison? Fact-finding? Any reason at all?"

Headleigh scratched his head. He was experiencing difficulty looking his chief in the eye. "I spoke at a seminar hosted by Alan Grady. That would have been in February. That's all."

A solemn pause was broken by a knock at the door. This time it was Inspector Colin Grant. "Sorry to interrupt, ma'am. There's an important call for you."

"Who is it? Can't it wait?"

"It's the chief, ma'am. He's waiting on the line. Shall I put it through to your office?"

Chief Supt Edwardes looked from Grant to Headleigh and quickly back to Headleigh again. "Yes please. I'll be right there. Please wait here for me, Henry."

She was grateful at the decision to bar telephones from the meeting room as she strode purposefully to her office. She managed to glimpse several detectives as she passed through an open plan room. There was one group in a huddle by a soft-drink machine; others had their heads down at their desks.

Chief Constable James McNish had been made aware of the Gazette story. He hadn't seen the paper but had received the shocking news from his opposite number in Kent, George Travis.

Kent Police's media office had informed Travis. They had received a call from a reporter on the Evening Gazette. The reporter had wanted an official reaction to the story about an investigation into an Essex officer. Wisely, Terry James had not called Essex.

The media officer had promised to look into the matter and get back to the reporter. When she discovered the details of the story, the chief constable was alerted. The paper would get no reaction that day. Travis and McNish were baffled by the story, the Essex man slightly more so

– Henry Headleigh was one of his finest officers with a blemish-free record of almost 30 years. They agreed to make no official comment until they had made their own enquiries. If they had a dirty copper they would nail him – even if it was Det Supt Headleigh with his string of prize catches behind him.

Edwardes and McNish spoke for five minutes before the female officer returned to the meeting room to see the crestfallen Headleigh.

"The chief wants you to phone him in five minutes, Henry. He's on his way home from Basildon so you can catch him on his mobile. I'm sorry to have to tell you that he intends to suspend you."

"Suspend me? Suspend me? But I've done nothing wrong!"

"He's no option, I'm afraid. I'm sure you will see that when you come round. Best go and give him a call."

Headleigh crept from the room like a thief. He managed not to catch the eyes of his colleagues as he made his way to his office, but he could sense an ugly feeling in the building. He had seen and heard enough in the line of duty to imagine the nature of the conversations taking place among policemen and women across the county.

Headleigh rang his chief constable and spoke softly into the phone; gone was the proud and powerful tone of a senior police officer. The old school demeanour was absent, too.

"Henry, perhaps you can enlighten me as to what the hell is going on?"

"Sir, as I have told Chief Superintendent Edwardes, I haven't the foggiest what this is all about."

"Nor do Travis and his Kent boys. Bloody strange business, Henry. I am sure you appreciate the seriousness of the matter. I have little choice but to ask you to take some leave for a while. Just while we get things sorted out."

"You're suspending me, sir?" Dejection rather than surprise in Headleigh's voice.

"Call it suspension if you like. What choice do I have?"

"But I've done nothing wrong, sir?"

"Come on now, Henry, don't treat me like an idiot. One of my senior officers is accused of being involved with paedophiles. You expect me to sit idly by and pray it will wash away? You're on leave for now. If I feel the need to make it an official suspension then, trust me, I will."

"I understand, sir."

"Listen, Henry. If, as you say, you have done nothing wrong, then there is nothing to worry about. We'll back you all the way. Let me and Travis deal with it for now. OK?"

"Yes, sir."

"Good. Now a few practicalities: is there somewhere you can take Jane and the children for a few days? The further away the better, and best not to relatives. The Press have ways and means of tracking people down. Is Jane aware of the news, by the way?"

"Not to my knowledge, sir. I'd best get home and see her. I'd rather be the one to break it to her."

"Well, good luck. The media office has been going crazy with calls for the past hour or so. Let me know where you end up going. I'll be at home all weekend if you need me. And have a good think about how this story came to be published. I'll let you know anything we dig up here or in Kent. Remember, you're off duty until I say otherwise. Goodbye."

Headleigh was hastily shoving a few pieces of paper into drawers in his desk when Inspector Grant entered his office.

"Just thought you should know, sir, I've blocked all direct calls to your line. I thought that was for the best. Jane's been onto the front desk a couple of times, though. Is there anything I can do to help?"

"No thanks, Colin. I'm going away for a few days while things calm down. Look after the shop for me." Headleigh managed a faint smile.

"Sure thing, sir. If there is anything, though, even if you just want a chat, I'm here as a friend as well as a fellow officer."

"Much appreciated, Colin. Truly. We need more like you. I'll try and keep you informed. Thanks for everything."

Headleigh arrived at his detached four-bedroomed home in Brentwood to find a tearful Jane and neighbour sitting in the kitchen drinking tea. His wife was clearly deeply distressed. She looked up and just stared at her husband. "Would you mind leaving me and Jane alone, Cathy?" said Headleigh, taking off his coat and placing his briefcase on a sideboard. "We need to talk."

"Sure, Henry. You know where I am if you want anything."

Cathy Hodges collected her things, patted her friend Jane's hand and left the couple to sort out the terrible, unbelievable mess.

"Henry! Henry!" blurted Jane. "What's happening? What's going on? You won't believe what people are saying. I've had to take the phone off the hook."

Headleigh sat by his wife and put his left arm round her shoulder. He could feel her whole body shuddering. She started sobbing uncontrollably, almost hysterically. He had seen witnesses to violent crimes react this way.

"Listen, Jane. It's all lies. Absolute lies; preposterous in the extreme. I am still shocked myself, so I know how you must be feeling. Do the children know?"

"Oh! I don't think so. Oh God! What will they think?" Jane Headleigh buried her face in her handkerchief once more; her sobs became more like convulsions.

"I'd better call them and prepare them for the worst. I'll do it, I think it is best coming from me. The chief has suggested it would be wise for us to go away for a few days to escape the Press frenzy. Makes sense; I don't want you to have to face that mob. Why don't you go and pack some things for us while I phone the children? Think where we should go. I was wondering about that hotel in Cambridge? At least we'd be near Sarah."

Sarah was the youngest member of the Headleigh household, having entered the world 37 minutes after her twin sister Theresa.

In appearance, the twins had little in common apart from their eager green eyes. Sarah had noticed in her early teens that she was approximately one inch shorter than her big sister. It had remained that way for nine years now.

Maybe it was desire to remain different that made Sarah keep her hair short, while Theresa kept hers long. Sarah preferred skirts, Theresa denims and tee-shirts, usually sporting the name of her latest musical favourites.

They inherited their modest good looks from their mother; they inherited a passion for learning from both parents. Star pupils at the renowned Chelmsford County High School for Girls, they passed their A Levels with top grades before going their separate ways into higher education.

Sarah plumped for Social & Political Sciences at Trinity College, Cambridge. She was delighted when her acceptance letter dropped through the letterbox. She would be following in the footsteps of major historical figures: Isaac Newton, Lord Byron, Earl Grey and a host of contemporary politicians.

Trinity also had its share of black sheep, most notably in recent times the traitors Kim Philby, Guy Burgess and Anthony Blunt. They added a certain mystique to the place in Sarah's eyes.

Sarah was approaching the end of her second year of studies and heading for an upper second-class honours degree. Her parents loved to visit her and tried to make the 40-mile trip at least once a term.

Henry and Jane Headleigh, both educated at red-brick universities, could walk around the splendid city for hours and hours. They loved to just stand and breathe in the atmosphere of the hallowed halls, or to stroll along the green banks of the River Cam. Henry had taken Jane and Sarah out on a punt the previous summer which left the daughter in stitches. "You're a wonderful copper, dad, but thank heavens the Royal Navy was spared your services."

Headleigh decided to break the distasteful news to Sarah first. He caught Sarah on her mobile a few minutes after she had arrived back at the 'double set' she shared with a fellow SocPol student.

Poor Sarah could hardly believe her ears as her father relayed the news. Of course she would ask her friend to book them into the King George III Hotel.

"Mr and Mrs Wallace, OK? You can square up the money when you get here. Suzie won't mind. See you soon."

"Thanks my darling girl. You're a treasure. Please don't contact

Theresa or Jon until I've had a chance to call them. Soon, precious."

He rang Theresa next. She was more than 350 miles north, studying French and Art History at Edinburgh University. Less practical than Sarah, she took the news harder than her sister; maybe it was the distance that made the situation seem worse. Headleigh again protested his innocence, he calmed down his daughter and stressed she try to concentrate on her studies. No, she must not head south. He and mum would visit her when they could.

Jonathan was three years older than his sisters. He had left Chelmsford's King Edward VI Grammar School with three decent A Levels and set about making his fortune in property. He possessed the business brains of the family.

He was just about to ring his parents from his Reading home when he took the call from his father. Jon had been showing prospective clients around some fine Berkshire country residences all day and returned to his more modest abode to read the disturbing story in the Evening Gazette.

"Sue the bastards, dad! Sue them for every bloody penny they have!" Jon positively screamed down the phone.

"Yes, Jon. It may come to that I have realised. For now it is important that my colleagues at work set about sorting this mess up. Believe me, it won't take them long. I do need them to clear this stain from my name firstly, and then we can take things from there."

Headleigh informed his raging son of his immediate plans.

"We'll try and see you as soon we can. For now, and I know it's difficult for you, but do try and keep a low profile." Headleigh tried to make light of the situation.

"Not a word out of place to any of your drinking chums, and avoid the Press like the plague. Any problems, ring me or Colin Grant at the office. You know Colin, one of my inspectors, he'll ensure the local bobbies will take any heat off your back."

Headleigh replaced the phone on the charger and, the worst of his family duties over, walked upstairs to join his wife. Jane was sat on the side of the bed. Her sobs had ceased but her face looked frightful.

What little make-up she wore had formed macabre streaks on her cheeks. An open suitcase lay on the bed with a few items of clothing scattered around it. That was as far as she had got with the packing.

"Here, darling, why don't you let me finish this. You go and tidy yourself up. Sarah's sorted the hotel and she'll meet us for supper after we've checked in. The sooner we get going, the better."

His compassion towards his wife was broken by the harsh shrill of the phone. "Don't answer it!" she cried. "It'll be them again. Damned Press! Bloody vultures! Take it off the hook, Henry! Please!"

Headleigh gently switched off the answer machine and let the call ring off. Then he did as his wife bade him and unhooked the phone.

Within 30 minutes they were packed and ready to depart. Henry had changed and would shower at the hotel. Jane had wiped away her tears and the mess of make-up. She looked better, though the rings around her eyes aged her by ten years. She stuffed a few personal items into a handbag and followed Henry down the stairs.

Henry had just turned round from locking the front door when a bright flash startled both he and his wife. He was blinded for a moment and came round to hear his wife shrieking once more: "Leave us alone! Leave us alone, you damned vulture."

He glimpsed the back of a photographer jogging back to a car parked 50 yards down the road. Headleigh swiftly ushered Jane into his Ford Mondeo ST220 and pointed the sleek vehicle towards Cambridge. He switched the radio to a classical music station. He wanted to avoid the news but needed some noise to block out the dreadful racket from the passenger seat.

Jane didn't stop sobbing until they arrived at their hotel 70 minutes later.

CHAPTER THREE

TERRY JAMES was wide awake bright and early as usual, even on a Saturday and even after a night on the town with his girlfriend. He had been seeing Annette Lindley for four years. She had moved into his Docklands apartment within six months of their dating. It was not exactly a typical residence for a self-styled Bohemian artist, but to hell with that: did artists really have to suffer in order to achieve greatness?

Like James, Annette loved to escape to the south coast, especially out of season. Brighton held special memories for the couple. James had spent many a childhood holiday there, and many of the buildings and the town's history inspired Annette's creative streak. More recently, they had consummated their relationship at The Grand Hotel; no expense spared for Terry James when he was trying to impress a lady, even a wacky one like Annette who was more at home in a paint-spattered apron than a frilly frock.

They were back at The Grand thanks to a two-nights-for-one special offered by the Evening Gazette. Staff were not supposed to take advantage of promotional deals, but James always had a way round minor technicalities. "Put it in Annette's name, will you, Ian," he had told his pal in promotions.

He left Annette in bed, still dead to the world. Caffeine and cigarettes were her regular wake-up call, even when there was a splendid breakfast available with no grease-stained kitchen to clear up. James breakfasted alone, rising to refill his coffee and to grab another newspaper from the rack. By the time he had finished a three-course feast, the 41-year-old stocky reporter had browsed through all the papers that mattered to him. He ran his fingers through his brown hair – almost shoulder length now but he would not waste a minute of his weekend by having a trim – and read again the two paragraphs in the Daily Mail.

Police in Essex were investigating claims that one of their officers may be involved with a child pornography ring. No mention of Headleigh; nor the rank of the officer. The other rags had given the story – James's big exclusive of the previous day – similar treatment.

The Independent, the Express and the Star had not even mentioned the county the copper was from. Strange, very strange. Looks like the cops had not yet released a statement.

He returned to the hotel room and snuggled up next to the still-dozing Annette. He would rest his eyes for a few minutes then rouse her for a frolic before they tackled the sea breeze.

✝

ONE WEEK EARLIER

Mr and Mrs Henry Headleigh were attending a charity ball for the benefit of the Brentwood Homeless on the Friday evening when a tall, black-clad figure darted stealthily over the wall and dropped lightly onto the path which surrounded their rear garden at 37 St Andrew's Avenue. Of course, the man knew that. He had planned his visit meticulously. He was a very thorough man.

Tape had been wrapped around his keys to prevent them jangling whenever he needed to use them for a job. It was approaching 11pm and had been dark for an hour, yet the intruder had little difficulty finding the key he required this night.

He would not use his torch until he was safely behind the curtains. Swiftly and silently he unlocked the French windows, took a deep breath before sliding open the door – again as quietly as a proverbial mouse. He stretched his hand around a wall and turned off the alarm; security code 747. He laid a sheet of plastic over a mat by the door before stepping inside. He was a very thorough intruder was George Lewis.

The door slid back silently, the curtains made a slight whisper as they were drawn together again. Lewis stood for a moment on the plastic sheet and took in his surroundings. He knew exactly where he needed to go but a few seconds to settle himself would do no harm.

The large lounge was as tidy as only a childless home could be. No dirty plates, cups, crisp packets lying around like back at his place. Even the TV remote control was carefully slotted into a holder that hung over one of the two leather three-seater sofas.

Lewis made sure his shoes were clean before he set foot on the thick pile carpet. Light-blue, if any confirmation was needed that the kids had indeed flown this coop.

He walked slowly to the hall before taking a large black torch from his rucksack. The torch helped him negotiate his way up the stairs. There was a fork in the stairway after he had climbed 15 steps; right led to the grand bedroom of the husband and wife, the left branched to the communal bathroom and the now unused rooms of their offspring.

Roughly ten feet from the fork there was another flight of stairs leading from the landing to the loft. The plush carpet gave way to bare wood, well-polished teak. The loft extension had been added when Jonathan Headleigh had been 13.

Thankfully, the Headleighs had decided to have it made so that the entrance was permanently open. How thoughtful of them, thought Lewis, as he entered the spacious room which covered the entire length and breadth of the house. It had served as a wonderful den for the Headleigh children: a toy room, a junk room, a study, a music room, a party room. There was just one wall dividing the loft space into one larger room with a second about one third of the size. There was an open archway providing simple access from one to the other.

Lewis kept the beam from his torch pointed downwards as he gazed around the loft. The junk some people just refuse to throw away, he mused. He moved silently to the smaller room, trying to ensure he did not disturb any of the junk. That wasn't an easy task.

He went through the archway and had reached his target: Henry Headleigh's den. Not to be confused with his study downstairs, you understand, Mrs Headleigh. The computer was situated in the back corner. Good, it was away from any window. He lifted the dust-sheet off and replaced it with a dark blue blanket from his rucksack. Why was it impossible to find a truly BLACK blanket?

Lewis powered up the computer, switched off his torch and sat down with his head under the blanket. The only light in the room was the blue haze from the computer screen which managed to sneak out between the blanket and Lewis's body. He was ever so thorough.

The intruder placed a CD-Rom from his sack of tricks into the D Drive and began to familiarise himself with the Dell Dimension home computer. He was acquainted with the model, naturally, even though it was rather an ancient model in these days of monthly upgrades.

A glut of teenage trash cluttered the desktop. Why wasn't it as spic and span as the lounge? No, this PC was at home in the loft. The haphazard array of downloaded MP3s, teen posters, trivia games, email folders and software applications – no doubt pirated – sat as appropriately on the desktop as the more material junk on the loft floor. The loft and this PC were made for each other.

Now where does our Henry keep his stuff, I wonder? Not on the desktop, no private folders for our man. So, I'll just have to put some on for him. Lewis had a few technical checks to make before he tackled the main part of his mission. His fingers flew expertly over the keyboard.

His impressive physique and rugged features belied a man well at ease in the technocratic age. He had a batch of detailed notes and instructions in his rucksack if he became bogged down; he wouldn't need them, however.

He checked the Internet connection. As promised, it worked. He disconnected and delved into the depths of the Dell's system files. Rows and rows of letters and numerals filled the screen. Pages and pages of them; enough to make Einstein shiver in his grave. Lewis wanted the registry and took several seconds to locate the necessary files.

A few dozen keystrokes later he was satisfied with his work. He closed down the system files and created a new folder titled 'HH'. He was not stupid enough to place it amid the children's stuff on the desktop but made it a hidden folder inside another folder which he titled 'Homework'. He added a blank word processing page to the 'Homework' folder and titled that 'test page'.

He placed his newly-created work inside the computer's standard 'My Documents' folder which the children had seemed to ignore. Anyone opening 'My Documents' would see a folder called 'Homework'. If they opened the 'Homework' folder they would just- see 'test page' – unless they knew they were looking for a hidden folder, of course.

Lewis began loading data from the CD-Rom and pasting it into the 'HH' folder. Images and Internet pages flew at lightning speed from the CD-Rom to 'HH'. They were not the sort of images and pages you would want decent folk to see.

While the transfer progressed, Lewis took out a thin notebook and flicked to a page containing a list of dates. The transfer took four minutes. Lewis ejected the CD-Rom and slipped it into his rucksack.

He went back into the system registry and made a few minor tweaks to his earlier work as he checked dates from his notebook against the Internet pages lying sneakily inside 'HH'. Lewis powered down the computer and waited until the screen light had faded before removing his blanket and replacing it with the dustsheet. He cursed himself for being unable to recall whether or not the computer had been switched on at the mains. He tossed an imaginary coin in his head and decided to switch the mains off, too. Not as bloody thorough as you think, smart-arse. Still, who's going to notice that?

He flicked on his torch – beam downwards, you know – and made his way carefully back to the loft opening.

"You dirty, dirty boy, Henry," he muttered to himself. "Such a dirty, smutty little schoolboy." He was happier once he had climbed down the wooden stairs. The Headleighs really should tidy up that room.

Once back on familiar ground, Lewis made a swift exit from the house. He collected his plastic sheet from the doormat, stepped outside and leaned back inside to switch the alarm on. He had closed the curtains and locked the door before even a hint of a beep could be heard.

The job had taken him less than 15 minutes. He walked the 400 yards to his blue Cavalier and was home within ten minutes.

Detective Sergeant George Lewis – frequent subordinate of Henry Headleigh and occasional visitor to his St Andrew's Avenue home – was sharing a nightcap in front of the TV with his heavily pregnant wife a good half hour before the Headleighs pulled into their drive.

✝

Terry James's story ruined many a weekend. While the reporter partied the night away by the seaside, James McNish and George Travis were forced to sideline their professional and social engagements. The chief constables of Essex and Kent had had a good score of their finest making enquiries into Henry Headleigh and possible unsavoury links with paedophiles.

Neither chief could enlighten the other when they spoke on the phone shortly before midnight. "At least we've managed to keep the Press hounds at bay for now," said McNish. "Your lot have any trouble?"

"Nothing they couldn't handle. They have been run off their feet, though. All the daily papers, a few regional and national agencies plus one or two foreign wire services, I am told. Bad news is big news, especially on this subject. I told them to issue a 'no comment' for the time being. So, you got nothing from Headleigh?"

"He strenuously denied it. He was still shocked when I spoke to him. But I think something like this would bring many of us down a peg or two. I've sent him away on indefinite leave. He's up in the Cambridge area – got a daughter at college. I warned him to expect an official suspension if I deemed it necessary."

"Fine, fine. All very bizarre and hard to believe. We can't keep stalling the Press forever. He's your man, so I'll be guided by you. How do you want to play it, James?"

"Well I have to agree – we need to do something about the Press. I have given it some thought and believe the best stalling tactic for now would be for us to issue a joint written statement tomorrow. I don't feel we should attempt to handle face-on questions for now. We could simply say our enquiries into the paper's claims are continuing and we will keep the media informed of any developments. I've spoken to the Home Office and they will issue a warning to all editors to keep Headleigh's name out of their publications. I've also let the Association know what's happening, out of courtesy to Headleigh. He may need their help soon."

"Yes, that sounds about right. My boys have compiled a list of sex offenders we could haul in for questioning. I thought I'd check with you first. A bit thorny this, but did Headleigh have any professional business going down on my patch that we didn't know about?"

"No! No, George, of course not! You know I would never tolerate that."

"Yes, of course. Sorry I had to ask."

"What about the paper? The Gazette? We need to speak to them I suppose. I was wondering…you still chummy with the porn baron?"

The Chief Constable of Kent raised a coarse laugh. "Chummy? Not quite the word I would have chosen, James. But, yes, I still have the misfortune to stumble into him from time to time. He has a palace a few miles down the road. Been there just the once and needed a map to find my way around the damned kitchen. Huge place, but oh so tasteless. Ask my Doreen. Want me to pay a call on the little shit in the morning? But please do me a favour and refrain from calling us chums."

McNish managed a tired laugh in reply. "That'd be most welcome, George. Best to go to the top rather than piss about with his underlings. I suggest you wait until you have returned home before showering. You'll probably feel like one then. I'll be home all day; the Newmarket bookies will have to survive without my money for once."

"One final thing, James; you're pretty convinced it's a stitch-up, right?"

"I truly don't know, George. I'm praying it is, or that it is some terrible blunder; for Headleigh's sake, for my force's sake and for all our sakes. But my boys have drawn a blank. No skeleton in his closet as far as anyone knows or is telling. A few of the lads know the reporter, and claim he is sound and highly regarded. They say he has covered a good few of Headleigh's cases in the past, but nothing for a while and there are no reports of any bad blood between them."

"OK. I'll ring you if I get to see Richardson. Oh, and he is very insistent on being referred to as a FORMER porn king these days. Good night."

✝

Le Chateau D'Or was indeed a palace fit for a king – of the realm or of porn. There was money in filth and Bryan Richardson had made a mighty pile of it before seeking respectability.

The chateau covered 200 acres of prime countryside on the south side of Maidstone. Richardson didn't really mind the locals calling it 'Chez Bry', but he seethed at his Press rivals for branding it 'Babe Hall', 'Raunch Ranch' or much cruder terms.

Chief Constable George Travis was pleased he had decided to phone the Evening Gazette owner early that Saturday morning. He caught Richardson preparing to depart on important business – golf, thought Travis, correctly – but of course he could spare the Chief Constable a few minutes. Anything to assist the wonderful Kent Constabulary. Yes, he could call round now. Would he like a bit of breakfast? No trouble at all for you, George. Travis graciously declined the kind offer. A cup of tea will do nicely.

He drove himself the four miles south, pressed the intercom on the huge wrought-iron security gates and admired the beautifully-kept gardens as he slowly approached the 30-bedroomed mansion.

The façade was thankfully protected by law. The hand of porn was not allowed to disfigure the ornate Georgian cratfmanship. Sadly, the inside provided a stark contrast and a shocking introduction into the world of Richardson's empire. He may insist on the use of FORMER these days, but the rooms of Babe Hall reflected in vivid colours the murky past of its owner. Surely the decorators had been on drugs?

"George! George! Splendid. Delighted to see you." Richardson opened the door himself for the police officer and proffered a warm smile and a vigorous handshake.

"You've met my Karen before, of course."

"Hello Bryan, hello Karen." Travis tried not to stare at Mrs Richardson. Or more accurately, he tried not to stare at her heaving bosom. Christ! It's not yet nine in the morning and she's dressed like that. Clearly, the missus was not planning to join her husband on his 'business' trip. She was wearing a pink, sequinned top. Travis reckoned there was more material used to make his socks.

He decided her breasts were about as real as her husband's smile. He asked her to excuse them for a few minutes but he really did need a few minutes of Bryan's time; dreadfully sorry for having to call on a Saturday.

A maid brought tea into the large study where Richardson had directed Travis for their little chat. Probably the most acceptable room in the building, thought the chief. A red and gold patterned rug lay on the original wooden floor; copies of Renaissance paintings adorned the cream painted walls. Travis assumed they were copies as he could not imagine the owner spending his ill-gotten gains on true art. A Rembrandt sat incongruously between two huge religious epics – Raphael probably.

When they were settled with their drinks he outlined his problem to Richardson and requested any information the Gazette proprietor could provide.

"Of course, if our man is guilty as your paper claims he is, I can assure you the full force of the law will be brought to bear on him. Let me stress, we have no room for rotten apples and are as anxious as the Press to rid the force and society at large of law-breakers."

The Chief Constable was glad he delivered his mini-sermon and hoped his host would not find it too ingratiating. Richardson had listened intently to the Kent chief. He stroked his chin as if in deep thought before replying:

"Hmm, wish I could help you, George. But I'm afraid I don't meddle in editorial affairs, unlike some Press barons, eh? But I can tell you that we regard Terry James extremely highly. He is an award-wining reporter with an impressive track record stretching back many years.

"I was reading his reports long before I ever imagined I would one day own a newspaper. And our editor Andrew Harvey has total trust in him. You ever met Andrew? Or Terry?"

"I've met your editor once or twice, just to shake hands sort of thing at a dinner or a function. Never met the reporter but, yes, I have heard good things about him. Listen, Bryan, I have no need to emphasise just how serious these allegations are for the police and for your paper. Very serious."

Richardson broke in before the Chief Constable could continue his emphasis. "Yes, of course. Now, why don't I give you Andrew's number and you can ring him? OK?"

"I have his number, but thanks. I wanted to speak to you first, but yes I will give him a call when I return home. Or maybe I should ask James McNish to ring him. You know James? Chief Constable of Essex? The officer concerned is one of his, so it may be better if he speaks to your editor."

"Sure thing, George. Believe me I want to do all I can to help. How about I call Andrew and tell him to expect a call from the Essex chief? I'll make sure Andrew gives him everything he asks for."

Richardson smiled all the way to the front door as he ushered Travis away. The smile vanished as soon as the Chief Constable's Rover was out of sight. Richardson slammed the door shut and hurried back to the study. He slammed that door shut, too, just in case his dozy wife needed to get the message. Bryan baby was not to be disturbed.

"Harvey! What the fuck is going on with this copper story? What the fuck, fuck, fuck?"

Gone for the next few minutes at least were the polite tones Richardson reserved for important business clients or notables such as the highest-ranking police officer in his county. In its place was the harsh south London growl of the Jack The Lad made good.

Andrew Harvey was shocked. Firstly because his chairman rarely called on weekends. Secondly, and more disturbingly,because he had never been bawled out by his surname since his school days.

"Bryan. Morning, Bryan, what do you mean about the copper story? What's happened?"

"Well my dear old Jock I've just had the fuckin' Chief Constable of fuckin' Kent round 'ere at a quarter to fuckin' nine on a Saturday morning. Not a very happy fuckin' chappy was he, either. Quizzed me rotten on this story we had yesterday. Didn't 'ave a bleedin' clue what he was on about; made me feel a right dickhead. Care to fill me in? After all, I am the fuckin' owner."

Harvey was tempted to fire back that he had phoned him the previous day but the owner had been more concerned with dashing out to lunch or his club.

"I've no idea, Bryan. Not heard a thing since yesterday. Mind you I wasn't home until late last night. What did George Travis say? Neighbour of yours, isn't he?"

"Yes, too bleedin' close for comfort some might say. He said the cops were shocked by the story, they weren't investigating this copper for kiddie fiddlin' and could we provide them with information to help their enquiries? He was ever so polite. But he did make it plain that we could be in deep, deep shit. Softly, softly for now, he was. But it was fuckin' obvious to me that he thinks we printed shit and could soon be covered in it."

"Did he mention legal action?" replied the editor.

"Not in so many words. I guess you get the nice guy if you donate three thousand fuckin' quid to the police victims fund. Just tell me we're sound Andrew? Sound, ain't we?"

The editor was relieved they were back on first name terms and that Richardson had appeared to have vented the worst of his anger.

"Terry James wouldn't mess up on something like this, Bryan. He's the best there is; we're lucky to have him. Want me to call him and probe a little deeper?"

"Yes, I bleedin' well do. ASAP. And I told my neighbourhood bobby that you would be happy to ring his pal in Essex and fill him in. Hang on, I've got the details 'ere."

"James McNish? The Chief Constable?"

"Yes, that's the geezer. Know him?"

"Vaguely. I'll have a chat with Terry and then give him a buzz. I'll keep you informed."

"Right, make sure you do. Don't call till five-ish. I'll be out till then and won't have the mobile on. Sort it, Andrew. Just sort it." Richardson ended the call as abruptly as he had started it.

Harvey sat back in his armchair. "Welcome to the weekend," he sighed. He hadn't arrived back at his Hampstead apartment until the early hours of the morning after his routine Friday night prowl around the West End.

He had slept in late – well 7.45 was late for Andrew Harvey. Unlike Terry James 50 miles away he had had a simple breakfast: juice and coffee. But, like his reporter, he had flicked through the morning papers and been equally surprised by the scant follow-ups to the Gazette scoop.

He walked around his tidy apartment for a few moments, thinking hard. He meandered in and out of the four rooms. They were surprisingly tidy considering the quantity of books and volumes upon volumes of magazines and papers Harvey hoarded. He settled in the kitchen and rang James as the kettle was boiling. He was aware that James was sunning himself on the south coast and cursed when there was no reply and he had to stutter out a voicemail.

Muttering curses, Harvey made himself another cup of coffee, returned to the lounge, switched on the radio and sank back into his armchair, his thinking chair. There was not much else he could do for now but sit and think and wait and worry. He ruled out calling the Gazette's lawyer; he knew less than himself about the story and would probably have a larger hangover, anyway.

Should he call Craig Butler, James's sidekick at the paper? No, best not for now. He was thinking, waiting and worrying when his phone rang. He darted up and grabbed the handset.

It was his eldest daughter phoning from Scotland. Moira Harvey just wanted to see how the old man was doing. Could she and her boyfriend spend a few days at his place next month? They wanted to see the bright lights of the big city.

"Sure love, be great to see you as always," Harvey tried to sound at his paternal best.

She was a red-headed beauty, his Moira. Should be settled down by 26, though. They exchanged some family tittle-tattle before Harvey told her he had to go as he was awaiting an important business call.

He wondered if Moira would be bringing the same boyfriend he had met at Christmas. No, knowing Moira, she would have some fresh stud in tow. He returned to his armchair; now definitely more of a worrying chair than a thinking chair.

Harvey had never had to contest a libel case. Sure, he had worked on papers that had been through the High Court. But not the Gazette. Not that the Gazette was a sissy paper, far from it. He had flown close to the wires many a time. A corrupt council official once tried to bluff his way out of a Gazette probe into his affairs with threats. The paper held firm and the official lost his job and his liberty for three years.

Terry James had experienced two close calls when chasing a cartel of businessmen in North London. They managed to slap injunctions on the Gazette before their bogus business covers were blown and three of them were jailed for drug offences. A fourth had managed to escape by jetting out of the country a few hours before the police raided his premises. He was last heard of hopping around Caribbean islands to elude the law.

No, Harvey trusted James. Didn't he? Course he did. Had he trusted him once too often? No, course not. Had the wily editor let his guard down yesterday? Christ! This bloody chair was annoying him.

He walked back into the kitchen, brewed more coffee and paced the floor. He recalled leaving the office yesterday. He'd been happy with the story – a good exclusive to end a mediocre week, news-wise. He just had a nagging doubt about jeopardising a possible police raid.

Funnily, Bryan hadn't mentioned anything about that. The Chief Constable of Kent hadn't said their man was innocent, just that they had no reason to investigate him. Strange. Harvey paced up and down some more. He hated waiting.

✝

James and Annette were heading for a sea front pub after their two-hour stroll up and down the Brighton prom. That had cleared away the cobwebs.

"Better just check if I've had any calls, sweetie."

Annette glowered at the man and unlinked her arm.

"C'mon, no pouting. You know us ace reporters. Always on the job." He winked and fished his mobile from inside his leather jacket.

"Phew!" he whistled.

"What's up, Superman? Does Metropolis miss you?" teased Annette.

"Eleven missed calls, two voicemails and 29 text messages. Am I Mr Popular or what? Let's get to the pub then you'd better give me a few minutes to see what all these are about."

James ordered a pint and a half of bitter at the Lion & Lobster and settled down to check his phone. He recognised seven of the missed calls; all from colleagues on Fleet Street, not that there were any papers operating out of Fleet Street these days.

His sister had texted him twice, saying she had taken a few calls from reporters trying to contact him. Three texts were junk. The rest were from hacks on rival papers; "Give us a buzz soonest" sort of thing. A couple of them mentioned the Headleigh story. One, sent at 7pm the previous night, read "Gud Wurk". He didn't recognise the sender. The first voicemail was from Craig Butler. People were looking for him. Headleigh story had caused a bit of a stir. Craig had just said he knew Terry had gone away for the weekend but he didn't know where.

The final check was on the voicemail from Andrew Harvey. His editor needed to speak to him URGENTLY. VERY URGENTLY. He'd be waiting at home for his call.

"Annette, real sorry love, but I have some important business calls to make. I need to get back to the hotel. Can you give me an hour, please?" Despite her occasional mocking of him, Annette Lindley was understanding about his work and his passion for it.

"Sure, off you go. I am more than capable of amusing myself. Don't shout if I spend too much."

Thrifty could have been Annette's middle name. James had no fears of his girl lashing out on a spending spree. "You're a doll. See you back here in an hour?"

James strode purposefully back to The Grand; not a mad dash but a quicker stride than he would use when promenading with Annette. He smiled as the commissionaire tipped his hat. He took the steps two at a time. The lobby and the bar were buzzing. He loved to watch people, and there were some sights worth seeing among the clientele of The Grand this weekend. But he requested his key and made straight for his room. He decided against using the room phone; he didn't want Harvey to know he was staying at The Grand unless he positively insisted on it. It was 25 minutes past mid-day when he rang the waiting editor. By that time, tough-as-old-boots Andrew Harvey was a nervous wreck.

"Where in God's name have you been?"

"Just out for a stroll with Annette, boss. Didn't realise until an hour ago that my mobile battery must have died in the night." He lied. "It's recharged now. What's the problem?"

"I'll tell you what the problem is, laddie. The problem is an irate Chief Constable of Kent called on our beloved leader this morning and demanded to know what your story was about. That's what the problem is."

James couldn't help smiling. Your story, not our story. "You mean he wanted to know where I got it from? I hope Bryan told him where to get off."

"No, not the source. He flatly denied the story, said there was no investigation into Henry Headleigh."

"That's bollocks, Andrew. Complete bollocks. You know that."

"Think, Terry. Would the top cop pop round to Babe Hall without good reason? On a Saturday morning? Before nine o'clock as our leader made clear to me. He wants me to check it out and make sure we are in the clear – legally he meant. We are, aren't we, Terry?"

"Sure, Andrew. Sound as a pound my source. You don't doubt that, do you?" James sounded upset.

Harvey hesitated before replying: "Terry, I just need to know so I can call the Essex Chief Constable. Bryan insisted I did as soon as possible. I've been waiting frantically for you to call. I guess you've seen the papers – not a bloody word on Headleigh. Smells like someone's shut up shop. Hate to ask this, but can you tell me who your source is? I'm assuming it's a cop, right?"

"Christ! I can't do that, Andrew! I'm staggered you would even ask me."

"Sorry. Of course, I understand. Maybe you can just tell me again: you're absolutely certain that he wasn't spinning you a yarn? You trust him implicitly?"

"Yes, never let me down and he was adamant about this when we spoke yesterday. One thought, anything on the raids due to happen today? I haven't listened to any news."

"No, now that's another worry. They either cancelled them 'cos of your story or, more disturbingly, they were never planned in the first place."

"Shit! But you do believe me, don't you, Andrew?"

"Course I do, Terry. I just need something to tell James McNish. Throw me a bone, any bloody thing just to get the police and Bryan off our backs for a while."

"Listen, Andrew, can you give me a few minutes to think? I'll call you back within 15, OK?"

"Go on, but no more than 15. It's more than three hours since I spoke with Bryan. Don't want him calling to find out I've made bugger all progress."

Harvey was sick of pacing so he settled down in his newly-baptised worrying chair and watched the grandfather clock in the corner tick away the minutes. Eight had ticked away when James rang back.

"Right, I've had a think and can only suggest that maybe you can let

McNish know some of the details we didn't publish? Best not to mention the raids or anything about me having a good source. But you could say we know he has been in Chatham and Maidstone. And you could let him know that we are aware Headleigh has been using child porn web sites outside work. Should give him something to think about. I won't be able to contact my source until Monday, but I should be able to deliver more info then."

"Better than nothing. You're 100 per cent certain of these facts, then?"

"Yes, I am."

"Ok. Thanks, Terry. Prepare yourself for a legal briefing and a verbal monstering from our leader on Monday morning."

Harvey's call to the Chief Constable of Essex could have gone much worse. He stressed that the paper stood by its story; he provided the extra details that his crime reporter had suggested.

McNish remained calm and polite but emphasised the police bewilderment. They were conducting their own investigation, of course, but were four square behind Henry Headleigh. Legal action could not be ruled out. The Home Office would be issuing a warning to editors. Essex Police would naturally appreciate any additional information the Evening Gazette could provide.

✢

Jane Headleigh was starting to come to terms with her predicament by Sunday. The Chinese meal with Sarah had been probably the hardest ordeal of the most horrible Friday of her life. Sarah had been unable to stem back the tears, too, and both weeping women aroused strange glances from the normally poker-faced waiters.

Henry Headleigh had spent most of the meal staring into his bowl. He possessed a healthy appetite usually. Sarah could shovel away her portion, too. But the three Headleighs merely nibbled at a succession of dishes. The waiters had cottoned on to some family grief and did not ask if there was a problem with the food as they took away the half full dishes. They all walked Sarah to Trinity, the air of depression hanging over them in stark contrast to the raucous yelps from the students leaving the pubs.

Total silence accompanied Jane and Henry on the 15-minute walk from Trinity to their hotel. Henry asked for the room key at The King George and handed it to his wife.

"I'll just have a nightcap and a cigarette at the bar, love. Join you in a few minutes." He kissed her gently on the cheek.

In fact, Headleigh took longer than he promised. He needed to be alone with his thoughts for a while and downed two large Cognacs and smoked three cigarettes while running through the hectic day's events.

He said a silent prayer that his wife would be asleep as he mounted the stairs to their first floor room. She wasn't. Jane was sobbing gently into her pillow as Henry crept between the sheets, her back to the centre of the bed.

Jane's sobs and his own private thoughts kept Headleigh awake through most of the dark hours. The husband and wife looked as if they had been to one hell of a party when they roused. Jane seemed calmer but would skip breakfast. Headleigh went down for coffee and a cigarette, and to escape Jane's presence.

They muddled their way through the Saturday. Headleigh had browsed through the papers in the hotel rack and been relieved at the scant coverage given to the Gazette story. He wondered how the boys at HQ were faring but decided against giving them a call. That could wait until Monday.

Lunch with Sarah proved a more amenable meal than at the Ding Ho. Dad managed to finish his steak pie and boiled potatoes; the women made a reasonable job of their salmon sandwiches.

Sarah had spoken to Theresa and Jon that morning. Jon had told his sister to persuade dad to take legal advice as soon as possible and to sue the backside off the bastards.

Headleigh said he would consider it over the weekend. Thanks for the advice. How was Theresa? Upset, but holding up.

Conversation between mum and dad came in fits and starts after

Sarah left them for the afternoon. They went shopping, or rather window-shopping. Cambridge was blessed with the finest bookstores and Headleigh did make one purchase: The Cambridgeshire Police In Victorian Times.

Their first visit to the cinema in at least 12 years came that evening. Headleigh had suggested it and made sure they didn't book into a weepy. One hundred minutes of adventure with Tom Cruise brought more welcome silence. They retired to bed with Headleigh telling his wife "try not to fret, darling, everything will be all right" for what seemed like the thousandth time in less than 36 hours.

Fatigue enabled them to sleep soundly and three hours past their customary waking time. Jane spent longer than usual in the bathroom. She emerged from her shower with some signs of normality on her face. Twenty minutes in front of the mirror, make-up applied for the first time since Friday morning and she was starting to resemble the woman Headleigh knew so well.

Rings still hung around her eyes and made her look older than her 48 years. But there was a glimmer back in the green – the green she had passed on to their daughters. Her short light-brown hair – with a few streaks of grey taking hold these days – could have used professional attention. The paisley frock suited her, disguising the extra stone she could have done with losing. But not bad for her age, thought Headleigh, not bad at all, really.

There was a bustling flea market a few hundred yards from the hotel. Jane suggested a stroll there; maybe buy a token for the children?

The Headleighs didn't notice the blue Fiesta parked opposite the hotel. The driver spotted them, though. The trained eye had been waiting three hours for them to emerge.

CHAPTER FOUR

"I'M DREADFULLY sorry, sir," the hotel manager forced out as he lightly gripped Headleigh's arm. Headleigh was at the reception desk, checking out. Sarah's friend Suzie had paid for the room in advance and 'Mr Wallace' just had a small phone bill to settle.

"I beg your pardon," said Headleigh, turning to face the man holding his arm. He wasn't used to being manhandled, and didn't like it; especially by subservient hotel employees. He read the badge on the man's lapel: Marcus Crowe, Manager. He vaguely recalled him from past visits to the King George. "Can I help you?"

"I'm sorry about the photograph, sir; the one in the paper."

"What photograph?"

The embarrassed hotel manager handed Headleigh that morning's Daily Mail. "Page seven, sir. If I find out any of my staff are responsible I assure you they will be disciplined."

Headleigh took his change from the receptionist and walked over to Jane who was standing with their bags by the entrance.

"Something wrong, love?"

Headleigh didn't answer but leafed over the first few pages of the newspaper. Page Seven featured a 'Mail Photo Exclusive'.

PROBE COP IN HIDING

Headleigh and his wife stared at the page. A brief article accompanied two large pictures. The top one showed the Headleighs leaving their Brentwood home. The second was taken yesterday as they left the hotel for the flea market. Their faces had been fuzzed on both images.

The Mail informed its readers that a senior Essex detective had gone into hiding while police investigated possible links with unsavoury characters. They had checked into a Cambridge hotel using fictitious names. A hotel employee told the Mail that the couple looked distracted and distressed.

That was it. Headleigh wasn't mentioned by name, nor was the hotel. There was no mention of child pornography.

"Good God!" cried Jane.

"Right, let's get into the car. The sooner we get back home I can sort this bloody mess out."

Jane's sobs returned. They were the only sounds Headleigh heard as he drove home.

✝

"That couple in 109, what they all about then?" said Mike Breach as he breezed into the staff room at the King George. "You know, the middle-aged folk – woman looks like she's been crying all the time."

"Yeah, I've noticed 'em," replied Mary Wells. "Here for a funeral or something if you ask me."

"Nah! Saw 'em at the Chinese last night with a younger woman, their daughter I reckon. Very mysterious, it was; hushed voices and all that. They left enough food to keep half of Africa going for a week.

"I caught something the daughter said. She kept touching the old woman and telling her not to worry, that dad's pals would sort it, that police always looked after their own. Weird, it was."

The chat in the room returned to football, the heated topic before Breach's entrance. Clarissa Hopkins had been interested in the news, however.

Hopkins was a 19-year-old catering student in Essex – at Harlow College of Further Education. She worked weekend shifts as a waitress at the King George as part of her course. She had read the Gazette story on the train the previous day. Later that day, she managed to grab Mike for a few private words. The 22-year-old porter grimaced. "Ewww, a paedo, is he? In our hotel?"

"Spike his food, shall I?"

They both laughed, then Mike added: "Listen, there may be a few bob in it for you. I've got a pal who works on the Mail. Well, the older brother of a pal actually. They pay for stuff like this. Why don't you give him a buzz? Tell him you are a friend of Davey's pal Mikey. Better still, ring Davey and I'm sure he'll let you have his private number. Gotta dash, have a football match to endure."

Davey took Clarissa's call and promised to pass on the tip-off to his brother, Harry. He took her home address and said he was sure his brother would sort out a few quid if the tip led to anything.

The tip led to Chris 'The Lens' Harris sitting outside the King George in his blue Fiesta for three hours that sunny Sunday morning. 'The Lens' could afford a much grander vehicle. But he had preferred Fiestas since his days among the London paparazzi. Semi-retired now, thanks largely to a series of lucrative photos of a young Royal tipsily leaving a nightclub with a married Premiership football star, the 43-year-old photographer liked to keep his hand in. Not too far from Saffron Walden, if you require my services, eh lads?

He had ended up at Headleigh's house in Brentwood by chance, having seen the Gazette story while shopping in Chelmsford with his mother. He was disappointed none of the papers used the photos he had spent a couple of hours of his precious time grabbing.

'The Lens' was surprised to receive the call from the Mail Picture Editor on a Saturday evening. They didn't want to waste sending a staff snapper up to Cambridge if it was a wild-goose chase.

It was a local job for 'The Lens' so he agreed to give the Mail five hours maximum of his precious time, but he wanted double-shift payment as it was a late call and a Sunday job an' all. He stayed sober that Saturday night, rose early and delivered the photos in good time for the Mail. Yes, he could confirm it was indeed Mr and Mrs Headleigh.

Clarissa Hopkins was overjoyed to receive a £500 cheque from the Daily Mail accounts department on the Wednesday. The invoice said 'Bent cop tip-off'. There was a second letter franked with the Mail logo. It was from Davey's brother, Harry Robinson. Thanks for the tip-off, he'd asked accounts to push through payment, and here was his private number if she ever had any further information for the paper.

Clarissa did a little jig in her kitchen. Whoopee; a month's salary for one little phone call. The following weekend she let slip news of her good fortune to a fellow waitress and asked her to keep her eyes and ears open for anything they could flog to the papers.

She was serving Saturday lunch when she received a summons to the manager's office. She didn't try to deny it. The 60-second interview ended with Marcus Crowe informing Hopkins her services would no longer be required. The King George had a reputation to protect and a duty to respect the privacy of its guests. Two messages she would do well to heed if she foresaw a future in the hotel trade.

The manager wrote a letter to Henry Headleigh, formally apologising for the incident and informing him of his decision. Of course, he had realised all along just who were the Mr and Mrs Wallace in 109. The Headleighs had stayed at his hotel on two previous occasions and Marcus Crowe was not a man to forget faces.

✝

The Mail photo exclusive spared Terry James from a verbal roasting in the Gazette's boardroom on the Monday morning.

Andrew Harvey had hosted an earlier meeting in his own office while the concerned parties awaited the arrival of their chairman. The smart money expected he would be in a little before his usual time of 11.15.

The smart money won by a good 75 minutes. Still, it left plenty of time for the editor to rally his troops. He began the day by addressing his staff on the office floor. He had decided not to pin up any notices about the Headleigh story in case they went missing and ended up in unfriendly hands.

"We have a problem, ladies and gentlemen of the Press. Some of you will already know that our exclusive on Friday has caused a stir. The police are not exactly denying the Henry Headleigh accusations as yet. But the chairman has had a visit from a senior officer and I have spoken with another. They are being cagey with their official statements.

But the Home Office has issued a warning against usage of Headleigh's name.

"Now please listen to me carefully. I want no mention of the Headleigh case to anyone outside this office. Loose tongues could prove very expensive. I know some of you like to keep certain stories in your personal folders. If you have Friday's story filed, delete it immediately this meeting is over. I want no record other than Terry's original and the production hands it went through. If any news about this story comes your way, you are to inform me at once. Me, OK? Not anyone else. You all should have my personal numbers. Right, get cracking. We still have papers to produce."

Harvey could hear the whispers begin before he had reached his office; too many of them to make anything out.

He had called several key members of staff inside his inner sanctum.

"First things, first; Conor, can you look after the paper today? I'm going to be tied up with this for a while. You can use Richard's office, if you like."

"Sure thing, Andrew," said Assistant Editor Conor O'Brien. The Irishman was still miffed that he had been kept in the dark during Friday's developments. But he would be happy to bask in Richard Long's office until the Deputy Editor returned from vacation.

O'Brien guessed it wasn't the best of days to ask Andrew when the partition would be erected for his own office.

"Lucy, you're in charge of the news desk. I think I'll need Phil with me today. Danny, get me a list of everyone who touched page one on Friday. Better leave us a single column somewhere for today's Headleigh news, not that I have a bloody clue what that will be yet. Page two should be fine."

O'Brien, Deputy News-Editor Lucy Atkinson and Chief Sub Danny Waddell left to perform their respective duties. Harvey was asking his secretary, Irene, to make coffee for the staff who remained in his office when Arthur Jacobs entered. The lawyer was breathless.

Harvey had phoned him to request his early arrival that day. Eight in the morning was an ungodly hour but Jacobs made it – almost.

"I'm impressed Arthur. Ten minutes late, not bad for a legal eagle."

"Thank you, Andrew, but I assume we are not here to discuss deadlines."

Terry James and News Editor Phil Calvin were the other men present. There was a melancholy atmosphere pervading the room, despite the trench humour between the editor and the lawyer.

"Well, we all know why we're here. I'm afraid there isn't much more I can tell you than I already have. But we need a few bright ideas before Bryan Richardson gets here. He wants us all in the boardroom at 10.15.

"Just to recap, since Friday's story broke, Bryan has met the Chief Constable of Kent and I have spoken on the phone with the Chief Constable of Essex. Both coppers spun us the same line. Naturally, they had conferred before contacting us.

"Both insisted there was no investigation into Henry Headleigh. There is now, of course. You will have seen the other papers over the weekend. They did not follow-up the story with a great deal of vigour, which did surprise me. I am assuming editors and owners were leaned on by the powers that be.

"For those of you who haven't seen today's Mail, have a look here."

Harvey already had a copy open at the relevant page. All except Jacobs had read the article and seen the photos.

"You will note that again there is no mention of our man. Over to you, Terry. You stand by your story, right?"

"Absolutely, Andrew. Absolutely. You gave James McNish the extra information?"

"Yes, I did. Not heard back from him. Of course you wish to protect your source, but have you any further information you can provide today? Any more contact with him?"

"What extra information?" asked Calvin. "Something I don't know?"

"Just a few details we thought wise to leave out of my original story, Phil. My contact tells me Headleigh has been surfing the Net for child porn outside his official duties. And he gave me names of a couple of towns in Kent the sick sod had visited. Gang meetings where they have their wicked ways with kids."

"Your source? When can you get more details from him?"

"I've left a message requesting a meeting ASAP; waiting for him to get back to me. Should be sometime today with luck."

"What about the raids, Terry? How come they didn't happen? Was it our story?" asked Calvin.

James had called Calvin out of courtesy on Sunday afternoon, as soon as he and Annette made their earlier than expected return from Brighton. They hadn't had the chance to discuss the story in detail as Calvin was heading out on family duty.

"Sorry, Phil. That bit puzzles me, too. I won't have a clearer picture till I meet my contact."

"Arthur, can you run us through how we stand legally? So far the cops have just dropped vague hints about possible action."

Arthur Jacobs looked up from the Mail article, flicked his thumbs behind his red braces and puffed out his chest before speaking.

"Well I don't think we need worry about the police force taking action as a body. As far as I can see the only one with a possible case is our Henry. Of course the police would probably back him if he convinced them of his innocence. But the action would have to come from him."

"Yes, I was hoping that was the case," said Harvey. "So what now, Arthur? Anything we could or should do to cover our tracks?"

"If we are standing by Terry's story we will just have to wait for Headleigh to determine the next step. As you young folk will recall – I hope – from journalism school, it is not a case of what we believe to be true, it is what we can PROVE to be true. I gather actual evidence is thin on the ground?"

"Very thin; non-existent, in fact. Terry, we really do need your man to come up with some concrete material we can use to nail Headleigh. You must stress that when you meet, OK?"

"Will do. I'm sure he will come up with the goods. He's never let me down yet."

"Fine, and you make sure Bryan understands that."

"How was he on Saturday, Andrew?"

"How was he? How was he? He was fine, Phil. Positively on his best behaviour. He was about to have the arse sued off him by some top cop we had branded a paedophile but, no, he took it all in good measure.

"He was FUCKING fuming! Jeeze, what did you expect, Phil? So, it is imperative we keep him as sweet as sweet can be. Got it? And if he calls me Harvey, would someone please restrain me from hitting him. You all know what he's like, so let's just pray there were fun and frolics at Tit City over the weekend."

Harvey had lapsed into his harsh Scottish accent and leaned back in his chair breathing heavily.

"Yeah! Sorry, Andrew, I get the picture. Anything else we should be doing to ease the situation, Arthur?"

"Damage limitation, you mean? Bit late for that. We've published and now must prepare to be damned if we can't fight our corner. Evidence, chaps, evidence is what we need above all else. Hard, tangible proof that our Henry is indeed in league with these perverts."

"Speaking of damage limitation," said the editor, "dare I ask for a ballpark figure on what the bugger could hit us for?"

"Oh, if it goes to court I wouldn't like to even hazard a guess. Juries are so fickle. If we fail to dig up any evidence and decide to settle out of court we would be looking at a sizeable figure. I'll have a browse through recent cases and let you know."

"What if Bryan asks?"

"For now it would be best to tell him the same. Off the top of my head I can only guess it will be very bad news. So one of us will have to break it to him gently, preferably when he is otherwise distracted. Maybe we could get the company solicitors to handle that. Far too delicate for an editorial legal adviser like myself."

"OK. I just like to be prepared. We've got just over an hour till his highness starts bouncing off walls."

Harvey turned to his two journalists. "I suggest you and Phil get your heads together and reel in any contacts who may be able to help. Be discreet please. No word on our chats with the cops for now. See you all in the boardroom 10.15 sharp. Wipe your feet before entering."

Bryan Richardson swept into the building like a whirlwind. His chauffeur, Alf, parked the Bentley right outside the entrance and Richardson sprung out with a cursory nod to a few faces who swiftly parted to allow him to enter. He took a private lift to the fourth floor, which was reserved for the B R Enterprises empire.

Richardson had sold off all his interests in pornography soon after buying the Evening Gazette from the troubled Max J Roberts Publications group. The Gazette was his flagship publication. But he had a multitude of publishing interests, ranging from dietary and heavy metal rock magazines to educational DVDs for children. BRE had come a long way since Horny Housewives On Your Doorstep. Respectability was what Bryan Richardson craved; and he feted the greats of the land in avid pursuit of it.

He had wined and dined with politicians, from the Prime Minister downward, members of the aristocracy, and a glut of TV and media celebrities. A call to Buckingham Palace could not be too far away. The last thing Bryan needed was a scurrilous legal case, especially back in the land of porn; kiddie porn at that. Bugger it. Why hadn't he paid more attention to what that damned Jock was rabbiting on about on Friday?

Money was not the issue. Sex had helped Richardson amass a personal fortune of £200m. He had celebrated his first million by relocating his parents from their south London council flat to a three-bedroomed bungalow in Cornwall – Mr and Mrs Harold Richardson were over the moon with their first garden.

No, Richardson was not concerned about the money; he could pay off this cop from his ready cash box. It was about being beaten and, above all, about respectability. He could not let this cop case ruin all his hard work over the past years and months. He was ready to fight the good fight and uphold the values and traditions of British journalism at its best. He would uncover the corruption and filth that enabled these paedophiles to lurk in the underclass. He would rid the police force of evil. He would emerge stronger and more powerful. These were the thoughts that accompanied Richardson as he entered the boardroom. He could not, in truth, claim them all as his own. His invaluable chief executive, Gary Chalmers, had popped round to the chateau and mapped out a vague battleplan with his chairman.

Chalmers was already sat at the large walnut table in the boardroom as Richardson walked in. He had a pile of papers in front of him.

"Mornin', Gary. Fine morning it is, too."

"Good morning, Bryan. Yes, a grand day. What a shame we have to ruin it with this mess."

"The price we have to pay for our fame and fortune, my good man."

They both laughed as Richardson settled himself in his seat at the head of the table and swung his feet onto the table.

"Right, our boys should be here in a few minutes. We play it just as we discussed yesterday. Rough and smooth. We just have to make sure they are solid on this. Let me do the talking to start with, OK?"

"Sure, Bryan. Have you spoke with Harvey since Saturday?"

"Nope. I'm sure he'll have his boys and girls all geared up."

A knock on the door heralded the arrival of Harvey and his three editorial staff. Richardson greeted them with a stony face. The pleasantries were brief as all sat around one end of the table. Harvey was relieved to find Richardson employing his business voice. He addressed the crime reporter first.

"Ah! The Great Terry James!" a half smile from the chairman. "I just know that our Terry is going to kick off this meeting of fine minds by confirming that we are one hundred per cent sound on this. Aren't you, Terry?"

"Yes, Mr Chairman."

"Oh, Bryan, please call me Bryan. We're all in this together and you know I'm not one for the formal crap. So if we're sound I wonder if you would care to explain why I received a most unwelcome visitor on Saturday morning?"

James had steeled himself to sound as efficient and assured as possible. He knew that he and his editor were the men on the spot.

"I can only assume Headleigh has somehow covered his tracks. But I am meeting my contact later today and I am certain he will provide the proof we need."

"Excellent, I adore words like 'certain'. So we are 'certain' we have a sound case. Excellent."

Harvey thought it best to add his certainty to the meeting. "We four will be working on getting the proof today, Bryan. I've put Conor in charge of the paper for the time being."

"Good. Good. Now what shall we do with this proof when we get it? That's a strange one, isn't it?"

Puzzled looks from the three journalists; Arthur Jacobs seemed to be deep in thought. It was a grand act. Richardson was the only person in the room on his feet. He leaned both hands on the table and looked hard at the journalists.

"I'll tell you what we do with it: we bring it all to me. If I'm not available, Gary here will do the honours."

Chalmers raised his head and let the room see a passive face. He lowered it again as the chairman continued with his instructions.

"What we do NOT do with this proof is publish a single bloody word of it until it has been okayed by myself or Gary. No loose cannons on this one. Call it editorial interference if you like, but this is my paper and I will not have Chief Constables disturbing my mornings; my SATURDAY mornings."

Harvey was desperately struggling to find the words he wanted to get out. He failed and decided silence was his best option.

"You've squared the Essex chief for now, right Andrew?"

"Yes, Bryan. I gave him a few details we didn't publish on Friday. He will hopefully be investigating those ends."

"Let's hope he's squared my neighbourhood cop then."

Richardson pressed his palms together and made a slow circle, staring at the walls before returning to his original position.

"OK, you two had better get after this proof then," he said to James and Calvin.

"Arthur, you'd better have a word with Gary about legal issues.

Andrew, a quick word before you go."

Calvin and James left the meeting. Once safely in the lift Calvin spoke for the first time.

"Christ! That bastard gives me the creeps. Think I prefer him when he's in rant-mode. I hope your contact comes up trumps, Terry."

"He will, Phil. He will. I'm sure of that."

"Sure? Is that the same as certain?"

Richardson placed his arm around Harvey and walked him to the far end of the room, leaving the lawyer and chief executive to pore over some papers.

"I'm feeling just a little bit better than I did on Saturday morning, Andrew," he said softly. "We just need to decide what we're going to do with our crime ace."

"What do you mean, Bryan? Do with him?"

"Well the cops have put this kiddie fiddler on gardening leave or whatever they call it. Not an official suspension from what I gather. What should we do with Terry James?"

Not for one second had Harvey considered suspending James.

"I don't think suspending him would be a good idea, Bryan. It would send out the wrong signals; look like he had done something wrong."

"Good point. Good point. But I don't think it is wise having him covering this story. Not officially anyway. In fact I think it would be sensible to keep him away from crime and cops altogether for a while; just until this blows over."

"Well, Bryan, I was planning to have him working purely on this case until it was sorted."

"Yes, of course. I have no problems with that at all. But, I do not want him under any circumstances talking to our friendly boys in blue. Most definitely not my neighbour, God bless him."

"I see," muttered the editor.

"So, I suggest you keep him in the office where you can keep a close eye on him. I want you to check all his movements. He is only to be allowed out to meet this bloody contact of his. Any idea who he is?"

"No, Bryan, and I wouldn't expect Terry to tell me. No editor would."

"Of course, I understand that. But do as I suggest, OK? A very close eye on our Terry. Keep me posted."

Gazette Editor Andrew Harvey left the boardroom a stooped figure. He felt like he was losing control of his paper. He called on his reserves of sheer willpower and just about managed to present his customary figure of authority as he walked through the journalists' floor to his office.

He called in James and gave him the bad news. The crime reporter looked shell-shocked at first, but a few curses at the walls brought him to his senses.

"Terry James, Press releases and general desk duties, at your service."

"Just while we get this sorted, my lad. Let me know as soon as you hear from your contact. Send Craig Butler in would you? He can handle crime while you're busy."

✝

Essex's finest were holding their own meeting 40 miles away from the Docklands luxury of BR Enterprises. The room at the Chelmsford HQ was more Spartan, but the atmosphere just as tense.

Chief Constable James McNish had assembled his most trusted officers. McNish kicked off by informing his eight colleagues of his phone conversation with the Gazette editor and the Kent summit.

"I can't believe it," said Assistant Chief Constable Derek Johnson. "Henry Headleigh a paedophile? Do me a favour?"

Johnson had worked with Headleigh on some big cases in the past. The pair were professionally close if not personal friends.

"Nor me," said Inspector Colin Grant. He had been instructed to attend the meeting as he was Headleigh's deputy in the anti-paedophile unit.

"Perhaps you can fill us in, Colin. You've worked closely with Henry for a few months now; anything suspicious to report?" asked McNish.

"Nothing at all, sir. This really is beyond belief."

"I find it hard to give the story any credence, too," said Chief Superintendent Mary Edwardes. "But we have to investigate the matter fully. This is a big, big issue as far as the public is concerned. They hate paedophiles more than any other kind of criminal."

"Very true, Mary. You and Colin were present when Headleigh was confronted with the story. Took it very badly you say?"

"Wouldn't anyone, sir? He was absolutely stunned. Stunned and then very, very angry. I wasn't able to get much out of him except a total denial. He was shattered."

"Well it's clear we have to clear him, the quicker the better," said Superintendent Michael Gray.

"We can do our bit at this end. I assume he's been onto the Association for legal advice?"

"I told him to keep a low profile for now. But it seems that didn't quite work out – if anyone hasn't seen today's Mail there is a copy on the desk behind me. As far as I know Henry's on his way home from Cambridge."

"What about these extra details you say the editor gave you, sir?" said Inspector Grant.

"Yes, I was coming to that. Don't like the sound of it at all, but I spoke with George Travis last night and we have an operation to plan for tomorrow. This stays in this room for now. No-one is to contact Henry, and you are to inform me if he attempts to contact you."

The senior Essex officers sat stone-faced as McNish outlined the combined operation to be carried out the following day by police teams in Essex and Kent.

✝

"Permission to leave the office, sir!" James snapped to attention, military-style as he addressed his editor.

"What is it, wise guy? I am in no mood for your wit, and I am surprised you can find anything funny in all this."

"Sorry, Andrew, gotta laugh or you'll cry. I've just had a call from my contact. He can meet me 3.30."

Harvey breathed a sigh of relief. "Thank heavens for that! At last! When do you need to leave?"

"Now, really. We have our own way of setting up meetings."

It was approaching 1.45.

"OK, Terry, off you jolly well go. Straight back here afterwards, please. I'll be waiting."

Harvey gave James ten minutes to clear the building before he rang Richardson. The owner was out to lunch with his chief executive. Harvey left a message; no details, just a worried editor covering his own back. He replaced the phone and looked again at the brief story sanctioned for that evening's paper. It was tucked away at the bottom of page two.

Essex Police have confirmed they are mounting an urgent investigation into claims made in Friday's Gazette against one of their officers.

Short and not so bloody sweet. He returned to the papers on his desk and shuffled them and shuffled them. He could hardly concentrate. Christ! He had a worry chair at home and now he had one in the office.

It was 5.15 when James returned. The office was eerily quiet. All the production staff had gone home, so had most of the reporters. Two reporters would man the office during the nighttime hours until the floor burst into life again at 7am. Phil Calvin had stayed behind with Harvey to await James's return. He was eager to hear any developments, and also to keep the editor company. Calvin sensed Harvey was in need of support.

"How'd it go? Tell me it's good news, Terry?"

"Yes, good news, boss. Headleigh's as guilty as sin, my contact assured me of that."

Harvey relaxed in his chair for the first time that day. "I'm all ears."

"First things, first. He seemed cagier than usual. He is getting worried about being found out. But he is adamant Headleigh's days are numbered."

"Proof, Terry? Evidence?" said Calvin.

"Let me finish, please Phil. He, like us, was baffled by the lack of action in Kent on Saturday but believes something has happened there, and says something is happening tomorrow. He isn't sure what exactly as his source is edgy, too. But he told me to expect developments down there.

"Now for the real good news. He told me to have a photographer outside the Headleigh home tomorrow morning. Seems the police are planning to pay him a visit. He said it wasn't to be a dawn job, but sometime in the morning."

James stood and waited for his editor's reaction.

Harvey took a few seconds before replying. "Well done, Terry. All rather cryptic but good work. No hard proof yet, though? Nothing tangible we could wave under the police noses?"

"Not yet, Andrew. I guess that is going to come out tomorrow. I stressed that our leader wanted reassuring and my man told me there is nothing to worry about."

"You saying we are looking at a police raid on Headleigh tomorrow?" said Calvin.

"Exactly. They're playing it by the book 'cos of the seriousness of the matter. He did say to make sure our snapper wasn't obvious. Best to wait down the road a couple of hundred yards till he sees the cops."

"I need to run this by Bryan, if I can bloody well get hold of him. I can't send you, Terry, and I don't want Craig there. Phil, if I get the nod from Bryan I want you there with Jack Barnston, OK?"

"Sure, Andrew, be nice to get back in the field again. Want me to call Jack?"

"Yes, but don't tell him what it's about. Nothing at all until the morning. Just put him on standby for an early morning job. Stand by your beds. I'll ring you at home tonight once I have spoken with Bryan. Good night."

Calvin and James collected their belongings and left the office side by side. "Sorry about this, Terry. I know it's your story."

"No problems, Phil. I know it does make sense, I suppose. Enjoy the Essex air."

"I'll try. You get anything else from your source?"

James threw his head back and laughed out loud. "Yes, I sure did. Thought it best to wait before telling the boss."

"What? What did he say?"

"He suggested we kindly double his tip-off fee as this was such a juicy story."

Calvin, too, burst into laughter. "Yes, Terry, choose a very appropriate time before raising that one."

CHAPTER FIVE

JACK BARNSTON picked up his news editor at 5am on the dot. Only then did Phil Calvin explain the reason for his secrecy on the phone the previous night.

Barnston had guessed it had something to do with the Headleigh case. The story was the talk of the Gazette office and all the Press pubs. Both men lived north of the Thames so it was no ordeal driving to Essex at that time of the morning. Barnston was a 29-year-old scruffy, skinny snapper. Medium height like Calvin, he had been on the Gazette for four years after launching his career on a weekly series of papers in Hertfordshire. He wore a pair of huge, heavy-framed spectacles which sat at a permanent angle on his thin face. The glasses had bent from too much camera contact. Barnston felt comfortable wearing them this way.

He had woken at 4.25 and driven the short journey from his single room flat in Barnet to Calvin's home in Walthamstow.

Calvin was always up early for his shift at the Gazette which started at 7am. He'd set his alarm for 90 minutes earlier than usual today. He had usually switched it off after two rings; he always tried to rise quietly so as not to wake his wife and two primary school children.

The 36-year-old was dressed casually, but sported a tie for once. He greeted Barnston in a whisper as he stepped into his Astra, a one-year-old company car already with 30,000 miles on the clock.

Office gossip and the Headleigh scandal kept them entertained as they headed up the A12 to Brentwood. They had little difficulty locating St Andrew's Avenue. It lay towards the south side of a small 1980s exclusive development. The journalists admired the houses as they slowly cruised around, seeking a suitable spot to park up and await the police. They had to settle for a place on the roadside about a hundred yards from No. 37; any further and the house would have been out of vision. Calvin wasn't entirely happy.

"We stick out like a sore thumb," he groaned.

"Problem with these posh folk – they all park on their drives, don't they?"

Barnston's Astra was one of just two cars parked roadside, the other was a blue Fiesta a similar distance from Headleigh's home in the opposite direction.

Barnston had come prepared for the job. Calvin hadn't. It had been six years since he'd been door-stepping. Barnston kindly allowed him to help with the crosswords.

They attracted glances from early risers on St Andrew's Avenue. It was just after 6am when they saw their first sign of life. An old dear's poodle was sniffing the Astra; maybe it had scented something emanating from Barnston's tatty jacket. The pair smiled kindly at the tiny pensioner.

They saw three more dog-walkers, several business types briskly heading off to catch their train probably, and a few cars, real smart cars, taking their owners to work.

They had completed two crosswords and were pondering a tricky clue on the third when Barnston nudged the news editor.

"Looks like our pals may be here."

Barnston dived into his bag and pulled out his three-month-old Nikon, a bang up to date digital model with a moderate zoom lens.

Barnston had decided on the lens for the job earlier and was well prepared. He continued watching the two vehicles as he made final checks by twiddling with dials.

"Ready to rumble, boss. You say when we get out."

Calvin had expected official police cars and was surprised to see the maroon Mondeo and white Bedford van stop outside No. 37.

"Let's just wait a few minutes and see what happens. Can you grab any snaps from here?"

Barnston went back into his bag and brought out his older camera, again a digital Nikon, and quickly fitted a 400m telephoto lens.

"I'll try a few with this old beauty."

After a few seconds, three uniformed officers emerged from the Mondeo – two men and one woman. They adjusted their uniforms and walked up the driveway to No. 37. There was no sign of movement from inside the white van.

The female officer rang the bell; Barnston rattled off a few shots as soon as the door opened. Sadly, it was Mrs rather than Mr Headleigh who answered. Still, Barnston had a good shot of her putting her hand to her mouth at the sight of her early morning visitors.

Henry Headleigh appeared moments later, alerted by his wife's cries. He was at the door just as Assistant Chief Constable Alison Hayes was entering his house. She had a piece of paper in her hand. Headleigh knew what was happening in an instant.

"Sorry, Henry. We have to do this. Here's the warrant if you need to see it."

"Jesus Christ! You're here to search MY home?" Headleigh ran his fingers through his uncombed hair and tugged at the belt on his dressing gown. "I don't bloody believe it."

"Please don't make this more difficult than it already is, Henry. Please get dressed. Steve will accompany you."

"What? You're not arresting me? Tell me you're not."

"We just need to ask you some questions; at the station please."

Jane Headleigh had moved a few feet further down the hall and was crying and muttering into a handkerchief. ACC Hayes walked towards her. "I know how this must seem, Jane. Come on, let's go into the kitchen. I need to have a few words."

"Now, let's go," said Calvin as he saw two figures get out of the van. Both were tall and wearing white boiler suits. Both were gloved. "Just hang back over there by that tree until they start coming out."

"Bloody hell! It's 'The Lens'," gasped Barnston. He pointed Calvin towards a figure crouched about 40 yards from No. 37. He was on one knee and snapping away at the scene.

"What the hell is he doing here?" said Calvin. "Fuck. Anyway, no time to worry about him. Don't let him steal a march Jack. Just don't get in the bloody cops' way."

Headleigh had spotted the boiler suits, too.

"What in hell's name are they doing here? He tried to block the door but DS Steve Wickford gently took him by the arm. "Please, Henry. This is a real bastard job for us all. Let's go and get you dressed."

The third officer was Inspector Grant. He was most pained of the trio to be involved in the raid. But he was the closest serving officer to the family and had the best knowledge of the house lay-out.

He waited until DS Wickford had taken Headleigh back up the stairs to his bedroom before directing the boiler-suited forensic boys to various rooms. They collected a computer, Headleigh's briefcase and several folders from his study.

Outside, 'The Lens' and Barnston bumped into each other in the middle of the road. Nosey neighbours had begun peering through windows. Two passers-by stopped and examined the commotion for several seconds before continuing on their hurried way.

"Now what brought you out here Lensy? Thought you were living the life of luxury?" said Barnston as they awaited the action.

"Hello, Jack," smiled the semi-retired photgrapher. "You know me; don't mind getting out of bed if the pay's good. Keep my hand in."

"Who you working for today, then?"

"Anybody who'll have me. Should be a pretty penny in this, as long as no-one else joins the party." He winked at Barnston just as one of the boiler suits emerged carrying a computer. The snappers snapped away.

"Couple of bleedin' Press boys outside," the boiler suit informed Inspector Grant as he returned inside to continue the search.

"Bugger it," said DS Wickford. "Give them a wide berth. I don't think the chief'll want us rattling their cage."

The search downstairs didn't take long. They found Headleigh's mobile phone in the lounge with a few more papers. They found nothing in the kitchen; the search there had been cursory, not wanting to lurk for too long in the presence of their boss and the clearly distressed Jane Headleigh.

"Right, upstairs then boys," said Inspector Grant.

DS Wickford had already checked the detective superintendent's bedroom and found a pile of papers which would need checking. The boiler suits didn't linger in the children's bedrooms before climbing into the loft. The junk piled in there took them longest to sift through. They removed some books and another computer.

They had a quick scan around the garage and garden shed before returning to the van and driving away. They avoided the temptation of V-signing the two photographers.

Five minutes later the three police officers left, accompanied by Headleigh, dressed in civvies. He made a pathetic attempt to shield his face from 'The Lens' and Barnston – too late, they had their photos before he had realised.

"See ya, mate," he shouted to Barnston as he darted to his Fiesta. "Happy snapping."

Barnston and Calvin returned to the Fiesta. Both were keen to find out how Lensy had come to be on the scene. But first Calvin had to relay the promising news of the raid to his editor. Barnston set up his wire equipment while Calvin spoke to the office. The photos beamed their way to the Gazette as Barnston drove back. It was rush-hour and the traffic heading into London was nightmarish as usual. "Harvey happy, is he?" asked Barnston.

"Yes, I think so; hard to tell with him since this started. He said they're getting reports of some action down in Kent. It looks like Terry's source is on the button. This thing got a third gear, Jack?"

✝

There had indeed been action in Kent, timed to coincide with the visit to Headleigh's home. Fifteen officers had been involved in three raids at premises in Maidstone and Rochester. They arrested a known sex

offender in Rochester and confiscated four large boxes of pornographic material. One of the Maidstone homes was empty, the second yield-
ed two offenders who were out on parole. More than 300 videos and
DVDs were discovered in a back room, which appeared to be used as
a screening room. A huge screen almost covered a whole wall, and a
dozen small tables and comfortable armchairs were scattered haphaz-
ardly around the room.

Three hours into questioning, one of the arrested Maidstone men gave
the police a name who just might know something about this copper
Headleigh. The squealer was a heroin addict who badly needed a fix.

He coughed out of desperation. There was a guy called Mr Teen who
lived Chatham way, Haymarket Street, not sure of the number. The
police interrogators thanked him for his wise decision to assist them.
Sadly, though, they had lied about letting him have a fix. They would
do their best to let him have medical attention as soon as possible.

A team was at Chatham by 11am. It didn't take them long to locate
the abode of Mr Teen. No-one answered their persistent rings on the
bell and raps on the door. They had had no time to arrange a warrant
and were about to phone HQ for advice when a neighbour approached
them.

"Something bloody funny going on in there. Crying all day and all
night. Mind you, he looks the type to beat his kids, he does."

Right! That was all the excuse the officer needed. The inspector in
charge ordered two of his constables to break in. The door offered
some resistance but the brawn of the coppers soon won the war. Three
of the team entered the perverted den of Mr Teen. It was not a scene
that would leave their memories quickly.

The two rooms that fronted onto the street were normal enough:
sofas, armchairs, TV, dining table. The three rooms at the back of the
house turned their stomachs.

The walls were painted in garish colours, from what they could see of
the walls that is. They were covered in photographs of the vilest kind.
All featured children, boys and girls. Some of the kids were hardly out
of nappies. Many showed adults abusing their victims. The shocked

officers walked slowly through the house of horrors. The third back room had a row of five computers against one wall. All the screens were blank but two of the monitors' screen lights were on. The inspector moved the mouse of one and the screen flickered to life. He turned away in disgust.

"Looks like some sicko left in a hurry," he said.

"What's that? Shush. I heard something," said one of the constables.

"Yes, me, too. It's coming from behind there I think," said the inspector, edging towards a side door.

He carefully opened the door and saw a tiny bare room with a trapdoor; it was fitted with a new twist-type lock. Yes, there was something down there. He gently twisted the lock and lifted the trapdoor. It was pitch black but he located a switch on a side wall. He flipped the switch and a red light illuminated the basement. The screams that greeted the light sent a chill down the collective spines of the three officers.

The screams refused to stop as the inspector led his shaking men down the stairs. He stopped at the foot of the stairs and stared openmouthed at three naked girls, huddled together, quivering and shrieking in a corner.

He held out his hands as if begging them to stop. "It's all right! It's all right. We're the police. It's all right! We're here to help you." He turned to the constables. "Get Christine in here quick."

The constable furthest up the stairs turned round, sprinted back up the stairs and dashed outside. He grabbed a startled WPC Christine Arnold and blurted out his message. "You're needed inside. It's terrible. It's horrible. Quick, the chief wants you...some girls. It's terrible."

WPC Arnold shook off her colleague's grasp and hurried inside. The constable stood in the garden with his hands on his knees and cried his eyes out.

The men in the white boiler suits were there within the hour. It didn't take them long to realise it was pointless searching the sick haunt of Mr Teen; they simply stripped the place bare. Two extra white vans were summoned to haul away their cargo of perversity.

The three terrified girls had been taken away earlier. WPC Arnold had borrowed some towels and blankets from a neighbour and the girls were ferried to hospital. Medical checks would discover a variety of bruises and injuries consistent with extensive sexual abuse.

It would be mid-afternoon before a lecturer in modern languages was able to help identify the girls as Bosnians. Two of them gave their age as 12, the other as 14. Their families had scraped together 30,000 euros to have them smuggled into Britain. They were supposed to meet up with relatives in Birmingham but had been kept in the cellar for at least a month, though they had no way of telling the time. Many old men had used them. The Child Protection Unit was given control of the material confiscated from Mr Teen's house. Mr Teen, real name Frederick Griffiths, was on record as having one conviction for affray. He had no history of sexual abuse. He was on no police database.

There was, however, a record of a Frederick Griffiths taking a British Airways flight from Heathrow that day to Antigua. He had booked a late one-way ticket.

It took the forensic department four days to sift through the sordid contents, and a further month to catalogue them.

Two scientists took the computers apart, discovering more than 200,000 explicit images of adults abusing minors. The scientists later told colleagues that they had become immune to the content of the images after filing away several hundred.

The computers also contained a few hundred hours of video and links to hundreds of web sites devoted to paedophilia – many of which, detectives were shocked to discover, were located within the UK.

More than three thousand email addresses were found. The British ones would be checked over the ensuing weeks. The Kent police had scored a minor success in the war against child pornographers. What they failed to find was any reference or link to Essex Detective Superintendent Henry Headleigh.

Four piles of magazines stood out from the others. The piles were tightly bound with plain string and had a label pasted onto the top mag-azine of each pile. The label revealed they had been confiscated by Kent Police and were earmarked for destruction. Further enquiries led to the arrest of a sergeant in the CPU who had been selling confiscated material to known paedophiles for several years. He was arrested, interrogated and charged.

He looked a tragic figure in the dock as Maidstone magistrates refused bail for his own protection. His face was pale as pale could be; his eyes red and his chin marked by spots and stubble.

The baggy jogging suit hid a hundred bruises from the beatings he had received from one-time trusting colleagues. Kent police finally believed him when he said he had never heard of nor seen Henry Headleigh in Kent.

✝

Andrew Harvey was smiling for the first time since his chat with Bryan Richardson on Saturday morning. It wasn't a full-blown smile, but at least it was utilising facial muscles in need of the exercise.

Terry James was by his side and they were stood behind Gazette Picture Editor Adam Franklyn.

"They're sending the best ten for now," said Franklyn. "Phil's choosing which to send as Jack's driving. They should be back within the hour so we can have a look at the others then. Jack says he rattled off about sixty."

Eight had arrived so far. It was a shame Jane Headleigh wasn't their target as Harvey thought the one where she opened the door to the officers was a cracker.

"Great stuff. Send them to me and I'll ask Bryan down to my office. You say 'The Lens' was just freelancing so these will be going the rounds?"

"That's what Jack said."

"Hmmm. Not sure if that is good news or bad."

Harvey rang the owner. He hadn't arrived yet but had called to say he was on his way, informed his secretary.

Christ! thought Harvey. He knows this is a big day and he can't even get here in good time. He hated having his hands shackled. Richardson would only have himself to blame if they missed deadlines.

Richardson arrived at work at 9.10am in time to accompany Barnston and Calvin up the steps and through the revolving door. They informed him of their morning's work and received congratulations and hearty pats on the back.

"Tell Andrew I'll be down on your floor in ten minutes."

Richardson had Chief Executive Gary Chalmers with him and they conferred for a few minutes before storming unannounced into Harvey's office. Calvin and James were with the editor; Barnston was over at the picture desk combing through the rest of his photos with Franklyn.

"So I hear they've arrested the bastard, then?"

"Morning, Bryan," said Harvey. "We're not sure if it is an official arrest yet, but Phil says it looked that way."

"No handcuffs and no big fuss," said Calvin. "But the Headleighs were shocked and clearly hadn't been told to expect a visit. It was an official police raid; they would need a warrant for that. So, yeah, it's an arrest in my book. Give me the nod and I'll call them for a state-ment."

Calvin looked at Harvey for guidance. Both men knew how they should act as journalists.

"Yes, get on it, Phil," said Harvey, not giving Richardson any time to interfere.

Harvey beckoned Richardson over to his computer so he could exam-ine the photos. "There was another snapper there, Bryan. You'll recall 'The Lens' – used to take Royals and celeb pics. He got that snap of the Headleighs leaving the hotel the other day. Neither myself nor Terry can think how he gets involved in this."

"Ahh that slimeball. We paid him some serious cash once, didn't we? Well that's good for us that others are working on the story, isn't it?"

"Yes, I think so," said Harvey, using his soft legal hat rather than his harder editor's one. "We just need to decide how to play these photos now. I've spoken with Arthur Jacobs and he says the only issue is whether identification could prove crucial in any trial. He thinks not as

Headleigh is such a well-known public figure."

"Where is our Arthur by the way?"

"Traffic."

"Now tell me about traffic. Been stuck in it all morning. Get the photos printed out and I'll be back in five minutes; important call to make before I forget."

There was no call to make; Richardson just wanted a few words alone with his sidekick. He had felt like he was being put on the editorial spot inside Harvey's office and hadn't felt comfortable.

"What d'yer think, Gary?" he said to his chief executive when they had left the Gazette floor and were in their private lift.

"Go for it," replied Chalmers without hesitating.

"Yeah, that's what I'd like to do."

"Page one pic – nice and big; few more inside. Let them know we are not backing down."

"That's my boy. Nothing fazes my Gary."

Chalmers was a good three inches taller than his employer. It was a strange sight but he had become accustomed to Richardson's hugs. He kept his arm wrapped around Chalmers as they walked back to the editor's office. "Just tell him to stick to the facts, Bryan. The facts, nothing but the damned facts. We need to see if the police have issued a statement yet. And we don't want any floss from his crime reporter and his mystery contact."

"You're a true hero, Gary."

Low-resolution photos were now scattered all over Harvey's table. High-res ones would take a while longer to print. The editor had put two to one side. The men were poring over the photos when Calvin returned, clutching a sheet of paper.

"Well this is it, and it looks like we are not going to get much out of Essex Police today."

Calvin had phoned the media office. They would tell him nothing over the phone but would fax a Press statement. There would be no Press Conference that day and none of the officers involved was available to answer questions.

'Essex Police this morning confiscated various items from the home of a senior officer. The officer is helping police with their enquiries into serious allegations.'

"Is that it? Why haven't they named him?" thundered Richardson.

"Par for the course at this stage," said Calvin.

"Yes," said Harvey. "They'll want to check out the material they took before going public."

"Another thing, Andrew," said Calvin. "There's a bulletin from Kent Police requesting a news blackout into ongoing operations in several towns. A statement can be expected later today."

"Good. At least there is action now."

"Arthur should be here any minute. I just want his advice on naming Headleigh in the light of that statement."

"Go for it. We bleedin' well go for it."

Harvey was surprised by Richardson's interjection. Surprised but pleased. Maybe an editor lurked inside the chairman's thick skin and head.

"Yes, we go for it! Let the buggers know we mean business. What you think, Gary?"

"I agree, Bryan. What were you planning, Andrew? Big page one photo and a few more inside? Pages two and three? Do you think we should use the wife pic?"

Now Harvey was truly startled but tried to hide it. Yes, that is exactly what he would like to do as the editor of this paper.

"You read my thoughts, Gary," he tested his facial muscles again.

"Great stuff. Hit 'em when they're down. Love it! Love it!" Harvey hadn't seen Richardson so happily animated in a long time. "Let's get cracking then, Andrew. Big pics, I love big pics. Pages one, two, three, yes, I love it. Let me know if that bloody lawyer throws any spanner in the works."

As soon as Richardson and Chalmers had left, Harvey summoned his backbench team in. Within 15 minutes the pages had been roughed out. Conor O'Brien was slightly taken aback as he had been told just to leave page one open, and room for a decent slot on page two.

There would be a short story on page one, and six photos with captions inside. Phil Calvin would do the writing; big by-line for Jack Barnston, if you please.

The professional outfit swung into operation and had almost finished by the time an exasperated Arthur Jacobs shuffled into the editor's office.

"Can anyone tell me why I chose to drive today of all days? Yes, I would love a coffee, Andrew."

"Better bloody late then never," growled Harvey. "Sit yourself down and then run your eyes over this."

"So the police haven't named him but we are? Fair enough, I suppose. They can hardly deny it. His image is too well known to be an issue. Just one thing, Andrew?"

"Yes, go on."

"We are happy to say these 'serious allegations' involve child pornographers?"

"Phil, you will note, has been extra careful to say the allegations involve paedos, not that Headleigh himself is one."

"A very moot point, Andrew. But the connection is there, legally speaking."

"Well even if the police aren't coming out with the details of the allegations, we do know what they are. I don't see a problem there. If there is, we already burned our boats on Friday."

"Quite, quite. Just doing my job, old boy."

"Our leader is happy."

"Oh, all's well and good then."

"Fine. Can you just check the headlines and captions for me and then we'll get this ball rolling."

The Gazette was rolling bang on time.

"You mind playing second fiddle to the great Jack Barnston?" said the photographer to Calvin as they examined the first edition.

"Not at all, Jack. You did a great job. I'm trying to remember the last time I had a page one by-line. Certainly not this century."

DRAMATIC RAID AT TOP COP'S HOME

EXCLUSIVE pictures by JACK BARNSTON

ESSEX Police this morning raided the home of one of their senior officers.

Detective Superintendent Henry Headleigh left with three officers and is helping with enquires into serious allegations involving child pornographers.

Two other officers, wearing white boiler suits and gloves, removed several items from the house, including computers.

Report by
PHIL CALVIN

The police raid clearly took the Headleighs by surprise, as our exclusive pictures reveal.

Neighbours in the exclusive Brentwood estate were shocked by the police activity.

A terse statement from the force said: 'Essex Police this morning confiscated various items from the home of a senior officer.

'The officer is helping police with their enquiries into serious allegations.'

Det Supt Headleigh, 51, has served with Essex Police for almost 30 years.

He currently is in charge of the Child Protection Unit's anti-paedophile squad.

He is married to Jane, 48, and they have three grown-up children.

CHAPTER SIX

CHIEF CONSTABLE James McNish decided that he and Assistant Chief Constable Alison Hayes should conduct the interview.

They would treat it as an official interview, even though their colleague was co-operating and not jumping up and down demanding legal representation. They left Headleigh alone with his thoughts for an hour before joining him. Headleigh was a seasoned officer, well accustomed to the interview routine.

"Well, Henry. Sorry about the visit this morning but you will understand I had little option," said McNish as he and Hayes settled down in chairs across the table from their colleague.

"No, sir, I don't understand why you had to do it. As I told you the other day I have done nothing wrong. Have you any idea of the distress you caused Jane?"

"We're looking after Jane. We've moved her to a safe house. You may join her once I am satisfied you have told us everything we need to know. These are very serious allegations, Henry. Very, very serious. The most serious in my time as chief."

McNish was no stranger to complaints and investigations into the activities of his officers. Since he had been appointed chief constable four years previously, he had seen two officers jailed for selling drugs, one for covering up a series of car thefts, and a group from Harlow kicked out of the force for extorting money from local businesses. They had escaped jail on a technicality. An inspector in Colchester had been accused of helping a gang member get off a murder charge. Nothing could be proved but the inspector could not expect promotion.

Headleigh, a year older than the chief, was the most senior officer he had been tasked to investigate; and his crime the most serious. Child pornography produced the most violent reaction in the public, understandably, claimed McNish.

"Sir, with all due respect, you have no need to tell me how serious this is. I have had to confront my wife and my children and swear till I am blue in the face that I have no idea what is going on."

"Henry, we all want to believe you. But where the hell have these allegations sprung from, then? Tell us that," said ACC Hayes.

"Thank you, ma'am, now I get it: No smoke without fire, eh? Old school myself: innocent until proven guilty."

"Don't get cute with me Superintendent Headleigh."

"Listen, the first I knew anything about this was that story in the paper. I was horrified. I've been racking my brains and I don't have a bloody clue. How many times do I have to say that? All I can think is that it is a set-up."

"Ok, Henry. Let's say it's a set-up. Any idea who?"

"No, I don't. Well, nothing firm. But you can check my record for a list of suitable candidates. I think you will find the list is quite lengthy. None of the people on there have ever sent me Christmas cards."

"I am well aware of your record, Henry. One of the best there is. Listen, I am not doubting your success and all the solid work you have done for this force. We are doing our duty and investigating serious allegations against you. I know you would do the same in my shoes. Try and remember that."

"Yes, sir, sorry. But I am sure for your part you will appreciate how stressful this has been for me and my family."

"Of course I do, we all realise that, Henry. That is why we shall try and keep our little talks off the record for now. But, believe me, when I feel the need to make things official I will do so.

"Let's go back to last Friday. You were at Mary Edwardes's meeting and the first you heard of this was when an officer brought in the paper?"

"Yes."

"And you're telling us this came completely out of the blue? You had

had no contact from the paper? And you've no idea how they got hold of the story."

"Correct, sir. The reporter concerned has covered past cases of mine, but I have not spoken to him privately; just at Press briefings."

"Has he been covering the CPU's activities?"

"Not to my knowledge. Colin Grant keeps a keener eye on the Press. He may know."

"OK, Henry. Now what about Kent? Tell us about Kent?"

"Again, sir, I can't tell you anything. I am totally in the dark. As I told Chief Superintendent Edwardes I have been down there just the once this year for a seminar, late February."

"How long were you there?"

"Overnight. There was a seminar, and a few senior officers had dinner that evening. Jane was with me the whole time. We stayed at the Gardens Hotel along with several other officers and their partners. We drove back here immediately after breakfast."

The two interrogators sat and stared at Headleigh. They looked like brother and sister, sat with their hands clasped on the table. Then McNish got up to leave. Hayes followed him in rising from her chair.

"We need you to stay here for a while, Henry," McNish stared around the small windowless room. "Not the most comfortable of places as you well know. Can I send you anything in? More coffee? An ashtray? Something to read?"

"Coffee and an ashtray would be fine, sir. Thanks. Jane's being looked after, you say?"

"Yes, she is."

"Good, thanks for that. One final thing, sir. The vultures outside my house this morning? Who told them to be there?"

ACC Hayes reddened slightly. "I don't know, Henry. Sorry about that. It was as much a surprise to me."

"What did you make of that?" McNish asked Hayes when they had reached his office.

"He's consistent, and very believable. I did manage to ask Jane about Kent this morning. She was in a state but what she said squares with what Henry just told us."

"So you're sold on the grudge theory?"

"Yes, sir. Until we have any more information I don't see what else we can do. Who's checking the suspects?"

"Inspector Grant. Give Henry one thing, he's right about the list. Very impressive number of suspects, we have. George Travis promised to ring if the raids down there revealed any news. Bloody horrible business. But we have to keep it straight with Henry, OK? Much as we admire and respect him, let's keep it official and polite and firm. Make sure everyone fully understands that. I'd rather have Henry getting mad at me than the anti-police mob claiming we go softly on our own."

It took the Hi-Tech Crime Unit five hours to find the hidden material on the third computer taken from Headleigh's home.

The officer who made the discovery was genuinely saddened and shocked. All those involved in the investigation hoped and prayed they would find nothing to pin on the respected detective. She relayed the information to ACC Hayes.

McNish had a copy of that day's Gazette on his desk when Hayes entered his office. He had intended to ask her if she knew who had tipped off the paper. Now he had more pressing concerns.

"They're copying the files they've found so far onto disc and it should be here soon. Pretty sick stuff, I am told."

"Holy shit! This was on a computer in the loft?"

"Yes, sir, well tucked away by all accounts."

"And we are sure it had nothing to do with his official work?"

"Not yet, but they believe so. I suggest we get one of his team to check it with us. Maybe they can confirm if it has anything to do with cases they are investigating."

"Yes, good idea. Grant's second in command, isn't he? Pull him off the grudge list and get him in here."

McNish was appalled by the images on his computer screen. Hayes's face betrayed her own disgust and anger. Grant could not believe his eyes. "This stuff was on a computer at the superintendent's home?"

"Yes, the one in the loft," said ACC Hayes.

"OK, that's the one his children used to use, I think."

"You recognise any of the stuff on here?" asked the chief constable. "Any cases you are involved with?"

"No, sir. Anyway, there are standing instructions not to take material home without permission – in writing – and then we're only allowed to use police lap-tops. Christ almighty! Excuse me, sir."

"That's all right, inspector. We share your feelings. Indeed, we do." McNish sat back in his chair and rested his hands on his stomach.

"The web sites, Colin? Your squad has closed down a good number of them, haven't you?"

"Yes, ma'am. But I don't recognise the names of any of these. These look more like amateur operations; just paedos hosting their own images for friends. The Hi-Tech Unit traced any yet?"

"Yes, they have traced them all."

"All? There must be 20-odd here?"

"They have traced them all to one computer and a single Internet connection. The one found in Henry's loft," said ACC Hayes solemnly.

"Bloody hell!"

McNish interrupted: "Forgive me, Alison. So that means all this...this...material originated on Henry's computer?"

"Well it may not have originated on there, sir. It may have been sent to him on disc. But it was all loaded onto the Internet from there, according to Michelle at HTU."

McNish looked away from the screen. He had seen enough. Give him a brutal slaying over this filth any day.

"I just can't believe it," muttered Inspector Grant. But the images would not disappear from the screen no matter how hard he rubbed his eyes and forehead. "This is just too incredible."

"You're closest to him on the team," said ACC Hayes. The 43-year-old spinster had taken charge of the meeting, as the chief constable appeared lost for words. "Have you ever suspected Headleigh may be involved with stuff like this?"

"Never. Never!" Inspector Grant was emphatic.

"We'll have to confront him with this. How do you want to play it?"

"I think I need some fresh air before we continue. Is there anything else I need to know for now?"

"There is a credit card account being checked out, sir. Seems it was just used for one set of payments. The HTU seem to think it was used to fund these sites."

"Right. Back here in 30 minutes. Enjoy lunch, if you can."

McNish changed into his civvies and went for a stroll along the River Chelmer. The Chelmer was a dirty brownish-grey, but that didn't seem to bother the ducks and Canada geese. McNish leaned over a bridge and wondered what he was to do. Henry Headleigh was a pervert. Christ Almighty!

"Anything else, Alison?" McNish asked as he invited the two officers back into his room.

"Some prints on the computer match Henry's, sir. There are lots of others, mainly partial. I would guess they are those of his children."

"Fine. Looks bad all round for our hero, doesn't it?" McNish decided that he and AAC Hayes should again do the follow-up interview. Headleigh said he had no problem with their latest 'little chat' being taped. No, he didn't need a solicitor, thank you. Was he being charged?

Inspector Grant listened to the interview in an adjacent room. Grant listened intently as Headleigh reacted in horror to the news of the find.

"What utter nonsense! That computer hasn't been used since the children were there at Chrismastime. What the hell is this?"

"Your prints are on the computer, Henry," said ACC Hayes.

"Well, yes. I was up there last Christmas with Theresa. She was showing me some of her college work. I'm sure you will find Theresa's prints there, too. I am sure she would have been the last person to use it. Are you going to accuse my daughter of being a paedophile?"

"What can you tell us about a credit card, Henry? A card found at your home, and used purely for a number of payments to a web hosting company."

"I don't know what you are talking about. I have just the two cards, the same as Jane. Both are issued by my bank. Can't you see it's obviously some kind of sick set-up?"

"Are you asking us to believe that someone broke into your house and planted this material?" said an incredulous McNish? "Come off it, Henry. You of all people should not treat us like idiots. Have you noticed any payments that you could not account for?"

"Well I confess I am not the most meticulous at checking my accounts. As long as I have enough for my needs."

"What about the computer then, Henry? Had any guests recently? Unwanted guests I mean."

"What, ma'am? What do you mean unwanted guests?"

"I mean, Henry, that if you are saying this sick stuff was planted," ACC Hayes leaned on the table and stared into his eyes, "then some-one must have planted it, mustn't they? Have you had a break-in?"

"No. No, we haven't."

"The house is alarmed, obviously. You would notice if someone had broken in, your neighbours would certainly hear something. Well?"

"I really don't have a clue."

"So a large quantity of child pornography just suddenly appeared on your computer, right? In a folder titled HH."

"Henry, I have no option but to suspend you from duty indefinitely. I intend to contact the Home Office to request an outside force be brought in to conduct an official investigation."

"Jeee-sus! Are you charging me? Arresting me?"

"No, well not yet, Henry. As a mark of respect for all the good things you have done here I will permit you and Jane to use the safe house for a while. I suggest you seek legal advice as soon as possible."

Before Headleigh had a chance to reply, McNish and ACC Hayes left the room. "Can you arrange a Press briefing for tomorrow Alison? I'd like you there with me, please. I want no further comment until then. I need to speak with the Home Office and catch up with how George Travis's boys are progressing. Let's say ten o'clock. Ah, Inspector Grant. Did you hear anything in there that rang any bells?"

"No, sir. He just seemed shell-shocked."

"Yes, it's a bad time all round. I want you to drive him to the safe house. Nothing too obvious, but see if you get anything out of him. Give him two hours alone in there and then go see him. Do it by yourself, no PCs involved, OK? I can't see Henry trying to do a runner."

WPC Carley Motson had tried her best to communicate with Jane Headleigh and given it up as a bad job. She offered the distraught wife tea and sympathy and received mumbled 'thanks' in between sobbing that stopped for a few seconds before commencing again.

She reckoned they had enjoyed a minute's silence at most at the thatched cottage in Witham. As safe houses go, this was one of the smarter; more a holiday cottage than a hide-out. WPC Motson relieved her boredom by checking the house and garden every 20 minutes. There was no sign of prying eyes outside.

The cottage had three bedrooms, a lounge with satellite TV, a smaller dining room and a fully-fitted kitchen. WPC Motson had arrived for her baby-sitting role with two bags of essential groceries; she would do any shopping Jane required later in the day.

She was surprised when Inspector Grant turned up at the door as she was expecting a fellow WPC to take over the shift. She was shocked at the sight of Detective Superintendent Headleigh. He looked drawn and tired; a haggard shambling figure rather than the authoritative officer seen marching around Chelmsford HQ.

The police officers left the Headleighs in the kitchen alone for a few minutes. Inspector Grant spoke first when they were in the hall: "Jane had anything to say?"

"No, sir. She's too upset. She's barely functioning if you ask me. How is Henry?" She surprised herself by using his Christian name.

"Well he's been suspended, in case you hadn't heard. I've just had the worst 30-minute drive of my life. Total silence with a bloke I've known and worked closely with for coming up 15 years; this is all too much to take in."

They were interrupted by a knock at the door. Another WPC – again in civvies – had arrived to take over from Motson. "You won't be needed, the superintendent is here now. Carley can stay with me while we let them settle." The officers stood in the hall a few minutes longer, Inspector Grant whispering details of the day's events to the WPC. They moved into the kitchen to find the Headleighs sat at the table, neither one looking at the other. At least Jane was no longer in tears.

"We'll be leaving now. Is there anything we can get you or Jane?"

"No, thanks Colin. We'll let you know in the morning."

"OK. I have to tell you, please don't leave the house. Feel free to use the phones or the computer, but you will be aware both are monitored. You have my number if you do want anything. You can call me anytime, night or day. Goodbye."

The officers left the Headleighs in silence; a deathly quiet that was to last a further two hours. Jane had indeed stopped crying as her husband informed her of his suspension and the reasons behind it. Shock had replaced her distress; shock and deep, dark thoughts.

Eventually Headleigh rose from the table and told his wife that he would go and make the painful calls to their children.

He returned from the lounge 30 minutes later to find Jane had at last risen from the table and was making tea. He let out a deep sigh of relief at the sign of normality at last. Jane passed her husband a cup of tea.

"What are you going to do, Henry?" She never asked about the children – she had no need to as she could sense their pain from many miles away. Headleigh mapped out the rough plans he had made. He shook his head and protested his innocence yet again.

Jane moved into the lounge and switched on the TV, careful to avoid the news channels, she selected a movie and stared at an old black and white film for an hour. "I'm going to bed, Henry," she suddenly announced. "I'll take the room at the back, if that's all right. I'd rather be alone tonight. Goodnight."

No kiss on the cheek, no ruffling his hair, Headleigh turned and watched his wife disappear slowly up the stairs. He could not recollect the last time they had taken separate beds, never mind separate rooms. No, it had never happened before; never in their 26 years of marriage.

Jane was definitely not old school, he thought.

No smoke without fire, no smoke without fire, he muttered.

CHAPTER SEVEN

MORE THAN 200 representatives of the Great British Press were crammed into the room at the Essex Police Force's HQ at Chelmsford. The flashes started as soon as Chief Constable James McNish and his assistant Alison Hayes took to the platform.

The two officers sat down at a table, sipped in harmony from the glasses before them and fiddled with their microphones. There were two other tables a few feet in front of theirs. They were sagging under the weight of a battery of recording devices.

McNish and Hayes were old hands at these briefings, but had never seen so many vultures assembled before them. They had never had to answer probing questions about a perverted colleague, either.

There had been no further statement from Essex since the brief announcement of the previous day's raid. The morning papers had had plenty to go at, however. 'The Lens' had touted his photos around the national papers. True, the Gazette had enjoyed the scoop, but how many read that rag anyway? Half a mill? Maybe threequarters?

'The Lens' had little difficulty persuading picture desks to cough up the grand total of £12,000 and rising. Single-use only, mind you. I'm insisting on repeat fees for this beautiful set, lads. After all, I had to get up ever so early.

'The Lens' operated a sliding scale; the Headleigh raid images would keep his account ticking over nicely for a few months. His photos – very similar to those grabbed by Jack Barnston – vied for prominence with details of the Kent raids on that morning's front pages.

George Travis's media department had issued a much lengthier statement, though they had yet to reveal information gleaned from the Chatham house of horrors.

The news dominated the TV and radio news programmes that morning. Many were set to broadcast live from the Press conference.

McNish, Hayes and several senior officers and lawyers had been agonising for two hours what information it would be wise to release to the vultures. Wise, to cover their own uncomfortable positions; and wise, to be fair to Headleigh.

Too little information and they would have the Press hounding them; too much and the Superintendents' Association would no doubt have loud protests to make.

"Treat it as you would any other investigation," said an unwitting lawyer.

"Don't be bloody ridiculous," McNish bellowed at him. "It isn't 'any other investigation', is it? It's a bloody senior officer accused of being heavily involved in a ring of paedophiles! That's why the bloody car park is full."

They had decided to ride out the storm and hope for the best. McNish and Hayes had a vague battleplan and took to the platform with their fingers crossed. McNish commenced by informing the ladies and gentlemen of the Press that Detective Superintendent Henry Headleigh had been suspended from duty pending the results of an investigation into serious allegations.

This was a good start, news of Headleigh's suspension had not leaked out. Impatient vultures began firing questions before the chief constable could continue. He restored order with a firm voice, reminding his guests that he had agreed to answer a few questions after his statement.

The Home Office had appointed Assistant Chief Constable Frederick Hill of Dorset Police to lead the investigation. He concluded by stressing Essex Police's keenness to have this matter investigated fully and promised that the public would be fully informed of the findings. After this meeting all further enquiries should be directed to ACC Hill's investigating team.

"Right, now I will take a few questions."

"Are these allegations about child pornography?" shouted a man at the front. He appeared to be with a television crew.

"I cannot confirm the nature of the allegations at present."

"Are they connected with the raids in Kent yesterday?" a woman waving a notebook above her head.

"Of course, we are aware of the activity in Kent and I am sure ACC Hill will want to question those involved. For now I can tell you that we have no information on any connection."

McNish was on shaky legal ground and tried not to let it show.

"Is Headleigh under arrest?" a middle-aged open-necked man to McNish's right.

"At present, Detective Superintendent Headleigh is not under arrest but is assisting with our enquiries." McNish made a point of emphasising his officer's rank. The vultures could kindly show some respect.

"Has he admitted anything? Where is he being held? Are you anticipating criminal charges soon?" The questions flew thick and fast.

McNish tried to calm the mob and motioned for them to restrain themselves. "Detective Superintendent Headleigh is not under arrest. As I have said, he is currently helping with our enquiries. I am sure ACC Hill will question him later today. It will be his decision on whether any criminal charges are in order."

"Are any other police officers involved? In Essex or other forces?"

"Not to my knowledge at present, but as I have …"

"What was taken from his house yesterday?"

"ACC Hayes, would you like to answer that one?" McNish gladly handed over the baton.

"Several personal items were taken from Detective Superintendent Headleigh's home yesterday. These included papers and computers and a few other personal effects. Preliminary checks have been made and all the material will be handed over to ACC Hill."

"Is his wife involved? Did you arrest her, too?"

ACC Hayes was not a violent woman, but she would happily have shattered the woman reporter's mouth.

"There have been no allegations whatsoever made against Mrs

Headleigh. I would remind you of the chief constable's comments: no charges have been pressed as yet and Detective Superintendent Headleigh is not under arrest. Those are decisions for ACC Hill to take if and when he feels the need."

"Has Mrs Headleigh been questioned? Jane, isn't it?"

ACC Hayes had no intention of helping the scruffy vulture confirm Mrs Headleigh's Christian name.

"I would like to emphasise that Mr and Mrs Headleigh had no knowledge of our visit yesterday morning. They were surprised by it but both co-operated fully with the requests of my officers."

McNish rose from the table. "Thank you, ladies and gentlemen. I think we have told you all we can for now. I am sure ACC Hill will hold a briefing as soon as he has something to report."

McNish was following Hayes off the platform when another question was shouted out.

"Is it true Headleigh was involved with smuggling young girls into Britain?"

McNish turned his head round just in time to glimpse the questioner. He turned back without replying and continued on his path.

Henry Headleigh watched the Press conference on television. He was alone, thankfully. Jane had been up early that morning and called the local police station with a request to go out. She needed a police escort to go and buy some groceries. Christ! What had happened to her life?

The broadcasters' microphones failed to pick up the last question fired at Chief Constable McNish. Headleigh had already switched off the TV, anyway, and was at the kitchen table with the telephone and some notepaper. He flicked through his address book and dialled the secretary of the Police Superintendents' Association's D District.

How ironic that he was calling on the Association for help in fighting child pornography charges! The Association had been instrumental in persuading Government to establish a national paedophile register a few years previously.

Chief Superintendent Martin Brewster of Bedfordshire Police was the secretary of D District, which took in Essex. "Henry, can't say I'm surprised to hear from you. I've spoken to James McNish and Mary Edwardes; they tell me you are strenuously denying these allegations. What's it all about?"

"Wish I could tell you, sir. Absolute nonsense, of course. I need your guidance to help me fight it. What would you recommend I do? Legally-speaking?"

"So you're going to take it to the courts?"

"Of course, what other choice do I have?"

"Good, can't argue with your decision. Right, got a pen? Here are the details for the legal boys we recommend."

Chief Supt Brewster gave Headleigh the address and phone numbers for Feuerstein, Savage and Amrein.

"You know them, Henry?"

"Can't say as I've had the pleasure."

"No, probably not, they operate outside your sphere of work. First class outfit. Feuerstein's the man you want, Michael Feuerstein. He's handled several defamation cases for us. Never failed yet."

Brewster wished he hadn't added 'yet' and hastily continued to impress on Headleigh the services offered by Feuerstein, Savage and Amrein.

"They'll get you a top notch barrister. Last I heard they were favouring Quentin Carel-Hobbs. He's the extrovert who was all over the papers a while back for getting that rock 'n roller a pretty packet. The gay one; well he wasn't gay as it turned out."

"Yes, I've heard of Carel-Hobbs. Who hasn't?"

"Feuerstein will also be able to offer some semi-official assistance, too; a useful lot."

"Semi-official? What does that mean?"

"Well, I think it's best if he explains that to you. Has the complete backing of the Association, naturally, but we prefer to keep it at arm's length. They do seem more efficient in difficult cases like this than the regular legal investigators."

"Fine. Thank you, sir. I'll phone Feuerstein and Co today."

"I'll email them now to say you'll be in touch. Oh, and it's Feuerstein,

Savage and Amrein, not Feuerstein and Co. You know how touchy some people can be. But it's Michael Feuerstein you want. Good luck, keep the Association up to date with your progress please."

Headleigh decided to wait an hour or two before calling Feuerstein, Savage and Amrein – not Feuerstein and Co. You pompous old tart, Brewster. So Headleigh sat and waited in silence. He didn't feel like watching TV or reading.

He was on the phone when Jane returned from shopping. "Yes, sir. Certainly, sir. Two o'clock will be fine."

"Who was that?" she asked, placing three bags on the kitchen table.

"Frederick Hill, an assistant chief constable from Dorset. He's been put in charge of the investigation. He's coming round to see me this afternoon."

"Oh!" Jane busied herself with the groceries. She could not bring herself to look at her husband, it seemed. "Do we know him?"

"I know of him, but, no, never met. Listen, darling, why don't you go out somewhere this afternoon while I speak with him? I know how painful this is for you."

The words were music to Jane's ears. She couldn't stomach the prospect of being alone with her husband in that house all day.

"Yes, I might do that. I'll let the station know I'll be going about quarter past one, all right? Not sure where yet. Want some lunch?"

ACC Hill spent two hours with Headleigh that afternoon. He had Inspector Roger Casely, also of Dorset Police, with him to take notes. They began with a stroll in the garden as Headleigh related the events to Hill, starting with the sudden and shock appearance of the story in the Evening Gazette.

Headleigh's story matched the version he had been given by Chief Constable James McNish at Chelmsford.

They adjourned to the kitchen and ACC Hill probed on. There was nothing Headleigh could tell him; he insisted yet once more that he was innocent of any crime.

The Dorset officer had not expected Headleigh to reveal much that day. It was more a case of getting acquainted with his adversary, for that is how Hill perceived Headleigh. No smoke without fire. Definitely new school.

Hill promised to return with more questions once the Hi-Tech Unit had completed their tests.

Jane was not expected back until mid-evening. She was meeting some friends out of town and told her husband she had stocked up so he had plenty of choice to fix his own dinner. She had made it sound like an instruction rather than 'would you awfully mind, darling?'

Headleigh didn't mind in the slightest. The peace helped him think. He would ring Feuerstein, Savage and Amrein and hope that the Michael he wanted was not the type to leave the office early. He decided to use his mobile, just to be on the safe side.

Michael Feuerstein, a solicitor for 20-odd years, was indeed still at work and expecting his call. He was very well prepared, which was a relief to Headleigh, with the rates these boys charged. He could probably claim some financial assistance from the Association, but civil cases generally relied on the individual's pockets.

It didn't take long to determine that he did want to sue the paper for defamation of character. Yes, he was fully prepared for an unwholesome appearance at the High Court with all the attendant publicity if that is what was required to clear his name.

Headleigh hadn't seen that day's newspapers, but had learned that details of the raid at his home had been all over them. Feuerstein informed him that two papers had 'sailed close to the wind' and left themselves open for possible libel action. The rest, while linking the raid at his home with those in Kent, had been careful to avoid an obvious paedophile link.

His company would send out faxes to all national news organisations warning them not to repeat the defamatory words used by the Gazette. Feuerstein rapidly informed Headleigh of the procedure; he was aware of most of it. Then, almost as an after-thought, he asked Headleigh if he would like to avail himself of the company's extra services. This, the detective assumed, referred to what Brewster had labelled 'semi-official assistance.'

"What extra services might they be?" Headleigh asked.

"Well we often employ the excellent services of a body which goes by the rather untidy name of PUD. I did once ask what PUD stood for but I never received a sensible reply and didn't ask again.

"PUD combines the experience and talents of former detectives across the United Kingdom. The organisation does not advertise its services and only works with legal offices guaranteed by the Association. That means ourselves at Feuerstein, Savage and Amrein plus just two other offices – one in Glasgow and the other in Cardiff."

"PUD? Never heard of it."

"No, few have; the ones that have are usually officers like yourself, officers who need help. I must stress that the body is entirely legal, though some of their tactics may be regarded as unconventional. I am sure a senior officer like yourself appreciates that.

"They can ask questions in places that we would not have access to. I recommend them, especially in a case like this. Would you like me to set up a meeting?"

"Why not? Please ring me back on this number only. Thank you, goodbye."

Headleigh was watching TV when Jane returned – eventually. It was almost 10pm and she had left nine hours ago.

The TV had kept Headleigh amused – he made a note to watch it more often. No cases to work on, no criminal masterminds to track, no never-ending piles of paperwork to shuffle from tray to tray. Yes, he could handle retirement, no problem. Once he'd cleared his name.

He had been watching a re-run of '24' – a VERY American adventure/action/thriller series. This was the third season. What had Headleigh being doing when the first two were screened? He even managed to laugh out loud at the amount of action these Yankee directors managed to cram into a 24-hour day, well a good bit less than that, if you included the adverts.

Thanks heavens for re-runs and compendiums. He would positively hate to have to wait a whole week to discover how the hero escaped the excruciating torture he was enduring. Of course, the hero always survived. Batman without the cape and the Batmobile and the Batphone, thought Headleigh, recalling TV epics from his youth.

He had just watched a dramatic episode which took place in a Santa Barbara library at 7am. Did Californian libraries really open that early?

The click of the door broke him away from his reverie. Dreadful shame; he was having the most fun he had had these last few days.

"Hello, love, been gone a long time. See the girls?"

"Yes," she lied.

Jane had told him that she was going out to see a few friends from her 'circle.' They were mainly bored housewives like her, in Henry's opinion, typical suburban set, kids grown up, hubby making a decent enough living, and too much time on their hands.

"How did the meeting go?"

"Hill? Oh, love, I told him the same as I told the chief and Hayes and Edwardes and everyone else who cared to listen."

"And?"

"And his reaction was the same as the others. I am a first-class officer with a first-class record but how do I explain...you have seen enough coppers to know how we work. Facts, facts, facts. Don't let emotion stand in the way."

"Yes. That's part of the problem, isn't it?"

"What, love?"

"Emotion."

"Oh."

"Well, it's true, isn't it? Always bottling up the sordid details of other people's messes that you have to try and clear up; day in, day out."

Headleigh had wanted to tell his wife of his day, the decisions he had formulated in his mind and would be finalising in the morning, once they had had a chance to talk. He was astute enough to realise she wanted an argument and had something to get off her chest. He played along.

"Jane? You want me to come home from work and tell you about the crap I have come across my desk, day after day? The sheer filth appalls me. Forgive me for not thinking it suitable dinner-table conversation."

Jane Headleigh did not want an argument. She found herself barely able to talk to her husband.

"Henry? I phoned Jon."

"Our Jon? Jonathan?"

"Yes, our Jon. He agreed to put me up for a while."

"You're leaving me?"

"I think...I need...I need to get away. Just for a bit...I'm...I'm not sure."

"Oh."

"Jon thinks it is for the best, too."

"He does, does he?"

"It makes sense, Henry. This is a police matter, not a family matter."

"Oh great! Forgive me for being a policeman."

Headleigh was stood up now, stalking around the kitchen, the TV screen long forgotten but still flickering away the '24' re-run: Jack Bauer fought dastardly terrorists; American President David Palmer wrestled with yet another moral dilemma. Six thousand miles west of Los Angeles, Mr and Mrs Headleigh, one-time pillars of Essex society, prepared to separate.

"I'll be off early, I have told the station. Goodnight."

And Jane Headleigh retired to the back bedroom.

CHAPTER EIGHT

"FEUERSTEIN, Savage and Amrein, eh? What do we know about this mob, eh?"

"Well-established firm, set up by Feuerstein's great-grandfather about 150 years ago," Arthur Jacobs told the Gazette owner. "Had dealings with them before, outside court, thankfully."

"And our paedophile has engaged their services to fight his corner. What do we make of that, eh?"

"They do not come cheap. I assume Headleigh will be receiving assistance from police bodies, but they are not generally prone to going out on a limb in civil cases. Letters such as these are often used as scare tactics. The late, not much lamented Robert Maxwell had a particular fondness for them."

"And," Richardson was jabbing his finger in the air, "once more, can someone tell me what the cops are playing at? Why haven't they come out and said what this bastard has been doing?"

Editor Andrew Harvey replied. "These things take time, Bryan. We'll have to wait for this guy from Dorset to get up to speed with the facts; the Essex lot have shut up shop."

"I don't like it. I don't like it. I really, fuckin' don't like it!"

Terry James had decided to speak only when spoken to. It was a wise decision, he told himself. Jacobs, pretended to search for something inside the pockets of his suit – grey pin-striped was his choice that day.

The chairman had calmed down in the last five minutes. He had burst into the editor's office after his shorter than usual lunch. He had been otherwise engaged until then, but now he demanded to know why the other papers were not following the Gazette's lead and outing this sick copper as a child pornographer; he wanted to know where the hard evidence was; he wanted them to tell him one more time that they had everything under control.

The fax warning from Feuerstein, Savage and Amrein had at least grabbed his attention and focussed his mind. He had been silent for a whole minute at least, some kind of personal best for him, thought James.

Now he was back on the warpath, a quieter warpath but his displeasure was obvious.

Some of the papers had even relegated the story to the inside pages that morning, though two had changed their final London editions to give Headleigh and the latest Kent revelations greater prominence.

There was a knock at the door. "Yes!" shouted Harvey and Richardson in not quite perfect harmony. Conor O'Brien entered. "Wire snap, Andrew – Headleigh's resigned."

Richardson clapped his hands above his head and beamed at O'Brien. "Finally, a messenger brings me tidings of great, fuckin' joy."

✝

Jane Headleigh had collected her few belongings early that morning and left her husband. The tears of recent days seemed to have all dried up and been replaced by a steely determination. Headleigh made a feeble attempt to persuade her to stay.

"Sorry. I'm going. A police car will take me to the house for my clothes and things and then drop me off at the station. They insisted on knowing where I was going. I told them even though it is none of their bloody business. I'll call you when I'm ready to talk."

That was it. No kiss, not even a goodbye. And certainly not a 'good luck I hope you clear your name…OUR name.' No, Jane Headleigh had left with the minimum of fuss. Headleigh wasn't quite sure what he felt. He felt alone to fight his battle, but that didn't unduly worry him. Jane would be a hindrance rather than a help. Flying solo was nothing new to him. He had long realised that he had few close friends outside police work; it came with the territory. He was a member of the golf club – an expensive membership for the handful of rounds he played each year. He was an occasional church visitor. He could be seen at his local public house now and then, just for a couple of lunchtime pints with the paper at weekends.

It was hardly surprising that no-one had contacted him to offer their commiserations and understanding during this dreadful time. He was branded.

Headleigh walked around in his dressing gown for a few minutes, then decided to shower before getting down to business. Suitably refreshed, he made himself coffee, switched on the computer and began typing. He sat back and read over his work. Happy with it, he was dismayed to find the printer was out of ink. "Bugger it! Well a hand-written one will have to do."

He sat down at the kitchen table and wrote two letters. He gave one to Assistant Chief Constable Frederick Hill when he arrived shortly before 10am.

"Sorry about the scrawl, the printer's not working. I couldn't find any envelopes, either. Can you pass the other one to the chief constable? Thank you."

"What's this?"

"Well, read it: it's my resignation."

Dear Chief Constable
I am resigning from the force in order to concentrate on legal action to clear my name of the malicious and very serious allegations made against me recently. I emphasise that the allegations are completely without foundation.
Any further correspondence on this subject should be directed to my solicitors Feuerstein, Savage and Amrein of Smithwick Road, London. Please pass on my best regards to all the fine officers I have served with during many rewarding years with Essex Police.
Regards
Henry Headleigh
(Detective Superintendent)

"I see," said ACC Hill, folding the sheet of paper and tucking it in a trouser pocket. "You think this is a wise move?"

"I can see no alternative, can you? Should I sit back and await public castration? Well, Fred?"

"The name is Frederick, and, to you, it is still 'sir'."

"Of course, sir. You can inform the chief that I have no wish to serve out my notice, unless he insists on it."

"And you are refusing to answer any of my questions today?"

"Oh, please fire away, sir! I will assist you all I can while I gather up my things. I deny, I deny, I deny."

"You're pushing it, Headleigh."

"No, sir, I am not pushing anything. I am taking the initiative in trying to clear my name – as it seems I am the only one who cares about doing so."

There was firmness in Headleigh's voice – a far cry from his demeanour the previous day when the Dorset officer called.

"I am leaving this hole. You may inform the chief that I intend to stay at my home. Hiding was his idea to start with, but I have nothing to hide."

"Right, you will be hearing from us, no doubt."

"Sir!" Very emphatic, and loud enough to startle Hill. "I have answered questions willingly from the chief, his assistant and yourself. For the last time: I deny any involvement with that crap found in my home. That's it. If you want to speak to me again you will have to arrest me."

"We shall see. Play it that way if you wish."

"May I ask the locals to drive me home, or should I call a taxi?"

ACC Hill's eyes blazed. "I will get the station to send round a car."

Headleigh had given Jane ample time to collect her things from St Andrew's Avenue. A friendly PC had driven him home. The Witham officer had said – off the record, of course – that they all believed he was innocent. He was, Headleigh discovered, a huge fan of '24' and in considerable detail told the detective of the extravagant plots in the first two seasons. No, he hadn't spotted the library gaffe in season three. "Maybe that's why you're a detective superintendent and I'm not, sir."

"Give it time, young man. Give it time. An eye for detail, always keep an eye on the detail. There's a tip from a FORMER detective superintendent."

"Will you come back when it's all over, sir?"

"Who knows? But I doubt it, at my age. I'll be fine, now, thank you."

"A pleasure, sir. Good luck."

"Goodbye. Oh, one thing. My wife stocked up at the safe house. Hate to see good food go to waste. Please tell your colleagues to help themselves."

What a decent chap that Headleigh – for a Super. Couldn't possibly be a pervert.

Headleigh entered the house and noted the signs of Jane's visit. A few items of mail had been taken and placed on the kitchen worktop where they always kept them until opened. She had even washed some cups left over from the day of the raid.

He stretched and took in the familiar surroundings; ever so empty without Jane. The children had flown the coop and now so had his wife. Think positive, he told himself. No distractions to bother you now, old chap.

He rang Feuerstein, Savage and Amrein and had to wait a few moments before he was put through to Michael. He was surprised to hear of his client's resignation and took his time before responding.

"A good move, on balance. Yes, a good move."

"I'm glad to hear you approve. Now can you tell me where we go from here? I'm keen to get this matter dealt with as speedily as possible."

"Well we can't rush these things, Henry. Is it all right to call you Henry? We prefer first name terms here."

"Yes, yes, no problems at all." Call me what the hell you like, just get on with it, he thought.

"Have you issued a Press release about your resignation?"

"No, I haven't; never thought of that. Should I?"

"Yes, I think so. Better coming from us rather than the police, unless they have already done so."

"I doubt it. Can you handle that for me?"

"Certainly, will do that right away. The next step for us would then be to issue a writ for libel, if that is what you wish?"

"Yes, I do."

"Good. Now, generally, civil action takes place after any criminal charges have been heard. Did the police give you any indication on whether or not they would be pressing charges? Do they intend to send a file to the CPS?"

"I have no idea what the police are planning. Naturally, if they have a file they think is worth sending to the CPS then that is the correct procedure. All I know is that they say they found some pornographic material on a computer at my home. They insist it is my material. I have told them in no uncertain terms that it is nothing to do with me."

"Yes. Good. Well I can issue a writ against the Evening Gazette, its editor and the publishers soonest. I suggest we hang fire on the other papers for now."

"And this would pre-empt any police charges?"

"No, it wouldn't. Leave that one with me; I will make some enquiries. The Lord Chancellor is most eager to speed up the course of justice these days, so we may be able to seek an early hearing."

"Please try your best."

"I'll be in touch, possibly later today. The good news is we have Quentin Carel-Hobbs on board. I still have to write to him officially but he seemed keen last night when I bumped into him."

"Good, I know of his reputation. I'm back at Brentwood now if you wish to contact me."

"Maybe you could pop into town and see me soon so we can run over the details?"

"Of course, you say when. I am not going anywhere."

"Will do. You should be getting a call from a Keith Whiteside soon. He'll want to meet you, too, to help his investigation."

"Is he with the privates you mentioned?"

"Yes, not come across him before, but he was recommended for this task. Formerly with Greater Manchester CID, do you know him?"

"No. I look forward to meeting him."

"Quite. Right, anything else before I get cracking?"

"Well, my wife has left me. I thought you should know."

"Oh, dear me! Now that is not so good. Not good at all. Is it an official separation? Does she seek a divorce?"

"She didn't say. She didn't say much at all, actually. I think it is just the strain of the last few days. She plans to stay with our son in Berkshire. For how long, I am not sure."

"I'm sorry about that, Henry. Great pity, a steadfast wife always looks good in court. She won't rock the boat will she?"

"No, no, of course not. Not Jane. It's just…it's just…well, you know what they say."

"What's that?"

"No smoke without fire."

✝

ACC Alison Hayes was surprised to see the Dorset investigator with her boss when she entered Chief Constable James McNish's office.

"Hello, Frederick. I thought you were interviewing Henry again this morning?"

"He was," said McNish, and handed Hayes the resignation letter.

"Well I must say this is a surprise. So we need to go through these solicitors if we wish to question him? Is that how he wants to play it?"

"So it seems," said McNish.

"I really don't see the point in contacting them yet," said ACC Hill. "Not until we have any further evidence to confront him with. He has flatly denied any knowledge so far. Any news on the tapes, Alison?"

"Not much, I'm afraid. Neither the videotapes nor the radio boys caught the question. Sorry, but I didn't hear it, either."

"Well let me assure you, I wasn't hearing funny voices," retorted McNish frostily.

"I didn't mean that, sir."

"Oh, I wasn't having a go at you, Alison. It's just such a funny, strange business. I can't get my head round it."

"I do have a possible ID on the reporter, however. I asked a friendly local Press guy. He was down in that section by the front and heard the questioner, but there was so much commotion with people packing up their gear."

"And?"

"He says he caught something about 'smuggling girls' and saw this freelance turn round and smile. A London freelance; has his own agency in the East End. Want me to chase it up?"

"We're assuming this is to do with the Kent raid?" said ACC Hill.

"Yes, unless anyone has any information about people smuggling in Essex. God forbid!"

"So, the leak is from Kent Police? Have you spoken with George Travis."

"Yes, he was surprised. They plan to release the information by the end of the week. They were hoping to find the man who owned the house, but he seems to have fled; left the country, they think."

McNish scratched his chin before turning to ACC Hill. "This is your inquiry, Frederick, do what you have to do. Sorry I can't be more help. Alison will continue to provide you with everything you need."

"I know it's tricky for you, sir. Alison is proving most helpful."

"My advice for what it's worth is to get more hard evidence before you seek a formal interview with solicitors present. When all's said and done, he's a damned fine copper, Henry Headleigh. Be very sure of your ground before you even attempt to put him on the spot. Purely my advice, of course; it's your ball game, Frederick."

"Thanks for the advice, sir. I'll take it onboard. For now, it seems pointless charging him when all he will do is deny everything."

"Right, I'd better write to Henry. I'll reluctantly accept his resignation, keep it formal. Send one of the lawyers in to give it the OK, would you, Alison?"

✝

Timothy Raines was hardly making a fortune on his patch these days. July and August to come, and they were deathly months for good hard news stories. Everyone flew off to seek the sun – parents, politicians, and even the bloody criminals.

The 36-year-old scrawny reporter sported his faded red bomber jacket, tight white jeans and tatty trainers as he strolled along Walthamstow High Street. It was 11am and there wasn't much life in the street, just a few women browsing in shop windows and a group of teenagers, obviously unemployed and probably unemployable, loitering by an amusement arcade. Raines hadn't bothered to shave that morning. What was the point? He had no outings scheduled.

He kicked away a crushed beer can and unlocked the door to his office – if you could call it an office; one-room at the top of a flight of stairs. There were two letters for him – an electricity bill and a cheque, 45 quid for covering a local council meeting. He almost missed the thick brown package that lay underneath a pile of leaflets and free newspapers. Raines detested free sheets, all advertising and no good for a working freelance like him.

Aha! Could this be? Yes, woo-hoo. Raines counted the notes quickly and then once more, very slowly while licking his lips. There were 75 of them – 75 lovely tenners. Why couldn't he get more work like this?

His mystery man was as good as his word. Seven hundred and fifty bleedin' quid; and all for asking a stupid question at a Press conference. Mind you, he had to time it right; the mystery man was very insistent on timing.

It looked like Timothy Raines had timed it to his customer's satisfaction. Such a shame the guy hadn't left a number – he'd be delighted to offer his services any time. Prompt payers were especially welcome. Raines didn't feel like working today. He pocketed the cash, relocked his door and headed for the pub.

✝

Henry Headleigh enjoyed his best night's sleep of the week that

Thursday. He'd considered delving into one of Jane's cookery books that filled a four-foot long shelf in their kitchen, but hunger convinced him to settle for a ready-made lasagne from the freezer.

He had spat out the first mouthful; it was still cold. He checked the knobs on the cooker; he was sure it said 25minutes at 200c. He checked the packaging again and discovered it was 45 minutes from frozen. Having finally come to terms with the mysteries of modern cooking, he enjoyed his first TV dinner since the children were in their early teens. What was the name of that stupid programme they always made him watch?

He had taken a call from Keith Whiteside and arranged to meet at the offices of Feuerstein, Savage and Amrein on Saturday morning. He was looking forward to meeting the 'semi-official' Whiteside.

The rest of the evening he spent flicking through TV channels. Not finding anything to grab his attention, he retired for the night at 10.30 and before dozing off managed to get through three chapters of an historical novel Sarah had bought him for his birthday four months ago. He enjoyed a cigarette in bed for the first time in his married life.

Eight solid hours sleep later, Headleigh felt as fresh as a daisy. He shaved, showered and dressed, and decided to brave the outside world. Yes, why not? No hiding for me, he thought. He would go and buy a bloody paper.

Headleigh rarely used the row of five businesses but had occasionally stopped off there while Jane collected something or other. He decided he would walk the two miles. He was a man of leisure, so why not enjoy some fresh air?

He genially greeted neighbours who looked surprised to see him out and about. He noticed a few who were desperate to avoid contact. At one point he amused himself by wondering whether he should yell out: You won't catch anything from me, you know?

I should try walking more often he mumbled to himself as he arrived at his destination slightly breathless. Jane was a regular at the drycleaner's. There was also a grocer's, a butcher's, a newsagent's and a shop that seemed to sell greeting cards for each and every occasion.

He browsed through a rack which was bulging with magazines. He was staggered at the variety on display, and deliberately avoided checking out the top shelf. He nodded to a couple of other customers, just being polite; he had not a damned clue who they were. He approached the counter and requested four national newspapers and the local rag.

The woman behind the counter was ever so pretty, called him 'sir' and seemed genuinely amused at his use of 'local rag.'

"Never can remember the name of the blasted thing," he joked as he took his change.

"Have a nice day, sir."

"Nice might be stretching it, young lady. Let's just hope for a better one. Good morning."

Had she recognised him? he wondered. He crossed the busy road before glancing at his papers. People always turn to the tabloids first. The headline and photograph on the front page of The Daily Mirror leapt out:

FIND THIS EVIL MONSTER!

Underneath the headline was a photo of a swarthy man, late 30s Headleigh would say. He had a smile which spelt depravity. Headleigh read the story quickly. A massive manhunt was being spearheaded by Kent Police...keen to interview...young girls...naked...cowering...cellar...illegal immigrants...

The three other papers had the ugly image splashed over the front pages, though the two broadsheets had led on a speech by the Chancellor about interest rates.

By the time he arrived back at St Andrew's Avenue, Headleigh had located his own story in all four papers. It was tucked away on the inside pages. He had resigned from the police and was planning civil action to clear his name. Yes indeed, he was.

He enjoyed two hours in the back garden, drinking tea, smoking cigarettes and reading the papers, actually reading them for once rather than just zipping through the items that caught his eye.

Frederick Griffiths – aka Mr Teen – was now Public Enemy Number One. Headleigh was glad to put that story behind him and move onto the economy, foreign affairs, letters, book reviews and even a smattering of sport. He would have some lunch and then maybe tackle a crossword.

He pottered around for the rest of day, dived into the historical novel, failed miserably with two crosswords, and made several sheets of notes for his meeting at the lawyers the next day.

After dining from the freezer again, he decided to call the children. He'd been surprised there had been no messages from them on the answer-machine.

The girls were as well as could be expected under the circumstances, tearful but bearing up. Yes, they had heard about mum, Jon had phoned. Really sorry, dad.

They seemed distant, which disturbed him. Even Sarah, who always had time to chat away with the old man on the blower, seemed in a rush to get to some meeting. "A meeting at 9.20 in the evening, Sarah?" he had felt like asking, but the father in him won over the detective.

He sorted his papers for the morning and went to bed with a heavy heart.

✝

Keith Whiteside? No, Chief Constable James McNish didn't know a Keith Whiteside.

"Formerly with the Manchester Force, you say, Alison?"

"Yes, sir. DCI Greater Manchester, retired two years ago. A real hard so-and-so. Impeccable record, officially. The word was, though, that he didn't mind who got trampled in his pursuit of villains; he had a particular brand of justice, so I am told: squeeze them till they squeal or keel."

"And now he's working for our Henry, eh? Interesting. You spoke with him?"

"Inspector Grant thought it best that he pass him onto me to give the OK. He's been employed by Headleigh's lawyers and wants to come here on Monday. I said 'yes' but said I would check with you first, sir. Or would you prefer me to go through Frederick?"

"Thanks for telling me first. I'll let Frederick know."

"Sir, I should point out that they have had similar dealings."

"Similar dealings?"

"Yes, Frederick was called upon several years ago to join another Dorset investigating team. Frederick was a DI at the time and Trevor Jones was his ACC. They looked into a complaint after a man died in custody. Whiteside was the last officer to interview him."

"And?"

"Whiteside busted a major protection racket during the investigation. Some drug gangs were 'dealt with', as he would put it, during the case. He was commended, the plaudits rolled in and no evidence was found by the investigators to warrant charges."

"I see. Thanks for that, Alison."

"I've emailed the file to you, sir, if you want to read it later. There is one thing that didn't make the file."

"Come on, Alison, it's not like you to be backward at coming forward."

"Well, sir, I hate tittle tattle, but I had a chance to talk with ACC Jones at the Solihull conference two years ago. I shared a table with him and two Yorkshire officers. Trevor got very drunk and let slip that they knew all along that Whiteside had beat the living daylights out of this guy in custody because he had battered his wife and child."

"And covered it up? Really?"

"No evidence. No hard evidence, sir. But he said the Manchester boys really knew how to make visitors feel unwelcome; even high-ranking police visitors."

"Let's make sure he gets a proper welcome here, but do let me know if he steps out of line."

CHAPTER NINE

RAY LAWRENCE was to Cheam what Timothy Raines was to Walthamstow – another freelance reporter searching for crumbs to sustain him through the summer months.

He managed to get by doing anything asked of him, the occasional advertising feature, or maybe a few reviews of amateur plays no other journalist wished to attend, and he'd knock into shape the editorial for the local racetrack's programmes.

He'd tried and failed to break into the Wimbledon tennis circuit; nothing doing there as the big boys had it sewn up.

He was enjoying a welcome tea-time pint at The Harrow when he was tapped on the shoulder. He turned round from the bar to peer slightly upwards at the dirty face of a man who had clearly seen better days. It was difficult to discern which held more dirt, the guy's face or his clothes. The guy was tallish, but Lawrence wouldn't like to guess his age; not unless he'd had a bloody good wash first.

"And what might you be after?" he said, not bothering to hide his contempt. Christ! This tramp didn't half stink, too.

"You're the reporter fella, ain't yer?" the tramp tried to push his glasses back on his nose but they slid back to an angle. The frame was held together by sellotape, and there was a crack in the corner of the left lens.

"I might be. Who wants to know?"

"Got summat yer'd be interested in."

"Oh yeah? Like what?"

"You know them guys on the nationals, eh? Don't yer?"

"What is it you want mate? I'm trying to have a pint, OK?"

"Picture. Good 'un. Worth a coupla ton I reckons, to them big papers wot pays."

Lawrence tried to remain indifferent, but his interest was aroused. It wasn't every day a smelly tramp came touting pictures down at The Harrow on Cheam High Street. Not pictures worth 'a coupla ton' for sure. "Well, how about we have a look at this picture, mate?"

"Not here. Too many geezers watching. See ya outside in a minute – in the car park round the back."

The tramp shuffled towards the door. Lawrence noticed his trousers were too small for him, and his shoes split and covered in dust. He waited a minute, wondering whether to follow or not. He took a healthy sup from his lager and called across to the barman.

"Watch my pint, Alf, would you? Just got to pop out a minute."

The tramp was waiting in a corner of the car park, trying to light a dog end he clearly just found there.

"Right, let's have a look at this picture, then."

The tramp pulled out a square Polaroid. He shook off a filthy piece of tissue paper and a sweet wrapper that were attached to it. He picked up the tissue and wiped the photograph with it. Rather than hand it over, he held it up for Lawrence to look at it.

"This guy 'ere," he said pointing to a man on the left of the photo, "he's the one whose mug was all over the papers yesterday. The one with those young girls down in Kent."

Lawrence peered at the photo. The quality was poor but, yes, he clocked Mr Teen.

"And this geezer over 'ere," said the tramp, his grimy finger pointing at a second figure. "You know who he is?"

The face looked familiar. Lawrence was wracking his brain for a name when the tramp came to his rescue.

"He's that copper who got the sack, innit? The one they says a pervert."

Yes, it was indeed that Essex detective – Headleigh.

"Not the best quality is it, mate? Got any more?"

"Naah. Just the one; me mate's it is. He asked me to flog it for him – reckons a coupla ton to a big paper. Wanna buy it, then?"

"Where and when was it taken? Your mate take it, did he?"

"Yeah, he found this camera. You know the ones with the picture coming out of the front?"

Lawrence nodded. Yes, a Polaroid; get on with you smelly creep.

"Well he took that snap down Maidstone way last year. September he said. Those geezers were at one of those places; you know, the ones where they 'ave the young 'uns."

Lawrence masked his disgust.

"I don't know, mate. If it was better quality maybe 200 quid, but not for that, sorry. Be nothing in it for me at that price; not if I had to take it into London and all that."

Lawrence made as if to walk away.

"Aww, go on, do a bloke a favour?" The tragic figure began polishing the photo with the filthy tissue, harder this time.

"Tell you what, mate. You look like you could do with some decent clothes on your back so I'll give you 50 for it." Lawrence pulled his wallet from his trouser back pocket.

"Fifty! Come on, guv, let's call it a ton? I've got to give me mate 'alf."

Lawrence stared at the tramp and felt a genuine pity. The pity was fleeting, as it usually is with reporters.

"Tell you what, I'll make it 70. That's the best I can do. The risk's all mine, don't forget."

He held out three 20s and a 10 for the tramp to see and smell. The mucky paws reached out and grabbed. He speedily stuffed them into his left hand pocket and handed over the photo and the tissue. The tissue made Lawrence recoil.

"You're a hard man, for sure," said the tramp and began shuffling away. He turned back to mutter at the reporter. "You didn't get it from me, mind you. Don't go saying that. I don't want no trouble with the law."

Lawrence walked back to the bar. No mate, I didn't get it from you, he smiled. Detective Sergeant George Lewis was smiling, too, as he discarded his rags.

✝

The tramp would not have got 70 quid from Keith Whiteside. No, indeed, the tramp would have been lucky to escape with the skin still on his back.

Whiteside, 48 but looking six or seven years younger on a good day, was as cosy as cosy could be for a man his size when Henry Headleigh was introduced to the office of Michael J Feuerstein of Feuerstein, Savage and Amrein.

"Two minutes, Henry. Call yourself a copper! Two minutes late. Keith Whiteside, former loyal and trustworthy servant of the Greater Manchester Police Force. Though why we should consider ourselves greater than the regular Manc cops is beyond me."

It was a joke, but almost lost on Headleigh as he gazed for a second at the daunting figure before him. They shook hands. The handshake lasted slightly longer than Headleigh was used to. If it had been a trial of strength, the Essex man would have conceded at first touch.

"Pleased to meet you, Keith. First name terms here, so I am told. You may call me Henry."

"Already have, squire, in case you didn't notice." Whiteside stood rocking on the balls of his feet as Headleigh turned to the oak desk.

"And you must be Michael. Pleased to meet you." Headleigh walked towards the desk and shook hands with his lawyer. He made sure that Michael J Feuerstein of Feuerstein, Savage and Amrein received the firmest Headleigh grip possible. Not in the Keith Whiteside class, but a no-nonsense handshake all the same. There was steel in Headleigh's spine that day. Steel in his spine and in his handshake.

Michael J Feuerstein, physically, was dwarfed by his two guests. They were of similar height, but the northern 'semi-official' one weighed at least three stone more. He was grateful for the arrival of his client, if only to spare him from the football chatter of Whiteside.

"Yes, Henry, I am Michael. Pleased to meet you. Thank you very much for coming on a Saturday, gentlemen. Open all hours here." His forced laughter was not reciprocated.

"I have been telling Keith that you want this matter resolved as speedily as possible, Henry. I suggest we start with you telling us the story from the very beginning."

Headleigh did as instructed, and it didn't take him long. He also handed his lawyer and the large 'semi-official' Whiteside copies of the notes he had printed out.

"Thank you, Henry. As we discussed, I have sent out notices to all major news outlets warning them not to repeat the libellous comments. So far, they are on their best behaviour, God bless them. You are fully aware of the consequences of going full tilt into court? The publicity?"

"Yes, I am. I just want this whole mess sorted out as soon as possible. I cannot stress strongly enough the sheer…sheer…outrage I feel. A whole week has gone by, well just over a week, and I have rarely felt so drained in 30 years. I realised last night, lying in bed, that I felt so shattered because everything I said was hitting a brick wall. I have told everyone that I have nothing to hide, that I have done nothing wrong, and all I see are my words bouncing back at me from this brick wall."

"Quite, Henry, I know this is a terrible ordeal for you."

Whiteside remained silent, allowing the lawyer to utter words of reassurance. But he was watching. He was watching the back of Headleigh's head; and the way his body sat; and the way he occasionally shuffled his feet.

"Right, gentlemen, I think this meeting has been fruitful. I will start things rolling on Monday, officially. The writs will go out and I will confirm Quentin's appointment as our Silk."

"Ahhh good, old Quentin! Have you heard this guy speak, Henry?"

"Not in person, Keith, can't say that I have."

"You're in for a treat, believe me."

"Thank you, Keith. But I'm not here for a treat. I've been accused of being a paedophile and I am here to clear my name. Kindly remember that, please."

Oh, you're good Henry Headleigh. Very good; but I'd heard that.

"Well, I think I have all I need for now, Henry," said Michael J Feuerstein, rising from his seat. "Keith here will be responsible for providing the detailed dossier, of course. Now, if you gentlemen will please excuse me, I have things to do. Please feel free to use Rachel's..."

"That won't be necessary, squire. Don't know about you, Henry, but I could murder a pint."

✝

"So, the wife's left you, then." A question or a statement?

"Yes," confirmed Headleigh.

"And it's purely because of this muck that started flying last week? There's nothing else I should know about is there?" said Whiteside, nestling a pint of best bitter in his hand. He preferred to do his drinking at the bar, but had steered Headleigh to a quiet alcove at the Royal Garter.

The pub would have been thriving during the working week, packed with various people, mostly from the legal world. It opened for several hours on Saturdays, and turned over a tidy profit from tourists and the few Saturday workers. The two former police officers had no difficulty finding a quiet spot that day.

"No, Keith, there is nothing else. No secret lovers, no blazing rows – well nothing on my part and I would be amazed if Jane had anything she was hiding from me."

"So she just upped and left because of these allegations, eh? Not very loyal if you ask me."

"I won't disagree with you. She took it all extremely badly. I think the raid did it, but, yes, I was surprised and disappointed. And sad, very sad that a woman I had lived with for more than 25 years seemed to distrust me. She couldn't speak to me, or she wouldn't speak to me. Not like I was used to. Her eyes seemed to freeze if they caught mine. A strange, sad and horrible feeling, Keith."

"I can imagine. You think she'll be back?"

"I don't know, Keith, and to be honest I am not sure if I care. I will wait for her to contact me."

"Have the police interviewed her yet?"

"Not formally, to my knowledge. They did look after her for a few hours on Tuesday after the raid."

"And she told them nothing?"

Headleigh leaned across the low bench and rested his hand on the muscled forearm of his questioner. "She told them nothing, Keith, because there is nothing to tell. Are we clear on that?"

Whiteside looked down at Headleigh's hand and then into his client's eyes. Headleigh let his hand remain there a second longer. He would not be intimidated by this giant.

"Yes, we're clear on that, Henry," said Whiteside and returned to the notes again. "Do me a favour, though, would you? Don't touch me again, OK?" He spoke offhand, but with a hidden menace that managed to force a muttered apology out of Headleigh.

"So when I visit your pals – or former pals – on Monday, what am I looking for? Someone with a grudge, is that it?"

"I can't think of anyone else who would do such a thing. And, believe me, I have been doing a lot of thinking these last few days."

"Let's start with personal enemies before we get to the cop work. Anyone outside the office who has it in for you? Or might have it in for you? Ever had an affair Henry?"

"No, I bloody well haven't."

"Keep your voice down. It's not unusual you know. Don't tell me our Essex police force is outside the national norm. All taken holy vows have they?"

"I have never had an affair, Keith, and nor has Jane. I am convinced of that."

"Fine. I had an affair once; messy business. But you don't want to hear about that. Anything else you can tell? Any non-police work I should be checking out?"

"Not that I can think of. I rarely socialised much; a few dinners and dances, generally to do with police functions or Jane's causes. Bit of a workaholic, I suppose."

"And you've no outside business interests?"

"None."

"Well we can rule out home life then. That's a start. Let's have another pint. Same again?"

"Sure. Thanks."

Whiteside returned from the bar clutching a full pint and his own, a third of it had already disappeared and froth remained round his mouth.

"Suppose this effluence grows on you after a few pints, eh? Cheers, Henry! Work then, let's talk about work."

"That's all I can think of; someone with a grudge, someone I've put down, I would say. I am hoping that Hill and his team are going through my records and checking names. But, as I have said, there will be a lot of names on my files."

"An impressive record, I am told. But, before we get to that, let's examine how this stuff got onto your computer. You say it was on a computer you seldom used?"

"That's right; a computer we kept in the loft. We had it converted a good few years ago and the children used it as a study, playroom, junk room. It's quite sizable; they would have friends up there all night sometimes. They loved that room," Headleigh's eyes seemed to be gazing far away, "and some bastard goes in and plants this filth."

"And you never used this computer, right?"

"Well, I never used it for anything of my own. I would sometimes go up there with the children and they would show me things; games they were playing or work they had done. This was the third computer they had gone through. Two and a bit years old. But, no, I never used it for myself. Never."

"Kids have left home now, haven't they? When was the last time any of them used it?"

"Last Christmas. As far as I am aware it hasn't been touched since. In fact, I haven't been up into the loft since Christmas."

"But someone has, Henry, someone has. An intruder, then. Yet you say you have had no break-in, and have seen no signs of a forced entry. You have a security alarm; fitted by the police was it?"

"No, a private firm. A local business run by the husband of one of Jane's friends."

"Would this husband have access to the security code?"

"No, he showed us how to work it and then made a point of telling us to change the code to something we could all easily remember. Jonathan chose the code. We had flown back from holiday three days earlier on a 747, so he suggested that as the code."

"And who knew this code?"

"Just the family; me, Jane and the children. I can't believe any of them would be stupid enough to hand it out, if that is what you may be thinking."

"Fine. So we've no forced entry and we've ruled out someone fixing the alarm – I would like to check the alarm, though – and let's assume these images were planted after Christmas."

"They were, the police did tell me that some of the web links were relatively recent. I am sure you will find out more about that when you visit them. You have the paperwork from the lawyers don't you? So the police know you're acting for them on my behalf?"

"Yes, of course, Henry. They are obliged to give me access. Bit of a grey area between the civil and criminal stuff. But I'm used to working in grey areas. I am sure they will co-operate fully."

"Yes, I like to think they will."

"Back to your computer; no break-in so we don't yet know how this bloke – or woman – got into your loft, do we? Had any parties at your place since Christmas? Any gatherings where people would be milling around?"

"No parties, no, nothing like that. We've had four or five small dinner parties; a maximum of three couples, mainly friends of Jane's. I can't for one moment believe any of them would be involved."

"What about workmen? Had any home improvements that would require giving access to workers? New windows are all the rage."

"No."

"Any plumbing? Electrical work? Anything like that?"

"Well there was a blockage in the kitchen sink a few weeks ago. I recall Jane being angry because she missed a train, I am sure she used a local plumber who she knew."

"So we're none the wiser how your visitor got access to this computer. I'll have a better idea when I see that lay-out. Monday morning all right with you? Nice and early before I go to HQ."

"Yes, Monday's fine."

"Thirsty work this. One for the road? Just a few more questions."

"Sure."

"Your shout, pint of best please."

Whiteside gazed around the darkened pub as he awaited his drink. Not a bad boozer, he thought. More upmarket than his local back in Stockport, but tasteful. The customers all seemed to be middle-aged. Whiteside liked that in a pub; no loud youngsters ruining a working bloke's ruminations.

A series of old pictures on a nearby wall caught his eye and he rose to have a closer look. A public execution at Newgate, a limp figure hanging from the gallows, a masked hangman and a baying crowd.

"Those were the days, eh, Henry?" Whiteside pointed to the wall as he took his pint.

Headleigh stole a brief look at the painting. He smiled at Whiteside and resumed his seat on the bench.

"Right, we don't know how they broke in, but let's have a think about who. We've decided it's got something to do with the job. Any particular bad lads who might have it in for you?"

"Take your pick," said Headleigh, waving his hand at nothing in particular.

"You know what I mean; anyone who swore revenge as he was led from the dock? Any special case? A nutcase?"

"Keith, I HAVE been thinking, bloody hard. Too many years, too many cases. I have been responsible for sending down murderers, muggers, rapists, drug dealers, robbers, thieves – you name it and I've done it."

"What about paedophiles, Henry? What about those sick bastards? How many of those have you nailed in your new role? Been at it almost a year now, haven't you?"

There was something in the way Whiteside phrased the question that Headleigh didn't like. But the Mancunian just looked at Headleigh from over the rim of his pint.

"Forget the past for now, Henry, and tell me about this role with the CPU. You must come across some pretty sick stuff every day, and some sick characters I bet?"

Headleigh leaned back. The bench was bloody uncomfortable and he soon regained his upright position.

"Yes, there's no shortage of sick people out there. We've had considerable success, but I can't think of anyone who would or could have done this. My role as senior officer was mainly above the serious dirty work, so to speak. My officers dealt with investigations at ground level."

"Lucky you."

Headleigh ignored the comment and continued. "I've appeared in court once or twice, usually to give evidence where an undercover officer needed protection. That sort of thing. I would present the police case, even though I hadn't been at the sharp end.

"My team has been finding its feet and most of our successes have involved child abusers rather than hardcore paedophile rings. I can't think I've made any deadly enemies, not compared to past villains I've had sent down."

"What about a pre-emptive strike?"

"Pre-emptive?"

"Any cases you were working on? Any cases where someone may think you were getting too close for comfort and wanted to halt your progress? Throw a spanner in the works."

"I see. Good call, but off the top of my head I can't think of any. Maybe you can check the ongoing files at the station?"

"Don't worry, I fully intend to." Whiteside sat back and enjoyed his pint. The hard back of the bench didn't seem to trouble him. Consciously or subconsciously his eyes returned to the Newgate hanging.

"Monday morning, then? About eight-ish?"

"Sure, I'll be there by eight. Let's have just the one more, eh, Henry? You wouldn't want to leave a poor northern boy down here all on his own with so much time to kill now, would you? Just a couple more questions. My shout."

Before Headleigh had time to reply Whiteside had reached the bar in five huge strides. Four points on Saturday lunchtime! Unheard of in the Headleigh family, but just a warming up session for Whiteside.

Whiteside didn't have any further questions, well not on the record. Headleigh spent an uncomfortable 20 minutes being quizzed on personalities. Whiteside wanted to know the tiniest details of those Headleigh worked with; friendly faces, ones he could trust, when to watch his back. What was McNish like? Was he a good chief? Loyal to his staff? Did he have any dark secrets?

Headleigh, of course, knew that office gossip made the world go round. He'd quite enjoyed it during his time as a DS. He was above that now, relying on his trusted subordinates to be his eyes and ears in the backrooms.

Having finished his pint, he visited the men's room and then told Whiteside he really did have a train to catch.

He walked a little light-headedly to Liverpool Street Station. He needed the walk and could always catch a later train. He wasn't sure whether or not he would have liked to work with Keith Whiteside 'officially' but he was a rather impressive character.

But what did he have against ACC Frederick Hill? No, Frederick 'Fucking' Hill, he had said. I'll have to check that out.

✝

Headleigh was feeling down as he stood in his kitchen, stirring a large pan which contained a bizarre concoction of vegetables and strips of beef. This was a big adventure for him, but he hadn't paid too much attention to the detail of the recipe in Jane's Chinese cook book. Still, it made a change from Sunday roast.

He'd had another excursion to the newsagent's that morning, and then enjoyed an afternoon in the garden with the thick papers and supplements; not a mention of his name in any of them.

He was down because he had left messages for his two beautiful, bright girls and they hadn't returned his calls. Maybe they were out having fun, he told himself. Yes, I hope so.

He had fought the urge to ring Jonathan. He didn't want Jane answering the phone. She could bloody well call him when she was ready. What price loyalty? Answer me that, would you?

The shrill of the phone interrupted his stirring. Ahh, Sarah or Theresa? He dashed over to the other side of the kitchen and picked up the extension.

"Hello." He never gave his name or number when taking calls at home. Training.

"Henry Headleigh? Is that Mr Headleigh?" He didn't recognise the voice.

"Yes. Who am I speaking to?"

"Good evening, sir, my name's Pete Grayson. I'm with The Daily Mirror and I'd just…"

"I have nothing to say to the Press. Please do not ring this number again."

"Can you just tell me how you know Frederick Griff…"

The phone went dead before the vulture could finish his question.

CHAPTER TEN

THE MIRROR had been careful. A small 'teaser' appeared on page one, luring the reader inside to page five and a four-column photograph; that was as big a blow-up as the art department had claimed possible, considering the quality of the Polaroid.

PICTURE EXCLUSIVE screamed The Mirror.

THE COP AND THE MISSING PERVE

The acting editor had had no qualms about branding Frederick Griffiths aka Mr Teen a pervert. He had a record and a well-documented file, according to the paper's sources in Kent Police. They had been careful not to label Henry Headleigh anything other than an 'Essex detective who sensationally retired last week to fight a legal battle.'

The connection was there, however, as any decent lawyer would tell them. It was a risk they were happy to take, and they handed over £2,500 to Cheam freelancer Ray Lawrence.

Gazette owner Bryan Richardson didn't like it, not one little bit. It was his story, his fuckin' story, wasn't it? Why didn't his paper have that picture? "Tell me that, Terry James, why didn't we have it? Your source dried up, has he?"

Andrew Harvey jumped to his reporter's defence. "You can't blame Terry? I took him off the story, and as he's already said his contact is scared of being discovered so he is keeping a low profile. Phil, you manage to find out how they got hold of it?"

"My friend says a freelance gave them first refusal," said Phil Calvin. "Seems it came out of Kent rather than Essex. They paid a pretty penny for it – out of our league."

"I'll determine what is out of our fuckin' league," shrieked Richardson. "Nothing is out of our league, not on this bleedin' story for certain."

"At least it strengthens our case, Bryan," said Harvey.

"Fair enough, Andrew. Small bleedin' mercies. But I still don't like it."

✝

Assistant Chief Constable Frederick Hill didn't like it either. "This is out of control," he complained to the room rather than the Chief Constable of Essex. "We're supposed to be running this investigation, not the damned newspapers."

"I know, I know. Bloody strange business. I had George Travis on ten minutes ago. That was the first he knew of the existence of the photograph. He says it could have come from the Chatham house; there were hundreds of Polaroids there. But he doesn't suspect any of his officers would have been responsible for selling – he was adamant about that."

"Some people would sell their souls for a few quid. We know for definite that they sell their kids." ACC Hill stalked around the room.

"How's your investigation going so far, Frederick? Care to share anything with me? Not that I wish to interfere."

"Slow, sir; nothing else to report. Well apart from this photograph. One of my men has a call in to the editor, requesting a meeting. I can't see them refusing to hand it over. Hopefully, he'll be able to find out how it ended up in their grubby hands."

"Looks bad for our Henry," sighed James McNish. "Bloody newspapers."

"Bloody newspapers indeed, sir. I'm still puzzled as to how the Evening Gazette could report that we were investigating Headleigh before we actually WERE investigating him."

"A leak you mean, Frederick? A leak from within my force?"

"I'm not saying that at all, sir. I mean there was nothing TO leak at that time. I hope to have an insight to that later in the week. I have a meeting scheduled with the Gazette editor. He told me I could speak with the reporter but only in the presence of a lawyer. They will willingly cooperate but he insisted their sources are sacrosanct."

"Sorry to push you out, Frederick, but I really have things I should be getting on with."

"Sure, sir. I will be out of the office most of the day. I gather we are expecting a visit from a private investigator employed by Headleigh's lawyers."

"Yes, I have been told. I said to go through you and you would make certain they had access to all our material."

"Well I know the investigator – there's a bit of history between us so I'll leave the men to deal with him."

✝

Christ! What time is it? Headleigh glanced at his alarm clock: 6.30, it informed him. He swung out of his bed and was putting on his dressing gown as he rushed down the stairs. Who on earth could be calling at this time? He opened the door to be greeted by the unshaven face of Keith Whiteside.

"Morning, Henry; bit earlier than I said, but I thought you wouldn't mind in the circumstances. May I come in?"

"It's half past six, Keith! What circumstances?" Whiteside walked through the hall into the kitchen, glancing left and right to take in his surroundings.

"Why don't I put the kettle on and then perhaps you can tell me what this is about?" He threw The Daily Mirror on the table and went to the sink to fill up the kettle. He turned to watch Headleigh flick inside to page five. He didn't bother to ask his host whether he preferred tea or coffee; he decided they both would have coffee and heaped generous spoonfuls into two mugs.

"Not exactly David Bailey, is it?"

"Bloody hell! This is...this is...I don't know what the hell this is!"

Whiteside waited silently while the kettle boiled. He peered through the window into the garden. There was a large patio area with potted plants, shrubs and a small flower circle in the centre. Whiteside wasn't what you would call green-fingered. He liked the look of the lawn. It stretched back 60 or 70 yards and was well-manicured. Looks like Henry had the lawn mower out yesterday. A six-foot high fence separated the home from one in the next street.

"There you go, Henry; hope you like it strong. I do." Headleigh was still looking at the paper and didn't bother to say thanks. "News to you, is it?"

"Yes...yes, it is. But I did get a call last night. Someone from the Press. But I just cut him off. I think he said he was from The Mirror. "Listen, Keith, this is a bolt from the blue. I have no idea who this...creature is."

"Are you telling me the photograph is a forgery?"

"It must be. What other explanation could there be?"

"You know what Henry? I believe you. I really believe you, and I am not a man who easily believes people."

"You've got to believe me. I'm counting on you...you and Feuerstein."

"Well our Michael may take a bit more persuading. It was he who called me last night. Dreadful panic he was in. I managed to calm him down and told him I'd be your personal paper boy. He'll be calling you later."

"What are we going to do?"

"Well you, Henry, are going to have a bloody good think while I have a look around this impressive place of yours. I assume you don't mind?"

"No, of course, not."

"Meanwhile, you, Henry, are going to think harder than you have ever had to think in a long while. Who the fuck has got it in for you? Who, Henry?"

"Don't you realise I have been doing little else? Do I look stupid? Isn't that what I have been saying all along? Christ Almighty!"

"Ok, Henry, calm down. There's no need to get riled at me, my friend. I've just told you I believe you. I believed you on Saturday, if you want to know. But this piece of shite confirmed it. All a bit too pat, isn't it? One of the finest detectives the grand old county of Essex has been blessed with suddenly turns into a raving pervert overnight. Pull the other one."

"Well it's a relief to know I am being finally heard. But, Christ, Keith! I don't have a clue!"

Whiteside drained his coffee and put the mug on the worktop by the sink. "Why don't you go and freshen up while I have a scout round? A good, really hot shower clears the mind, I find. You need to think, Henry. I can't do that for you. Alarmed front and back, I see. Where's the box?"

✝

All the officers at the Essex Police HQ had been forewarned. They were to co-operate fully with their guest, but watch your back, your front, your sides. Inspector Roger Casely apologised for his chief's absence but ACC Hill had important business to attend to out of town.

"Such a shame! I was looking forward to meeting old Frederick again. Please pass on my best wishes."

Casely showed Keith Whiteside around the investigating room, and introduced him to the officers who were assisting the Dorset duo. "Just ask and we'll be glad to help. There's a desk and a telephone over there for you. If you require any material copying one of the officers will oblige," said Casely in his most formal tones.

"I should hope they jolly well will; after all, we're all in the same boat, aren't we?"

"Sorry? What do you mean?"

"I mean we're all trying our damnedest to clear a first-class cop, aren't we?"

Casely did not reply. He turned away and busied himself with a small bundle of papers on his desk.

"Well aren't we?" Whiteside shouted at his loudest, and that was loud. His voice carried out of the room and down the hall, making a few of the clerical workers stop and look up. "Heaven help us! Or more accurately, heaven help poor Henry. With friends like you lot who needs enemies, eh?"

Inspector Casely replied over his shoulder: "If you could get on with what you have to do Mr Whiteside and let us get on with ours."

Casely returned to his work. He felt uncomfortable enough on jobs like this, his second investigation into an officer from another force. The locals were on their best behaviour, especially when ACC Hill was around, but the atmosphere was formal and polite; none of the usual banter in crime rooms up and down the land. The presence of the brawny Mancunian only added to his unease. Was his boss really being diplomatic in avoiding this Whiteside? Or was he scared? Casely had not been in the company of the former detective long before he realised he could indeed be quite scary.

Whiteside plonked his briefcase down on his allotted desk and walked around the room, mimicking a silent-movie cop with his hands behind his back. He glanced rather than inspected a large noticeboard that dominated one wall of the room. He treated the wall covered with photographs equally casually.

"I really hate windowless rooms," he said to no-one in particular. "Still, we don't want people peeping in do we? Not with all this mucky stuff in here."

The lack of response amused him. He knew, he just knew that none of the officers were concentrating on their work. He'd let it all sink in, a couple more circles, and then he'd get down to business. He made his two tours of the room very slowly. "Right, Roger, I've cased the joint and now let's crack on. First things first, I'd like to have a little chat with all the officers who were involved in the visit to our Henry's home last Tuesday. Please."

For a fleeting moment, Casely considered reminding Whiteside that he preferred to be addressed by his rank. He wisely thought the better of it. The sooner this brute was out of his hair, the better. The little chats took up the remainder of the morning. As expected, they provided Whiteside with no new evidence but added to his overall picture. He was polite and grateful for the officer's time; and he actually managed to make it sound as if he meant it.

Even his meeting with ACC Alison Hayes – the stuck-up cow insisted on having a witness – failed to spark his natural sarcasm and disrespect. Until he was leaving her room, that is.

"One last thing, old girl, the boys in the other room are a bit sheepish. You DO believe Henry's in the clear, don't you?"

"Mr Whiteside, nobody but NOBODY calls me old girl. As for your question, you should need no reminding that the officers are involved in a serious inquiry. A professional inquiry."

"Sorry. Won't happen again, love."

Whiteside was enjoying his day, even if no-one else was. It was going to be difficult restricting his lunchtime to just two pints.

✝

"Hello."

"Henry, sorry it took so long to get back to you – dreadfully busy," said Michael Feuerstein.

"Busy on my case I do hope."

"Of course, well just one other tiny matter to tidy up. All done and dusted now."

"Have you issued the writs yet?"

"Henry, please try and slow down; these things take time."

"Yes, I am aware of that. I appreciate they take time. They also cost money – in this case MY money hence my eagerness to press on."

"Have faith Henry. I am pressing on. I have contacted the Evening Gazette solicitors, which is the first step in cases like this. I am obliged to give them the opportunity of making a suitable apology and correction, and offering compensation for damage caused."

"You can take it from me they have caused some damage, all right!"

"Indeed they have. Now we are rather in their hands. Until they respond I cannot officially make requests of the court."

"So they can bloody well draw it out as long as they wish. I can't have that."

"Exactly. Bear with me while I go through a few suggestions. A lot will depend on what our Keith can find out in Chelmsford today."

"Well I must say Keith does seem on the ball. And it was a welcome relief to actually hear a human voice say he believed me this morning."

"Ah, yes, The Mirror photograph. Keith and I did speak about that and his reasoning is sound indeed; it usually is, according to a few mutual acquaintances."

"So, please tell me what we can do if the paper plays for time?"

"You could force their hand, Henry? You could embarrass them by making a Press statement."

"I'm not exactly keen on the Press right now."

"Wait, wait. I'm not talking about a conference; I won't have anyone questioning you. No, not at all. That won't do. If they do delay proceedings, I think it would be a good idea for you to try and get the public on your side."

Headleigh laughed, not a full-throated laugh, of course. "Get the public on my side? That's the funniest thing I've heard…"

"Henry, hear me out. You make a public statement – no questions, remember – and you proclaim your innocence. Naturally you just stick to 'serious allegations' for now. You pile it on – the thicker the better. You tell the fair-minded British public that you have lost your job because of totally unfounded serious allegations."

"Hmmm, Michael…"

"You could also say you have lost your wife – think about that one –

and you briefly tell them about how loyally you have served the British Police for all these years. British Police, mind – not Essex – we don't want to parochialise the issue.

"You want to have your day in court and defend your honour and your reputation. You will call upon the law to expedite matters and not allow a humble public servant to suffer longer than absolutely necessary under the shadow of these slurs etc etc…what do you think?"

"I'll give it some thought. Not sure about it, to be honest, but I will give it some thought."

"Please do, Henry. It's a good tactic, in my professional opinion, especially with the Lord Chancellor being so keen on speeding up the judicial process these days."

"When would you suggest I make this statement, if I do agree to it?"

"Well you just consider it for now. I would give the newspaper's solicitors at least a week to respond. Meantime, I'll have words in friendly ears and see what strings can be pulled."

"Fine, thank you."

"I should point out that it is highly unusual for a civil case to be heard while possible criminal charges are pending, but there are precedents. That may be a tricky hurdle. Hopefully, Mr Whiteside will return with an indication of how the police are planning to proceed. If you can have a discreet word with anyone with connections it would not go amiss. Goodbye for now, Henry."

"I'll see what I can do. Goodbye."

✝

Keith Whiteside returned to his task, suitably refreshed from a couple of lunchtime pints. He chose a recommended hostelry, packed with office types, that was on the site of a former jail. Garish colours and trendy food was now the order of the day. He enjoyed a pleasant stroll around the cathedral – even a hard-nosed ex-cop like him appreciated a modest intake of culture – and was suitably inspired for his afternoon tasks. Inspector Roger Casely managed to stay clear of his barbs as Whiteside quizzed the locals. He wanted to see everything – EVERYTHING – taken from the Headleigh household. He whizzed through the paperwork, requesting just a handful of photocopies, please. He spent most of his last two hours in Chelmsford browsing through the files on the computer. The computer that Henry Headleigh hadn't touched since Christmas. The computer that contained hundreds of his fingerprints – digitally-speaking.

"Can you run me off a copy of all these files on disc, please, young man?"

"Certainly, sir. Take about 20 minutes, OK."

"Yes, fine." Sir. Long time since anyone called me SIR. What a pleasant officer; must have some northern blood in him.

"You know Henry well, sergeant?"

"Yes, sir, quite well. He brought me onto this team."

Whiteside was almost in the officer's lap, but he managed to sidle up even closer. "Tell me what a bright young sergeant like you thinks," whispered Whiteside. "Is the great man a paedophile?"

The sergeant shuffled as close to the edge of his chair as he could manage without falling off. "We're not supposed to talk about it to outsiders, sir, with all due respect."

"Oh please don't think of me as an outsider. Who had it in for him? You must have some idea?"

"Is there anything else you need while this is finishing? Henry's official papers and diary are in there if you need them."

"Let's have a look at them, shall we?" Whiteside dismissed the papers and flicked through the diary, a list of meetings, lunch dates, dinner dates, seminars and the like.

"Come on, sergeant, between you and me?"

"Please stop asking sir? Would you like any photocopies from the diary?" A slight emphasis at the end of the sentence.

"Go on, then," yes, thought Whiteside. "Pages for the last six months, please, well let's say since January 1st."

"The last six months? Is he taking the piss?" said the WPC after the sergeant left the diary with her by the photocopier. The disc was just finishing as he returned to his desk.

"Might be another ten minutes with all those pages, sir. You've delayed WPC Withers's tea break and she's got a fiery streak in her so watch out when she comes through." The sergeant raised his eyes and smiled at the private investigator before returning to his desk.

Whiteside sat at his own desk and fiddled with his pen before the WPC came in and handed the sergeant a thick wad of papers. "Don't mention it, sarge," and she wiggled off for her cuppa.

"I'll escort you to the door, sir, if you're ready to leave."

"Thank you but I can find my own way out; I used to be a detective, you know."

"Oh it's no problem, sir."

They walked down a corridor to the reception. They had passed into the public reception area when Whiteside felt a faint tug on his sleeve. "No sir, most of us don't think he is a ruddy paedo," said the sergeant softly, and then louder: "Here's the disc and the diary. Not had time to check the diary yet myself. Have a safe journey, sir."

Before Whiteside could reply the sergeant had returned police-side and was briskly walking down the corridor. He was a very thorough man was Detective Sergeant George Lewis.

✝

Michael Feuerstein sounded quite excited when he phoned Headleigh. It was not quite four hours since their morning conversation. "Well it didn't take them long, Henry."

"What didn't take who long?"

"The paper's solicitors have responded to my letter, hand delivered less than 15 minutes ago."

"And?"

"Cutting out the legal jargon – and they're very scant with that – Jefferson, Franzeb & Kisseber say the paper will definitely not contemplate an apology, nor a correction and most certainly not compensation. Basically, it's 'see you in court'. I must say I'm surprised."

"So now you can go to the court?"

"Technically, yes. But please be patient, Henry. I do know this is a huge strain for you but trust me on this. I can only push people so hard. Sleep on what we have spoken about and we'll talk in the morning."

✝

Bryan Richardson's laugh could be heard well outside the heavy, closed doors to the boardroom. He threw his head back and clutched his sides and then his stomach. It was all for effect, of course.

"An apology, a correction and compensation. Henry 'Raving Pervert' Headleigh wants the Gazette to say sorry and line his pockets, does he?"

John Franzeb had met the owner of the Evening Gazette on just one previous occasion. His two partners at Jefferson, Franzeb & Kisseber – solicitors to the very wealthy – usually had the pleasure. But the slender, bespectacled Franzeb, as the firm's defamation specialist, found himself enjoying the raucous good humour of their client this lunchtime. He could have passed for Arthur Jacobs's younger brother. He stood to attention in his pin-striped suit – always black or blue, unlike Jacobs's choice of many colours – and waited for Richardson's laughter to peter away.

"I thought I'd bring it round in person, sir. If you or Mr Chalmers could let the office know when you wish us to formulate a response?"

This brought on more hysterical laughter from Richardson. It was really rather unbecoming, thought Franzeb, but then again he didn't know the proprietor that well.

"Oh, you can formulate a response right now, John. You can formulate a response which tells Henry Fuckin' Headleigh that he has more chance of seeing my bare arse at the top of Nelson's Fuckin' Column than getting a fuckin' apology out of me."

"I see," coughed Franzeb.

"No fuckin' apology; no fuckin' correction; and no fuckin' compensation. Can you believe the bleedin' cheek of some people?" He addressed the last part to Gary Chalmers who sat at the board table, toadily smiling along with his boss.

"Shall I send the response right away, sir? Are you sure you wouldn't like to think the matter over?"

"No, I wouldn't like to think the matter over, thank you very much. Make sure these fuckers know we will fight them all the way. And we will win. Thank you for making my day."

✝

Headleigh had decided he would go along with his solicitors' suggestion and planned to call him that morning and ask when they meet the vultures. He had slept well the previous night. After a day stuck indoors he found himself surprisingly tired without having exerted himself in the slightest. He had decided against walking to the newsgents; the Daily Mirror had been enough for him that day. So he spent some time in the garden, plucking out weeds, and flowers that to him looked weedy. He finished his historical novel, cooked – here, he was slowly improving – and watched television with little interest.

He was tucking into a hearty breakfast at ten o'clock – normally he would have at least two hours of work under his belt – when the phone rang.

"Dad? It's Jon."

"Jonathan! How are…"

"It's mum, dad. She's all right, but she's in hospital."

"Hospital? Why? What's happened?"

"She took some pills to help her sleep. I couldn't wake her this morning so I called an ambulance. She's all right. The doctor said they would let her leave after some tests."

"Which hospital, Jonathan? I'll get there as soon as I can."

"Go to my home, dad. We should be there in time to meet you."

CHAPTER ELEVEN

HENRY HEADLEIGH drained the coffee mug and scraped the food from his plate into the bin under the kitchen sink. He placed his cutlery and crockery in their allotted sections in the dishwasher – it would hold a good week's dishes for a single man. He went upstairs to shower and dress, and decided against tempting fate by packing an overnight bag.

He collected some papers from the kitchen table and put them in his briefcase. He was easing the Mondeo off the drive within 40 minutes of Jonathan's call.

Jonathan Headleigh had chosen to launch his property career just short of 70 miles away from the family home; not a great distance for any parents to be concerned about losing touch with their beloved. His Reading home, however, lay the opposite side of the monstrous motorway that circled London – the M25.

If you were lucky, which meant travelling between 3-4am, the journey from Brentwood could be done in just over an hour; slightly quicker if you pushed it, but you had to watch out for the speed cameras that were lurking everywhere these days.

As the south east of England woke from its slumber each day, rain or shine, the M25 woke with it. If the M25 possessed a grin, it would be a fiendish one. New lanes had been added, old ones widened, yet at rush-hour the traffic resembled a giant metallic snake, its head and tail not quite meeting at the River Thames junction which separated Kent and Essex.

The worst had passed by the time Headleigh acknowledged a courteous fellow motorist who allowed him to slip into the nearside lane, but the cars and huge trucks were idling along. Roadworks, perennial roadworks were the reason for the slow...stop...slow-slow...stop rhythm for the next five or six miles. Headleigh drummed his fingers on the dashboard and wound down the window so he could enjoy a cigarette. No Jane to nag him about that. What had she done? Had the silly cow really attempted suicide?

Headleigh reached the modern estate which was now Jonathan's home shortly before noon. Was it really a year since he was last there? This was his second visit and he drove around the maze of cul-de-sacs, drives and avenues. Eventually he gave up and stopped to ask directions.

Jane and Jonathan had arrived an hour earlier. Jonathan was doing well for himself to afford a mortgage in this area, even on a humble two-bedroomed terrace. Headleigh had to park four houses away, and that was a damned tight squeeze for his saloon. Modern planners!

They were expecting him. The door was slightly ajar; Henry knocked to announce his arrival and walked right in. His wife and son were in the kitchen. "Jane, darling? What happened?" Headleigh outstretched his arms in an attempt to embrace Jane, but she turned abruptly to the sink, a reliable refuge for many a woman, as the detective in Headleigh was acutely aware.

"I didn't try to kill myself, if that's what you think."

It was a terrible ordeal for poor Jonathan; his father's concerned face in stark contrast to the brutally dismissive body language of his mother. "Hi, dad," he said, offering a sweaty handshake.

"Jonathan!" Headleigh almost crushed his boy with his hug; he noticed the emotion and intensity was not reciprocated.

"I'll make some tea, dad, then I'll leave you and mum alone for a while." As he waited for the kettle to boil, Jonathan noticed there was a new message on his answer machine. He pressed 'play'. "Hello, my name is Keith Whiteside. I work for Feuerstein, Savage and Amrein, your father's solicitors. I'd just like to ask Mrs Headleigh a few questions, please. I can pop over at your convenience..."

Christ! thought Headleigh senior.

"Oh just what I need!" said Jane, not wishing to keep her thoughts to herself.

Jonathan switched the message off. The only bit they'd missed was the polite Mr Whiteside suggesting they check his credentials with the lawyers to reassure themselves he wasn't a reporter. Jonathan handed his parents two cups of tea – white, no sugar.

"I'll just pop down to the shops; be back in about half an hour. OK?"

"Fine, Jonathan. Thank you," replied the father. Jane had moved from the sink to the furthest point from Headleigh in the kitchen. He would still be able to reach out and touch her as the kitchen seemed no larger than his pathetic parking space. Three was definitely a crowd in there. Headleigh broke the chilly silence as soon as he heard Jonathan close the front door.

"Tell me, Jane, tell me what happened?" She looked paler than he had ever seen her. The absence of make-up emphasised the puffiness of her eyes.

"I'll tell you what happened. I haven't been able to sleep for days, so dear Jon got me some pills. I took a few too many, that's what happened – an accident, simple as that."

"And you're all right now?"

"All right? Yes, I am absolutely tip-top. God Almighty, Henry!" She still had a hospital blanket around her shoulders and hugged it closer to her body. She was shivering slightly, though it was a fine June day.

"What can I do? Why are you treating me like this?" pleaded Headleigh.

"Why the hell do you think? Come on, you're the great detective."

Headleigh did not at that precise moment look like a great detective: Columbo, minus the raincoat, at best.

"Here's a clue!" Jane had taken a paper from behind some jars. She flung it on the table and the photograph of Headleigh and the Kent pervert stared back at him.

"Jane? How many times do I have to tell you? I have done nothing wrong! You're my wife! My wife of 26 years. You know me better than anyone, and you're...you're telling me you don't believe me? You don't trust me?"

Jane had her arms folded tightly across her chest now. If she squeezed the blanket any more tightly it would end up under her skin. "So you want me to believe that you're being picked on because you're a policeman. Is that it? Our children's computer, Henry! In our loft! A place of happy memories and happy children. And now this." She pointed in disgust at the paper.

Headleigh had never struck a woman in his life, and he wasn't going to start now. "I am fighting to clear my name, Jane. I want you to believe me. I…"

"I want a divorce." There, it was out in the open. Headleigh took hold of the back of a flimsy wooden chair. He turned it around so he could sit down. The chair was not designed for a man Headleigh's size.

"After all I have done for you, Jane; after all I have done for OUR family…you want a divorce." He slammed the palm of his hand down hard on the table. The table was not designed either to take the wrath of hands like Headleigh's. There was a sharp crack, the legs wobbled but the table managed to remain upright. Headleigh rose from his chair.

"Well I am fed up, Jane. Fed up of wasting my breath on you. I've worked every hour God sends to make a decent living for you and the children. Do I bugger off to the golf club when I've finished work? Do I nip down to some boozer for a few jars with the boys? No, I work my…my…socks off and then I come home to my family. The family that I cherish so much."

His words had little if any affect on his wife. "Fine. You can have a divorce, Jane. Fine. I'll wait outside so I can say goodbye to Jonathan."

✝

Keith Whiteside studied his rough features in the bathroom mirror. The worn face and shattered eyes convinced him he should shower before bed, not that he had any lady in his hotel room to prettify himself for. He needed to wash away the grime of the last four hours. It had just turned midnight and the constant buzz on the street outside the Ryan Hotel had not abated. King's Cross was like the M25; it did not enjoy many peaceful hours.

Whiteside had returned from Chelmsford and enjoyed a pleasant stroll down by the Thames embankment. He refreshed himself at two pubs packed with office workers winding down after a 'bloody boring day' or a 'bloody non-stop, crazy day.' The chatterers seemed to know no grey areas. He bought two bottles of Rioja at an off-licence on his way back up King's Cross Road to the Ryan. He ordered a coronation chicken sandwich – make that two – from room service. He wolfed down his evening meal while the files from the disk were loading onto his lap top computer. Then he settled down for an evening's viewing.

This is what paedophiles do, he told himself. Maybe not in the relative luxury of a hundred quid a night hotel, but in some dingy bedsit with black curtains tightly drawn. Or maybe tucked away in a loft? No, Headleigh hadn't been sneaking up into that loft to feast his eyes on this supreme example of degradation. Whiteside was convinced of that, wasn't he? Whiteside got up every hour for a minute or so, to stretch his mighty legs and to clear his mind.

The image files seemed to be primarily stills from videos, but there were a good number of high-resolution photos – almost certainly taken by digital cameras. He wasn't sure what he was looking for and none of the images caught his attention, professionally speaking.

He was into his second bottle of the Spanish red when he turned to the Internet files. Essex Police had taken the web sites down off the World Wide Web, so the Headleigh computer and this disc were the only sources to view the sites which invited viewers to enjoy the delights of the youngest 'talent' on the Net. The Essex officers had told Whiteside that Headleigh probably received the material via disc – none was found at the house during the raid – or downloaded the stuff from elsewhere on the Internet.

There was second folder on the disk, entitled 'LOG'. It contained notes on the police investigation. One document listed the dates the web pages had been accessed. There were just six over the past four months, not what you would call a daily paedo then, was he, our Henry?

Another document contained a report by the WPC who had looked after Jane Headleigh when her husband was taken to the station. Mrs Headleigh said little but was in a state of extreme distress. Whiteside read the transcript of the interview conducted by Chief Constable James McNish and Assistant Chief Constable Alison Hayes most carefully.

He had finished the second Rioja. He made himself a cup of coffee and decided he would have a nightcap from the mini-bar. The choice was brandy or vodka – he went for brandy and returned to finish his nighttime reading.

There were a few notes from the Dorset officers, yet it appeared ACC Hill and Inspector Casely had not yet filed any proper reports. Finally, there was a list of useful contacts: Headleigh's home numbers, his and his wife's mobiles, those for his children and a few friends.

Whiteside switched off the computer, left his chair and walked around the room. What the fuck was that lot doing in Henry's loft? The shower didn't yield the answer, nor did it clear away the grime. But it did clear his mind of Rioja. You dozy bastard, Whiteside! You dozy bastard! He hurriedly washed away the soap suds and grabbed a towel. He switched back on the computer while he dried himself.

Even though he had felt shattered earlier after being on the go since before the crack of dawn, Whiteside spent a further hour examining the material he had been given in Essex.

Should he call, Henry? Don't be daft. Mrs Headleigh, Mrs Jane Headleigh. Yes, I'll call Mrs Headleigh in the morning. With that son of theirs, isn't she? It was 1.30am. He set his alarm for six and drifted off, thinking…thinking…

✝

"Good morning."

"Morning, morning. Assistant Chief Constable Hill, I presume. Please come in and take a seat."

"Thank you for seeing me so promptly, Mr Murphy."

"Always available for the police. The Headleigh case, messy business. How can I help you?"

Duncan Murphy's office was probably as large as the Dorset officer's back home in the south-west. ACC Hill thought it was, especially if you tidied up a bit and removed some of these books.

He studied the walls and the shelves crammed to bursting point with books. Crime books: Inside The Criminal Mind, Interviews With A Serial Killer, Why I Did It. He smiled. "Have you read all these, Mr Murphy? Some tales in there I would bet."

"Oh yes, once upon a time I have read them. I really should have a clear-out. But you never know when you just might need something checking. The problem, as you can see, is finding the blasted thing." Both men laughed.

"I joke, sir. Believe it or not I do have an excellent filing system. The problem is, only I know it."

Murphy was the same age as Henry Headleigh, 51. They both shared a fascination with police work and the criminal mind. There the similarity stopped. Murphy was two inches shorter than the former detective superintendent and weighed in upwards of four stone heavier. He had curly, greasy brown hair which he occasionally swept back to reveal an equally greasy forehead. His belly bulged over his trouser belt, displaying a green vest underneath the white shirt. Thankfully, ACC Hill was not there to discuss dress code, otherwise Murphy would be under arrest.

"Yes the Headleigh case. I would like your professional opinion?" The criminal psychologist folded his hands across his vast stomach.

"Well I don't claim to know him personally."

"You have worked with him, though?"

"Not for, oh, must be four years. And then I had more contact with his inspector; forget the name. A murder down Southend; like to think I did my small bit in achieving a conviction."

"Well please tell me what you can about him. You are aware of the details of the case?"

"Yes, yes. I received the files the other day."

"And do you think he could be a paedophile?"

"Why don't you tell me what you think first, Assistant Chief Constable? Do YOU think he is guilty?"

"I'm really not sure. Everything I know about him, his record and the words of his colleagues, seems to cry 'no'; the evidence screams out 'yes'. I'm a copper, and don't mind admitting an old-fashioned one, same as Headleigh – hard evidence, hard cold evidence matters more than anything. The Archbishop of Canterbury could stand up in court and tell the jury you are the finest, most decent, church-going, lawabiding citizen he has ever met. But if your prints are on the murder weapon..."

"Aha! Well put, sir. I can see the dilemma."

"So, do you think it is possible that a man like Headleigh could be involved in paedophilia?"

"Oh yes, of course. A man, any man, is capable of anything. It doesn't take much to trigger an unusual reaction. But generally, well let's say OFTEN, there is a straw that broke the camel's back."

"Meaning?"

"Our police officers, as you well know, have the most stressful job. Some cope well, some not so well. A young bobby on the beat can exorcise his demons over a few pints, some athletic activity, for example. Or, sadly, he can go home and take it out on the wife or children. Thankfully, the former is most common."

"So you are saying Headleigh could be exorcising his demons?"

"He could be. But I doubt it."

"What then?"

"Could be one of a number of things. Again, speaking in general terms, it is not uncommon for the nature of the job to affect an officer's personal life. You recall the case only a few months ago, an officer in Scotland dismissed for being in possession of heroin? He was addicted. Now that officer had worked in the drug squad for six years. Medical tests showed that he had been taking drugs for less than a year. The connection is obvious."

"So Headleigh turned to child pornography for entertainment because he was working for the CPU?"

"Do you have any evidence that he was doing such things before his appointment?"

"No; just over the past few months."

Murphy browsed through some papers on his untidy desk. "And he was appointed...hmmm, about ten months ago, according to the file?"

"Yes, that's about right."

"Clearly there is a connection. I am not saying they ARE connected, but, yes, you can see the connection." Murphy checked the papers once more. "Of course, there are other factors which could prompt such unusual behaviour. His home life, perhaps?"

"What about his home life? From what I know and hear he was a middle-aged, happily-married man with three wonderful children."

"Three children who had left home. And who really knows whether or not a couple are happily married? If, and I must emphasise IF, sir, IF he is guilty, somewhere there will be a straw which broke the poor camel's back.

"The children leave home for university or whatever – that is a massive change. Both for him and his wife, I would add. He returns home from work; to a home missing the exuberance of voices, even rowdy teenage voices. Some men will breathe a sigh of relief, others will be saddened."

"I see. Yes, I can see Headleigh in the saddened role."

"As for the marriage, well there is many a marriage held together by the presence of children. Now, I have no knowledge of the Headleighs' marriage. I am merely providing my expert advice here."

"Yes, I understand. Please continue."

"What I am saying, Assistant Chief Constable, is that perhaps the Headleighs had little in common apart from their children. I have no idea whether they shared mutual hobbies or interests, or whether everything was hunky-dory in the Headleigh bedroom. I can merely suggest reasons why the officer may have done what they say he has done. Not an absolute science, my field. I am afraid. The straw and the camel, though; very common. Now, do you have any further questions?"

"No, thank you Mr Murphy; you have been most helpful."

✝

The editor's office was very quiet for 11 o'clock in the morning. Andrew Harvey had held conference that day, managing to focus briefly on other stories besides this pervert cop.

Yes, the EastEnders cast row on page one: something light for a change. Who was slagging off whom? Oh, never mind. A good cross reference to the cricket, please. England set to win again: well, well, well. Weather on page two: who says we're in for the hottest summer since records began? Oh, never mind. Easy on the Middle East on three: readers don't care, really, do they? How many dead? Oh, never mind. Details, details, details.

He appeared interested as the feature articles to be used and those suitable for holding over until a rainy day were discussed; he appeared interested, but wasn't. Right, off you go. Knock 'em dead.

The four defenders of the truth remained in his office: Harvey, lawyer Arthur Jacobs, News Editor Phil Calvin, and Crime Reporter Terry James, temporarily on desk duties but digging hard for evidence. Evidence that would get the four men off the hook.

Just Harvey and James were technically on the hook; Jacobs had given his legal advice with the customary provisos – lawyers are not stupid – and Calvin had been roped in to help out. His numerous contacts had drawn a blank.

"So then, Arthur, to use BR-speak, he simply told Headleigh's lawyers to fuck off? And he didn't bother to consult either you or me."

"The first I heard was an hour ago. I received a call from John Franzeb. He didn't seem to want to go into details, but in a nutshell, yes. The response was back in the hands of Headleigh's lawyers by teatime."

"And now Franzeb wants you to compile a dossier for the defence. Decent of someone to tell me – I'm only the bloody editor, after all."

No table-thumping punctuated Harvey's whines; he was beyond that. He seemed melancholy, more than anything, thought James. Like a man staring down into his last scotch after the wife had upped and left.

"I came to you immediately, Andrew. Well I waited for conference to finish. I'm very surprised the chairman hasn't informed you."

"Not a dickey bird for more than 24 hours now. Normally I would be delighted at that."

"There's no rush from my point of view, old boy. But I did get the impression from Franzeb that they wanted as much information soonest, to appease their client more than for preparing our case. BRE is a lucrative, high-profile client."

"What about the police? What are they doing? Are they going to charge him? Shouldn't we be waiting for them to take the lead?" said Calvin, trying to be helpful.

"Yes, you are perfectly correct, Phil," said Jacobs. "Criminal charges come first. That is why Franzeb was surprised to receive a claim from Headleigh's lawyers so soon. A friend did tell me last night that he wouldn't be surprised if this Dorset chief was taken off the case soon; now that Headleigh has resigned from the force it should be just a routine investigation by the local force."

"Not in a case like this, Arthur," said Harvey. "This is a senior officer – or former senior officer – we are talking about. And it's not like we've simply accused him of nicking a few quid from a crime scene."

"I don't see what the problem is, Andrew?" said James. "The cops have Headleigh's computer and porn files, so we believe, and now they have the Mirror photo. Maybe they don't have the photo yet, but I'm told the Mirror editor has agreed to hand it over and co-operate fully with them. Naturally. Same as we are doing. When is this Freddie Hill coming? That been sorted yet?"

"Thursday – early afternoon."

"Has it been decided whether or not I'm being interviewed?"

"I said 'yes' but we wanted a lawyer present. That would mean you, Arthur, and Franzeb or one of his chums. I've not had a reply yet from the cops."

"I don't think we should do anything until then. Let's see what they have on Headleigh."

"I doubt very much they'll give anything away during an investigation; least of all to us, Terry. For now I am more concerned with our leader and his great expectations. You'd better starting knocking those notes you showed me the other day into some sort of shape that a lawyer will understand. I mean Franzeb, not you, Arthur." The editorial lawyer nodded gravely.

"Any news from your contact, Terry?"

"No. He said he wouldn't be in touch until he had something new."

"No news. Is that good or bad? Oh, never mind."

When Harvey was alone, he rang around a few contacts on other papers. He was dismayed to discover that the Gazette was the only paper which had received a letter from Headleigh's lawyers. The Gazette had broken the story, after all. How proud Harvey had felt a week last Friday, was it? Seemed like a lifetime to the editor. Headleigh's team was clearly gunning for the Gazette first and, if successful, would settle up with the others later.

He opened up his Headleigh folder and ran through all the stories that had appeared since Terry James's exclusive had hit the streets. The rival rags had been more cautious. Maybe two or, at a pinch three, were on unfirm ground, legally. But the Gazette was well and truly scuppered if they couldn't come up with the evidence. Harvey told himself to think positive. Terry James had never let him down. He wished he had an inkling who the source was.

✝

"Fine, Jonathan. I understand your desire to protect your mother. It's only natural. If she won't meet me would you please ask her if I might have a minute or two of her time on the phone? Please?"

"I really don't know, Mr Whiteside."

"I'll be very quick, Jonathan. I promise not to say anything to upset her."

"Hang on, I'll see what she says. But she has been under a terrible strain."

"All very understandable, Jonathan."

Jane Headleigh took the phone a few seconds later. "What do you want, Mr Whiteside? I am in no frame of mind to face questions."

"I apologise, ma'am. Won't take a minute of your time."

Whiteside took precisely one minute and 25 seconds of Mrs Headleigh's time before expressing his gratitude and hanging up. The brief chat had been more fruitful than he had expected; much more fruitful.

CHAPTER TWELVE

HENRY HEADLEIGH addressed the British Press, plus two foreign correspondents, in the rear garden at St Andrew's Avenue. He had not needed police advice to move the throng from the front. Ever dutiful, he had requested they not disturb his neighbours more than necessary.

Michael Feuerstein had enrolled three casual helpers to deal with the proceedings. Keith Whiteside was there, too. The reporters, photographers and TV crews were ushered down a side alley into the garden where their host had provided four large tables. Six plates of sandwiches, four-dozen sausage rolls, two-dozen pork pies, three bowls of cocktail sausages, four supersize sacks of crisps, six pounds of cheese and three boxes of crackers were demolished in a matter of minutes.

"At least real vultures leave the bones," said Headleigh, watching his new friends from behind the curtain of an upstairs window.

"The Press pack hunt like wolves but eat like pigs," said Feuerstein. "I've witnessed it all before. It is a good idea to feed them, though. But still don't expect an easy ride. Play it straight as we discussed. No questions; not one. We're almost ready. Keith will signal when he wants you down there."

Feuerstein had limited attendance to a hundred, politely refusing requests from several agencies but informing them that the statement would be available by fax or email shortly after the meeting. Feuerstein had been concerned the previous day when he could not contact his client. Headleigh's mobile battery had died when he went to Reading, and it was late in the day when he arrived home to answer the lawyer's messages.

"The divorce was bad news, Henry, but perhaps we can turn it to our advantage. Sorry if that sounds callous."

Headleigh entered the garden through the French windows in the lounge. He stood on a low patio wall so that the massed ranks of the media were looking slightly up at him. This was much appreciated by the photographers; the hanging baskets made a good backdrop, too. Feuerstein coughed, Whiteside coughed louder and quickly there was a peace over the garden.

"Mr Headleigh and I thank you for your attendance today. Mr Headleigh will make a short statement. Printed copies will be available on the table over there as you leave. Mr Headleigh will not be answering any questions. Mr Headleigh."

Headleigh was accustomed to public speaking, and had handled many Press conferences with considerable verbal dexterity. This was the first, and hopefully last, in his garden. He spoke in a voice loud and distinguished:

As you will all know, serious allegations have been made against me; very serious and totally unfounded allegations.

I cannot stress strongly enough the complete absurdity of these wicked slurs on my character. I have served Essex Police and the county's community at large to the best of my ability for 30 years.

Not once in those 30 years have I ever committed a criminal act. Not once have I been in the slightest tempted to commit a criminal act.

It was with great sadness that I tendered my resignation as detective superintendent last week. I believe that was the honourable decision to take for the sake of Essex Police, and to free me for my fight to clear my name through the courts.

I believe in a free Press. The Press is one of the great bastions of freedom in this country. But the Press must realise that it has to act with decency and integrity. It cannot publish lies with impunity.

I call on the Lord Chief Justice to prove good his intention of speeding up justice for the little man. I do not have the funds to contest a drawn out legal battle with the media moguls of this world. The fair-minded British public demands that every citizen be given the opportunity to defend himself. That is a fundamental principle upon which our nation

*is founded: fair play. I have always played fair as a police officer, hard
though that sometimes proved. Now I call on the law to play fair with me.
Not purely for my sake and my reputation as an individual. But for the
sake of ridding this stain from the Essex Police Force.*

*And, finally, I implore you all to respect the privacy of my family. This has
been a terrible strain on my wife and our three children. Thank you.*

The questions rang out before he had both feet off the patio wall. Is it
true you are separated from your wife? What happened in Kent?

Feuerstein put a gentle hand on Headleigh's shoulder and guided him
back through the French windows and closed the curtains. Two vultures dared to climb onto the patio and were approaching the windows. Whiteside placed a huge hand on the shoulder of one, gave him
a gentle shake to the side so that he collided with his colleague and
sent him tumbling into the wall. The vulture grimaced and rubbed his
behind and back.

"Please don't come onto the patio," said Whiteside to the gazing
media folk who were contemplating whether or not to follow the two
hardy souls. "Mr Headleigh was watering his plants this morning and
it may be still wet and slippery."

Whiteside picked up the fallen vulture by the scruff of his neck. He
was still holding onto the other one and walked both towards the alley.

"Don't forget there are printed statements here if you require them.
Please keep the noise down on your way out. Thanks for coming."
Whiteside stayed rooted to his spot as the guests walked to the alley-
way. A few looked at him, but only from the corners of their eyes.

When they had all departed, he told Feuerstein's assistants to clear the
tables and to try and do something with the lawn. Poor lawn! It was
strewn with empty crisp packets and plastic cups; crusts from sandwiches and pies were trampled into the grass Headleigh had lovingly
mowed only the other day.

✝

Two days later: Assistant Chief Constable Frederick Hill was in the private office he had been allocated at the police HQ when he took a call from Chief Superintendent Martin Brewster.

"Hello, Martin. I was wondering if and when I would hear from you? How are things at the Association?"

"We do our bit, sir, to keep the country on the straight and narrow," laughed the secretary of D Division of the Police Superintendents' Association. "How are you liking the Essex air, sir? Managed any sight-seeing? All somewhat flat for many, but there are some interesting walks outside the new carbuncles."

"As you know, Martin, I'm not here to go rambling." And stop rambling yourself and get to the point.

"Quite. Shame as I'd recommend Maldon for a good afternoon; avoid the weekends though, in the summer. Just a friendly call to see how the Headleigh case is progressing. Did you see his statement on television? Imagine allowing all those monsters in your back garden."

"Yes, of course, I saw the television footage, watched it several times. Did you notice a Mr Keith Whiteside prowling the grounds? I didn't realise he was one of yours?"

"One of ours? Oh, no, sir, he's not one of ours; never made superintendent. I do believe he's working for Henry's solicitors; an excellent firm by the name of Feuerstein, Savage and Amrein. I can recommend them if you ever..."

"If I ever find myself defending serious allegations? Yes I may give them a call should such a situation arise."

"Can't help but feel sorry for Henry, what with the cost of engaging expensive lawyers. I do hope he gets his wish of a speedy trial. As he said: Fair Play. How's your investigation coming along? Must be a tiresome process."

"Now it wouldn't be the first tiresome process any of us have been saddled with, would it?"

Brewster gave a slight chuckle. "Any inkling of when a file might go to the CPS? I suspect you have to check out all the potentially VERY serious villains who could be involved; you might still be in Essex at

Christmas." Brewster laughed more heartily this time.

"Sorry, Martin, have to dash, there's another call been waiting. I promise to call you soon for a chat. Take care and best wishes to all at the Association."

There was no call waiting, of course. ACC Hill didn't really mind Martin Brewster. He had a great deal of respect for the superintendents' body. He just needed time to think before answering the secretary's not-so-subtle questions.

That was the third call he had received in less than 30 hours. All had mentioned the length of his investigation; all had mentioned widening his inquiry to take in other villains – and that was not exactly within his remit. He was investigating an officer; the locals could pick up on any trails he left behind. Two of the calls had mentioned Christmas. He lunched with his thoughts. Fair play won the day, even if the rules of this particular game were a trifle irregular.

Before close of play for the day, he phoned the Home Office and the Crown Prosecution Service. If they wanted him to stay on in Essex and widen his inquiry he could really do with at least two more local officers assisting him full time; and, yes, it would probably be late in the year before his report was ready. He returned to his hotel and broke the 'good' news to Inspector Roger Casely.

To be fair to his deputy and what family life he was permitted, they agreed to work four-day shifts. One of them would be in Essex at all times, while the other enjoyed three days in their Dorset haven. "Is that all right, Roger?"

"Can't argue with that. Fair play to you, sir."

ACC Hill phoned Brewster early evening from his hotel room. "Hope you don't mind me calling you at home, Martin? Sorry we were interrupted today."

"Immaculate timing, sir. I have just one minute ago finished dining. I do hate having my evening meal disturbed, even by my superiors. Ha-ha-ha."

"Dorset duck a la Mrs Hill, you can't beat it; a speciality sadly unavailable in this part of the world. I shall look forward to tucking into mine for Christmas dinner. I shall enjoy my Christmas dinner; and Boxing Day, too – probably a bracing 20 miles by the coast. After that I shall have the pleasure of writing up this sordid story. I have told the powers-that-be it will be delivered between Christmas and the New Year. I thought you'd like to know."

"Well thank you very much for informing me, sir. Good luck to your good self and, Casely, is it?"

"Yes, Inspector Roger Casely – first-rate chap and it won't be long before he's one of yours."

"I look forward to his promotion then. Sir, if there is any way the Association can help, don't hesitate to ask."

"Thank you. Maybe you could ask Headleigh for all his private contacts? It seems I am taking over his old job for a few months."

✝

"November? November? That's more than four months away!"

Michael Feuerstein waited for his client to let the information sink in; and to calm down.

"November, Michael? November?"

Feuerstein waited a few seconds more and then replied: "Believe me, Henry, in our circles that is a miracle on a par with the Second Coming. It has several benefits…"

"Benefits? Forgive me for not seeing right now the benefits of having this hanging over me for another four months. You told me the statement and all that nonsense in my garden would speed things up?"

"Please listen to me, Henry. It may be hard for you to believe but that 'nonsense' has speeded things up. As I was saying, it was several benefits. One: we have sufficient time to prepare, based on your briefings and Keith's investigations. Two: the defendants have ample time, too. Now that is the key here. They can hardly call for more time to prepare because they would lose face. And, I am told that is something the proprietor of the paper would never allow. Three: Quentin Carel-Hobbs is available."

"But four months! Four months, Michael?"

"I had to pull a few strings to get a date then. Fortunately there is an opening for a trial lasting up to three weeks. You may not have heard of Wiggins vs MRH Holdings, but that took five years to get to court. I would never dream of claiming the Lord Chancellor or Lord Chief Justice played a role in our case, but, yes, I am sure your statement led to a few words in the right places.

"And, as I have told you, it is irregular for civil hearings to take place with possible criminal charges pending, but again...a few strings. It seems the CPS will not be ready until early in the New Year and will not object to an earlier High Court trial.

"Finally, if – no, WHEN – when we win our case, it will make it all the more difficult – not to say IMPOSSIBLE – for criminal charges to be laid against you."

"OK, Michael. You must forgive my impatience, but what am I supposed to do for four months? Wait in shame? That is not me."

"I know, I really do know. Just try and keep a low profile. At least you will be out of the spotlight for the time being. Perhaps you could take a vacation? Deal with the family affairs? Just keep us informed of your movements, please, in case we need to contact you."

"I'll try. Keith has made progress I hear? Any details for me?"

"No, not yet. All he said was that he had some promising avenues to explore. He said he has probably two more weeks of inquiries. I suggested we then regroup in September and get stuck into the details. Trust me, the timetable is the best we could expect. Enjoy the summer. That's an order, superintendent."

✝

There was an isolated disruption to Feuerstein's plans. The Gazette owner wanted the world to know that he planned to fight Henry Headleigh with no punches pulled.

John Franzeb was given the task of dissuading Bryan Richardson from holding a live televised Press conference. It took the intervention of chief executive Gary Chalmers for the owner to concede that the lawyer was talking sense. If the world could not know, Richardson was damn well sure the Gazette readers would know.

He brushed aside more objections from Franzeb, sent him packing and marched down to the editor's office. He demanded Harvey obtain the photograph from the Mirror – money no object – and told him to leave a full page open for an article penned by himself for the following day's paper. He would have it ready by 10am.

There was no problem acquiring the photo from the Mirror – they'd had the exclusive, and it was common practice for picture desks to share material. You owe us one. Harvey told his staff to get on with filling the paper but to leave page five open for words of wisdom from on high. True to his word, Richardson emailed the story to the editor two minutes before ten and was in the office on the dot.

"Read it yet, Andrew? What do you think?" Harvey was sat at his desk with his fellow defenders behind him peering at his computer screen. The three journalists – Harvey, Calvin and James – had already speed-read the article. Arthur Jacobs was, as usual, taking his time. The journalists were reading it again, more slowly. They still could not believe their eyes.

"Big type, Andrew. I want a bloody B-I-G type size on it; for impact." The owner handed Harvey a sheet of A4 paper on which he had roughed out a design for his hard-hitting piece.

Harvey barely glanced at the paper, turning instead to face Richardson. "Bryan, are you serious? You want me to publish this?"

"Why ever not, old boy?" he said, slapping Harvey heartily on the back and joining the foursome reading his epic defence of the Press against perverts.

"For one, it's repeating the defamatory words in no uncertain terms. It's exacerbating the matter, and…"

"It's making our stance fuckin' plain, Andrew. That is what it is doing. It is letting these tossers know they don't fuck with Bryan Richardson and they don't fuck with my paper – OUR paper. They don't fuckin' mess with us, right chaps?"

"I have to agree with Andrew," said Jacobs, having finished his lawyerly perusal of the epic defence. "We could no longer claim we published the original article in good faith."

"Bollocks! What do you think, Terry James? Your source is 100 per cent kosher, isn't he?"

"Sure, he says the computer is riddled with child porn – all bearing the prints of Headleigh. The police will have to hand it over once your lawyers request access to prepare the defence."

"That's that sorted then," he beamed, clapping his hands. "Let me see a proof soon as it's done, Andrew. Which page is it earmarked for?"

"Page five."

"Hmmm, OK. Fine, you're the editor. I assume you're doing a nice cross ref from page one. Right, things to do. A proof when it's ready, Andrew."

Harvey slowly counted to five in his head after Richardson had left his office. "Don't say a bloody word any of you. Let's just do what he wants. Madness; absolute madness."

The backbench thought it was madness, too. Harvey left them the owner's rough scheme and told them to bring a proof asap. Big type, lads. Bloody big type.

"We working for the bleedin' Sun these days?" said Chief Sub-Editor Danny Waddell. "Two Paedos In A Pod? He wants that as the headline? Jee-sus Christ!"

Look at the two wicked faces in this photograph. Don't they make you sick? They bloody well should do.

The one on the left is on the run from the police. He goes by the name of Mr Teen. He lures young children – boys and girls – into this country by promising them a life of riches.

There is no life of luxury waiting for the poor kids, just one of total depravity at the hands of scumbag paedophiles who pay Mr Teen hard cash for the privilege of putting their paws all over the wretches. I won't go into the sordid details of what else these monsters get up to in their filthy dens.

Three young girls from Eastern Europe – their ages ranged from 12-

14 – were found naked, shivering and scared out of their wits at the home of Mr Teen. The police also discovered mountains of the sickest child pornography.

What are the police doing to catch Mr Teen? Why haven't they caught the bastard already? Come on, policemen of Kent! Wake up and let the people know.

The fiend on the right of our photograph is also not in police hands. Maybe Essex police can tell us why not? Perhaps it is because he was until recently one of their senior officers?

His name is Henry Headleigh, who resigned as a detective superintendent recently. He resigned – he loftily told the Press – in order to fight to clear his name of serious allegations.

These 'allegations' involve child pornography. The Gazette had led the way in exposing this man.

Sickeningly, Headleigh was the senior officer in a unit established to bring paedophiles to justice. Now this pervert has had the nerve to launch legal action against the Evening Gazette.

Let me assure our readers, the Gazette will defend our position with fairness and ferocity. Make no mistake, Henry Headleigh, you are not just fighting a newspaper. You are fighting our legions of fair-minded readers.

Many of those readers will have young children. They are sickened by the disgusting activities of you and your kind. The Press has a duty to ensure that people like you are kept off the streets. We will fight to bring you to justice, and to make this land a cleaner one to live in.

Bryan Richardson
(Chairman, Evening Gazette)

The battle lines were drawn.

CHAPTER THIRTEEN

NOVEMBER – Day One

GEORGE EDMUND STREET, like Henry Headleigh, was a native of Essex. Headleigh stood outside Street's masterpiece one overcast morning and admired the sheer extravagance of the design and structure. Headleigh was neither a great scholar nor a lover of architecture, but he could appreciate the majesty of the many fine castles and churches to be found in Britain.

He must have wandered around London many times with the children, but it was generally Jane and Theresa who had examined the detail of the places they visited: the parks, the bridges, the churches and the cathedrals, but not until this day the Royal Courts Of Justice. The father of the family was more of a coastal or countryside man; give him Walton-on-the-Naze or Dedham any day.

The Royal Courts Of Justice were impressive, though. Or maybe it was just that he had lingered outside on The Strand longer than expected. Where were the lawyers?

So this place was to yield his salvation or to compound his disgrace. Yes, it was a suitable setting for the great trials of the land; preferable to the Crown Courts Headleigh was more accustomed to.

G E Street died the year before Queen Victoria opened the Royal Courts Of Justice in 1882. The great architect, author, scholar and traveller had spent the best part of a decade overseeing the construction of the massive, neo-gothic building on the site of an old slum. The stress brought on by the project caused his premature death, it has been claimed. The Royal Courts Of Justice occupy a 500-foot stretch of The Strand. It is a veritable warren, containing three and a half miles of corridors and a thousand-plus rooms – 88 of which are used to try a myriad of cases.

The High Court is responsible for hearing the majority of the cases. The rich and the famous, the good and the bad, the honourable and the corrupt have passed through the Great Hall, mingling with an interminable line of officials and tourists.

Tradition still reigns supreme, powdered wigs and gowns providing an aura at once authoritarian and intimidatory. There are divisions dealing with a wide range of civil disputes such as divorce and commerce. The Queens Bench Division handles the most high-profile trials. Former Detective Superintendent Headleigh was joining their ranks that day.

He had rested up during the summer, spending as much time as possible away from the Brentwood home. He had managed to see Jane and the children. Jane had confirmed she would wait until after the trial before starting divorce proceedings.

Jonathan was friendly but cool towards him during two outings in July. Diplomatically, the father had booked into a hotel at nearby Henley-on-Thames to avoid the embarrassment of having both estranged parents under the son's roof. They had spoken just the once since then; Jonathan phoning a week ago to wish him good luck. It was a brief call, the catch in his son's voice betraying a lack of conviction in his well-wishes.

Sarah and Theresa hooked up for the summer vacation; that pleased dad. They had landed posts with a work-study project in York. The pay was poor, but accommodation and food were provided. Headleigh spent a week there in August. He toured the Yorkshire Dales, reminiscing over long-ago walking trips and discovering new ones. He was particularly impressed by Wharfedale. He enjoyed the brisk sea air of Robin Hood's Bay – a small, relatively quiet cove which was new to him. He lunched twice with his beautiful, wonderful girls and they said their goodbyes over evening dinner. They had been warmer than Jonathan, but there had been tears; and there was something about the twins that he could not quite put his finger on. Their eyes, their voices, their whole body language was not as it should be, he thought. Not as it used to be. At his insistence, for which they were all probably grateful, no family member would attend court.

Four weeks before the trial was scheduled to start, he'd flown to Italy and spent a fortnight on the Mediterranean island of Ischia. Headleigh enjoyed being a solo traveller. He could walk at his own pace, rest when he wanted to, and read when he wanted to. He had heeded Michael Feuerstein's advice and raided his local library for a bunch of legal books. He was no stranger to the courts and their mechanism, baffling to many outsiders but not to him. He would not, however, claim to be an expert in the field of civil law. But he felt much wiser after the fortnight.

Recalling the last night on Ischia made him smile; he had had to fight off the amorous advances of a touchy-feely German lady who had par-taken of a glass too many at a 'typical island dinner.' Did the friendly frau not realise he was Henry Headleigh? The notorious English pae-dophile? She may have been fun, but even though he, too, had enjoyed more than his usual intake of wine, the advice of Keith Whiteside had stuck with him: Beware of vultures in the guise of angels.

He re-read a lighter tome on his flight home. It detailed many of the famous British libel trials. Headleigh was familiar with most. Former trade minister and Tory Party vice-chairman Lord Aldington's £1.5 million vitory over Count Nikolai Tolstoy who had accused him of war crimes. The brashness and arrogance of other Conservatives: Neil Hamilton, Jonathan Aitken and Jeffrey Archer.

Hamilton was declared bankrupt after failing in his bid for damages against the owner of Harrods, Mohammed Al-Fayed, over a scandal involving payments for asking questions in Parliament.

Aitken's claim against The Guardian newspaper collapsed and he was later jailed for perjury.

Archer, another former Conservative vice-chairman, won £500,000 from The Daily Star who had reported that the novelist had slept with a prostitute. What was it with Tories and the courts?

The saga of disputes between rock singer Elton John and Britain's tabloid Press caught his attention. Both The Sun and The Daily Mirror came unstuck in the High Court against the singer, who readily admitted he was bisexual. The Sun especially waged a vendetta which brought forth numerous writs and resulted in John winning £1 million and a front page apology. A million? Headleigh would settle for that.

Other celebrities had not been so fortunate. A TV actress and two England cricket legends were left nursing astronomical legal bills after failing with claims which Headleigh considered petty in the extreme.

The Headleigh trial was to be held in court 14. Hollywood stars Tom Cruise and wife Nicole Kidman had triumphed over Express Newspapers in that courtroom, a good sign Headleigh hoped. The Sunday Express magazine had published a report making several slurs on their marriage. Cruise had emerged from court 14 to tell the world that legal action had been "the last recourse against those that published vicious lies about me and my family. I have to protect them. This was certainly not about money. Every penny of this very substantial sum will be donated to charities." Charity starts at home, thought Headleigh.

"Ah, Keith. What's happening? Where are they?"

"They're on their way. A breakdown in communications; they expected us at the offices and were getting worried."

"Well that's a fine start, I must say. The enemy has gone in. They just walked right on by, not bothering to even acknowledge my presence. Quite an impressive team, I must say."

"Numbers mean bugger all, Henry. Quality, my friend, quality and of course righteousness. Where would we be without that, eh?"

"How very true."

"I heard their top man was raging that we'd already nabbed Carel-Hobbs. Now that is a good sign, Henry. Our Quentin doesn't back many losers."

"How is our flamboyant barrister? I hope he is dressed for the occasion and hiding those hideous ties he fancies?"

"He's fighting fit, raring to go."

"Here, he comes. Christ, Quentin! Take your bloody hand off your hip. I'd nick him if he tried walking round Manchester like that."

The great, legendary, spectacularly flamboyant Quentin Carel-Hobbs did not hear Whiteside's asides to Headleigh. If he had heard them he would not have batted an eyelid. He had heard them all before. The wolf whistles enchanted him. The outrageous mannerisms were all part of the act for Carel-Hobbs, part of the grand theatre of the Bar.

It was a travesty of justice that the legal profession had no equivalent of the Oscars; Carel-Hobbs would scoop the board year upon year. The left hand stayed on the hip as the right jetted forward to greet Headleigh. The former policeman had met his brief four times previously and knew now to keep the handshake delicate.

"Sorry about the confusion, Quentin. Seems we were both worried. Can't say I'm looking forward to this, but…guide me. I am in your hands."

"No problems, Henry, dear chap. I passed the time well. I discovered that ANOTHER of Feuerstein's paintings is a COPY. Ha-ha-ha! Let's go join the party!" With a twirl he was off and leading his troops into the hallowed halls he knew so well.

Quentin was his mother's choice. His father – the late Radislav Carel – preferred George: an excellent, regal, solid first name, very English. Radislav had landed in Britain shortly after the Second World War as a young orphan. A British colonel had taken the boy under his wing after rescuing him from the blaze that killed his mother, father and four siblings. The blaze had been started by German troops fleeing Yugoslavia to escape Allied advances.

Radislav was given a modest, very Army upbringing in Hampshire. Colonel Edward Verity was not wealthy. He and his wife had two teenage children of their own and were stunned when daddy returned home after the war with a refugee in tow. He would hand over Radislav to the authorities, but he's a bright little chap and well, would you like an addition to the family?

When they heard daddy's story the die was cast. Radislav gradually became a master of all things British, though he preferred to say English. He had no choice but to hurdle the language barrier at a brisk rate, if he wanted communication. Within two years his accent had almost disappeared.

He studied harder than his classmates and was destined for higher education. But he decided to leave school at 16 and seek work to help repay the Veritys for all their kindness. A son or daughter of his would have the best that England could offer; he promised himself that.

Radislav and Susan Chisholm were blessed with just one child, a boy who was very sickly for the first two years of his life. The medical staff was surprised that the scrawny kid survived; he had contracted many killer infantile ailments and spent day after day lying in a tiny cot with an amazing number of tubes running through his wretched body. He survived but was never likely to play Rugby for England.

Hobbs was the insistence of Quentin's wife. Caroline Hobbs was, Quentin supposed, a partial feminist. Not that she promoted the advancement of women in any respect other than the steadfast decision that if they were to marry they should keep her surname, too.

Caroline and Quentin met at a Cambridge dance. Caroline was a first year history student, Quentin a second year lawyer. Not just any second year lawyer, but the outstanding scholar of his generation. Very pale, very thin, very interesting. Already he was creating a stir. He was the master of the Law Studies Department debating society, acknowledged by his under-graduate friends and post-graduate students alike; he impressed his professors and tutors.

His masterly defence of Stalin had first brought him to Caroline's attention. Quentin won a highly-charged debate. He was tasked with defending the Soviet dictator against charges of crimes against humanity. His closing address to the debating society brought the house down – the applause was thunderous. Stalin got off, justification, pleaded Quentin. His pogroms were unavoidable in his bid to drag Russia kicking and screaming into the modern era.

Caroline, struggling to grasp the Russian section of her course, joined in the standing ovation. She was amazed that a second-year lawyer could have such an incredible knowledge of history. Where did they find the time?

Quentin never had any trouble mastering a brief; he read, read and read some more. The pleasures of a youth to whom sport was an alien concept, brought on by the fragility of his physical frame. Just talking to him entranced Caroline. The theatrical side was yet to be unveiled.

Quentin Carel was simply a young man who was determined to make the best of himself to honour his father who was slowly ebbing away due to the ravages of cancer. His father lived in time to see his son wed.

Yes, the old man had no problem with Carel-Hobbs – very British – he quite liked it. In fact, he really liked it.

Quentin Carel-Hobbs quickly rose through the legal ranks as a member of Lincoln's Inn – the oldest of the four inns of court – and his reputation grew at a steady pace until he was propelled onto the front pages of the newspapers by successfully defending a Government minister accused of corruption.

The evidence against the Junior Minister For Health had seemed damning but he emerged from the High Court with his reputation restored and almost half a million pounds the richer. The case saw the debut of Carel-Hobbs of stage fame. The flamboyance stuck and increased in campness over the years, but it never took precedence over the brief. Quentin Carel-Hobbs was still as sedulous as the day he defended Stalin – though, personally, he would have happily strangled the monster, strength permitting.

Carel-Hobbs led the way into court as they were called, amiably acknowledging the defendants. Whiteside had already secured a suitable spot on the public benches thanks to a word with a friendly court official. The QC, Headleigh, Feuerstein and one of his assistants sat at their tables and prepared their notes. Sheafs of paper were brought from briefcases and assembled into some sort of order.

Benjamin Smith QC sat a few yards away with a four-strong legal team, plus the owner, editor and crime ace of the Evening Gazette.

All rose as Mr Justice Grant entered the court, a picture of history, tradition and wisdom in his white powdered wig and brilliant scarlet gown. Documents had been lodged with the court, the formalities, legal and traditional, were over; the jury had been chosen and sworn in.

Headleigh glanced across at his accusers. Bryan Richardson and Andrew Harvey he had never seen previously in the flesh but was familiar with their photographs by now. Both looked comfortable in their suits – one black, one blue. Crime Reporter Terry James rarely wore suits and his grey pin-striped looked new. There was a slight clash with editorial lawyer Arthur Jacobs who was seated behind them. Headleigh's eyes flitted between judge and jury as Carel-Hobbs addressed the court, or rather the jury. He was fully aware who mattered most in this historic room.

It was a modest address by his standards: his client was a fine – not to say one of the finest – police officers ever to serve this country of ours. He had to deal with the dregs of society on OUR behalf on a daily basis. He ensured those of us with clean consciences could sleep at night. He had been commended on numerous occasions. He had an unblemished record, and Carel-Hobbs remarked on a few notable triumphs that could be explored later.

Henry Headleigh was here to defend himself against the most outrageous allegations, that he, a father of three, was involved in the sordid world of child pornography. There are few charges you can lay at a man that would prompt greater revulsion in the British public. He is innocent of those charges.

Benjamin Smith QC would never possess the physical extravagances of his courtroom rival. Outside the court, the barristers were, at best, on nodding terms. There existed, perhaps, a tinge of envy in Smith. He was in his late 50s and looked it. Like Carel-Hobbs, he was skinny to the point of sickness. But he could speak loud and strong. And long. He, too, could master a brief superbly. His major flaw, according to contemporaries, was that all had to listen to every miniscule detail of his briefing – no matter how tedious and off-point his speeches. He rambled, but he rambled well to those willing to listen. He ambled to his feet and rambled to the defence of the Great British Press in general, and then specifically to the defendants here today – the three men of the Evening Gazette, who daily kept their readers in London and its surroundings up to date with all that was happening in the South East of England.

Yes, there was tittle-tattle in the paper. They reported on the trivia of celebrities, they reported on sport, the theatre, but they also devoted much time and energy, physical and intellectual, on recording the actions and deeds of national and regional officials.

This was a great duty of the British Press (no longer Great British Press, Headleigh noted) to act as a check on the servants of the crown; on politicians and council officials; on medical bodies; on bodies that dealt with our roads and trains; on those that dealt with our children's schooling.

And, yes, members of the jury, the police forces that are so vital to the good health of this land. They report the heroics of this devoted body of brave men and women who risk life and limb to protect us all.

Now and then, sadly, they are duty-bound – duty-bound by their own consciences and professional code – to inform us of the rotten apples; of those who disgrace their calling and the uniform they bear in its name. This is their duty. Do not confuse it with the tittle-tattle that they readily confess is a means of selling newspapers. Their duty.

My clients were performing their duty when they informed the public of the despicable private activities of the plaintiff. They are here to prove to you that their reports were accurate, honest and truthful. And that there is no place in the British police for officers who conduct themselves in such an indecent manner.

Probably a 2-2 draw, Terry James told himself. He was fascinated by Carel-Hobbs. Like all journalists, especially those who worked in the realm of police and courts, he was aware of the legend but he had never seen it at work.

Headleigh's advocate scored some good points and was fittingly to the point and succinct. He could make a good sub-editor. Smith was thoroughness personified; no stone unturned. He had made the Press seem like a most solemn body of men and just dropped in neatly the fact that they also dealt in the world of trivia and nonsense. Well some did, but not your Terry James. He wondered if the jury of eight men and four women – two of them grandparents, six parents and four childless – would be able to cope with his droning on and on. Smith would not make a good sub-editor.

"That will do for today, gentlemen," said Mr Justice Grant. "Tomorrow you may commence calling your witnesses Mr Carel-Hobbs. I notice from the files you have handed to me that you wish to call three police witnesses."

"That is correct My Lord."

"But you have not specified any order. An order would be useful to myself and the court officials."

"I think your Lordship will discover that I added a note last week respectfully suggesting that we call them in order of rank."

"Starting at the top or the bottom?"

"Starting with the lowest rank – if that is what My Lord meant to convey by top and bottom." Mr Justice Grant ignored the smile that flashed across the face of Carel-Hobbs. The advocate made sure the jury saw it; fleeting as it was.

"So that would be DS Lewis?"

"Yes My Lord, Detective Sergeant George Lewis."

CHAPTER FOURTEEN

Day Two

BENJAMIN SMITH dined late but well that evening at the Inner Temple; just the starter, mind you. Japanese Green Tea Cured Salmon with a Celeriac and Dill Salad, was sufficient for a nibbler like him. He washed it down with a half bottle of Chassagne Montrachet. He had already shared three bottles of middling white wine with John Franzeb, Andrew Harvey and Arthur Jacobs at a crowded, refurbished bar on Fleet Street. How times had changed since the glory days, thought Harvey. Even Smith readily admitted the taste in décor these days was not of his particular preference.

Franzeb had sipped and watched the editor and the lawyer from the Evening Gazette join their brief in running through the proceedings on opening day. Bryan Richardson had dashed off to deal with 'important business' as soon as the trial adjourned for the day. He was not expected to give evidence, hated being there but thought he should, as it would be he, have no fear, who would take the spotlight when victory had been assured. Oh yes, victory would be acclaimed from the rooftops.

Benjamin Smith breakfasted frugally, too. The grapefruit had to be chilled but not bloody freezing with ice clinging to the sides. The first nibble of the day was taken in his casual attire. Few saw him dressed in such a way in the city. He read the quality papers in detail and skimmed through the tabloids; just part of the job he would inform anyone who needed to know. The qualities had given his address pride of place. That was natural as, for most, this was their first bite at the sleaze of the story.

He enjoyed a brisk autumnal walk along the Thames Embankment before returning to shower and prepare for the day ahead. The 57-year-old lived in Aylesbury with his wife, Anne, but spent most of his weekdays in London, especially during a big trial. He was Oxford-educated and proud of it: Magdalen College. Oscar Wilde and Lord Alfred Douglas had studied there, but Smith preferred to view Lord Alfred Thompson Denning as a mentor. Magdalen had served the late Master Of The Rolls well, and it hadn't done too badly by Benjamin Smith. Benjamin, not Ben. Not even Anne called him Ben. It was a family thing, imbued in him at an early age by his mother in Durham and had stuck. He was glad it had. Ben Smith did not exactly sound like a name one of Britain's finest advocates should possess.

Smith had crossed swords with Quentin Carel-Hobbs before. He wouldn't say he liked the man, but there was a mutual admiration and respect between the pair. Smith took his hat off to the new star of the legal stage. He knew he could never match the youngster in terms of free-flowing eloquence or theatrics more befitting a TV court drama, but they shared a passion for getting to grips with their cases inside and out.

As he walked along Inner Temple Lane that morning, he wondered why Carel-Hobbs had been so keen to take the police officer's case. At such an early stage in the legal proceedings, too, by all accounts. Smith had been keen to take the paper's side. Like most barristers, he had a penchant for affluent clients, but, no, this was too good an opportunity to let pass. It was a first class chance to make the score between he and Carel-Hobbs a shade more even. Presently, it stood at Carel-Hobbs 4, Smith 1 with one honourable draw.

To be fair to Smith, two of the defeats had been lost causes from the outset. Why his clients hadn't been prepared to settle out of court was beyond him. He reached Fleet Street where he met the journalists from the Gazette, his assistant and the Franzeb team outside the old Express Newspapers building. The Gazette owner was to meet them outside the court. He preferred to arrive in chauffeur-driven style.

"Not a bad morning for November, gentlemen," said Smith, shaking hands with all. "Seen the papers?" Yes, all had seen the papers. A fair start.

"How do you expect today to go?" asked Harvey out of politeness rather than genuine interest or concern.

"Aha! A quiet day for me I expect. But don't tell your proprietor; I still charge by the day. Ho-ho. A lot will depend on how long young Quentin keeps his character witnesses on the go. I won't try and push the police too far unless I feel the need. But I have gargled just in case. Ho-ho."

That was exactly how Arthur Jacobs laughed, thought Harvey; maybe it is a legal laugh. Did Carel-Hobbs laugh that way?

Mr Justice Grant: "You may proceed Mr Carel-Hobbs"

"Thank you, My Lord. I must firstly inform the court that unfortunately my first witness is unable to attend today. I was only made aware of it myself about an hour ago; some family tragedy. However, the Chief Constable kindly sent me a letter by fax from Detective Sergeant George Lewis. If it please your Lordship I can read the letter and lodge it with the court. Naturally, if Mr Smith wishes to cross examine I am sure the sergeant will be able to attend at a later date, family concerns permitting."

"I see," nodded the judge. "I think it best for you to read the statement and then Mr Smith can decide if he wishes the police officer to attend."

"Thank you, My Lord. Here is the statement from DS Lewis as faxed to me by Chief Constable James McNish this morning:

Dear Mr Carel-Hobbs,

I will be unable to attend court today owing to a serious illness in the family which I only heard of late last night. I contacted the Chief Constable first thing this morning as I was due to travel to London with him. He suggested that I prepare a statement which I did and dictated over the telephone to one of the secretaries at Chelmsford.

Statement of DS George Lewis: I have known Henry Headleigh for just over six years. I have worked closely with him, particularly over the last few months within his team at the CPU.

Carel-Hobbs interrupted his reading to inform the members of the jury that CPU referred to the Child Protection Unit.

Despite the differences in our ages, I always thought we got along well. Detective Superintendent Headleigh was a highly-regarded senior officer. I came to learn that regard was fully justified.

He had a keen eye for detail and managed to keep abreast of the dozens of incidents which passed the way of our department. Some would be relatively minor, but he always stressed to me and others the need to treat each incident as individual and have respect for the victims.

He encouraged me to forward my career within the force. He was helping me prepare to seek promotion to an inspectorship and he was willing to offer advice and support well outside what you would call office hours.

I would like to consider him as a friend as well as a great boss.

I have not been directly involved in the police inquiry into the material taken from his home, as that is being dealt with by officers outside the force. I have, however, helped the Dorset officers conducting the inquiry, mainly on the running of our department and taking them through our detailed files.

I am obviously restricted in what I can say as the police inquiry is ongoing. But I can say that all within our department were shocked and dismayed when the allegations came to light.

I can tell the court that there has been no hint of any unseemly activities in Detective Superintendent Headleigh's behaviour while I have known him. None whatsoever.

Once again, my apologies to yourself, the judge and the court for my absence today. I hope you understand.

Yours respectfully.

George Lewis (Detective Sergeant, Essex Police)

"That ends the statement from DS Lewis. I understand, My Lord, that the family business concerns his wife's brother who was involved in a serious car accident yesterday. Mr and Mrs Lewis have a daughter, just a few months old, and I am sure the court will appreciate his desire to support his family during this sad time."

"Thank you, Mr Carel-Hobbs. Yes, of course, we appreciate the officer's concerns and wish the family well. Mr Smith, would you be wishing to call DS Lewis for cross examination at a later date?"

Benjamin Smith rose slowly to his feet. "No, thank you, My Lord. We are fully aware that Mr Headleigh – as he is now known – has a very loyal staff. Loyalty is to be commended where appropriate. We are also aware that he has a first-rate track record as a servant of Essex Police. Until now."

"Good shot," muttered Bryan Richardson and felt like applauding.

"Mr Carel-Hobbs?"

"I would like to call Inspector Colin Grant."

Grant looked a fine, smart figure in full uniform dress as he was sworn in. But his face betrayed a surprising nervousness for a man familiar with giving evidence in a courtroom. Carel-Hobbs had noticed and slowly and gently brought him to ease. The officer coughed a couple of times while even giving his personal details. He came more into his own as he and Carel-Hobbs guided the jury through the workings of Essex Police.

How long had he been in the force? Happy in your work? How long had you worked with Detective Superintendent Headleigh? Benjamin Smith could call the former officer plain, old Mister but Carel-Hobbs would not be sidetracked. "Fourteen years? That's a considerable length of time for someone to be acquainted with a work colleague these days. You can get to know a man well during that amount of time."

"Yes, sir, very well, I would say."

"And, Inspector Grant. Would it be fair to say that you knew Detective Superintendent Headleigh better than any other officer cur-rently serving with Essex Police?"

"Probably, sir. I can't think of any fellow officer who has known or worked with Henry as much. We are both Clacton lads, too, so we have a little in common from there. The Chief and maybe one or two offi-cers more senior than myself will have known of Henry longer than myself, but I don't know anyone who has worked as closely."

"You were as thick as thieves, so to say? Ha-ha-ha!"

No, it was a totally different laugh to Benjamin Smith's, thought

Harvey. It seemed…more genuine. Inspector Grant raised a smile. He was relaxing finally.

"You could say that, sir. We did work on a lot of cases together. Successful cases in the main. And I would like to put on record my gratitude for Henry's advice, experience and support on some of my own so-called successes. Being the man he is, though, he was happy to let me take the plaudits."

"Quite. The sign of a good boss, I say." Don't rush, inspector, thought Carel-Hobbs, relax, but don't rush.

"You knew the family well, I understand?"

"Yes, sir. To be honest I would say good acquaintances rather than lifelong buddies or whatever. But, yes, we spent a fair amount of time outside work in each other's company. Our wives got along well..." Grant stole a quick look at Headleigh as he mentioned their wives. Poor Jane. Grant tried not to blush and wanted to continue but had lost his thread. Carel-Hobbs leapt to the rescue.

"You visited the Headleigh home on a number of occasions. Was it a happy household?"

"Most definitely. He had three great kids. Chatty, intelligent, polite – what more could a dad want? We went there mainly in the summer – drinks and the odd barbecue in the garden; twice over the Christmas period for dinner; and now and then I would just stop by for coffee if I needed Henry's advice. He was always most insistent that I should feel free to drop by if I ever needed him. We live about two miles apart."

"Now, inspector, when you were at the Headleigh home – for a barbecue, dinner or just dropping in for coffee – did you ever suspect your superior was up to no good? Did you ever think you had interrupted some nasty hobby he may have had?"

"No, sir. Nothing of the kind."

"Did he ever look flustered or upset to see you? As if he had been occupied – in his, ahem, loft, perhaps?"

"Absolutely not, sir."

Ten more minutes and Carel-Hobbs, with minor assistance from the witness – had painted the jury a quaint picture of the Happy Headleigh Home. The birds sang, flowers bloomed, the children skipped with songs in their hearts – and Inspector Grant was always welcome to drop by. No problem, Colin, I was only going through my collection of child pornography – want to come up to the loft and see the new stuff just in? Absolutely not, ladies and gentlemen of the jury.

"Now let's return to police work, Inspector Grant. What was Detective Superintendent Headleigh like there?"

"A top notch professional. Ask anyone who's worked with him. Quiet and efficient. A few I know could learn from him. Hardly ever needed to raise his voice; he was a class act at making a point firmly. I can't recall him ever making a wrong call – I guess it was that that made him so well liked. That and the fact that he wasn't a ranter and a raver."

Carel-Hobbs insisted Grant take the jury through some of the celebrated cases he and Headleigh had worked on. The drug peddlers, rapists and murders they had put away. They were responsible for bringing to justice some real bad villains – they dealt with them politely and firmly, naturally. Sure, a few doors had been kicked in and villains wrestled to the ground. Wrestled was a grand word, inspector, just don't mention the occasional kick to the groin. You're doing fine.

"Ha-ha-ha! I simply cannot imagine Detective Superintendent Headleigh kicking in a door. Dear me." Carel-Hobbs turned and smiled at his client – long enough for the jury to see, of course.

"It's not something he did every day, sir. And despite what you see on TV it is not something any of us do every day. The last time I saw Henry do it was about eight, maybe nine, years ago. Was quite funny.

"We were on this murder investigation and had a warrant to search a known drug dealer's premises. Myself, Henry and a DC went to the flat. Henry knocked on the door twice and called the guy's name. He counted to ten and then told the DC to break in. Well, the constable tried the softest shoulder charge you have ever seen. Henry gently edged him aside and with one size 12 the door was open and we caught the guy trying to flush some crack down the lavatory."

"Ha-ha-ha!" You wouldn't catch Quentin Carel-Hobbs shoulder

charging a door. No way, inspector. One more, inspector, tell the jury about the big drug bust – the major haul – and then we can get back onto the grimy matter.

"That was quite a feather in Henry's cap – and you played a far from minor role yourself, Inspector Grant. We are all grateful to you for helping to keep this menace off the streets. Shortly after that, Detective Superintendent Headleigh was appointed to take charge of the new team tracking down paedophiles, wasn't he?" There, it was out in the open, that most hated species: PAEDOPHILES.

"Yes, sir. There had been some bad Press and the authorities wanted a senior officer to take over the detection side of things."

"And there was no more suitable senior officer with no more impressive a record than Detective Superintendent Headleigh for such a key role. Is that fair?"

"Certainly. I think it is indeed fair to say Henry was the top detective on the force."

Good, good. Carel-Hobbs was pleased with the way things were going. He thought the balance they were striking was paying off slowly. They had decided that he was to refer to his client by his rank, and the inspector by his Christian name. Just don't make it sound like you two were chums.

"You were assigned to the team investigating these paedophiles, too?"

"Not exactly, sir. Well, not officially, is the best way to put it. I was still officially CID, on the drug squad – something to do with paperwork and allocation of resources – but, yes, I did work with Henry's team mostly. Myself and DS Lewis were the main officers Henry relied on for the field work. I handled the uniform side."

Inspector Grant told the jury how the unit operated, what kind of disgusting material they uncovered; the revolting people they were trying to apprehend or run out of Essex. He toned it down as much as possible – this, too, had been previously determined.

"So Detective Superintendent Headleigh, yourself and other officers had to deal with this utterly sickening material daily. You had to examine photographs and video footage of very young children being abused – physically and sexually; young children being kept in the most appalling squalour. Sometimes, these young children would be killed, murdered for the ENTERTAINMENT of these sick pae-dophiles. Is that correct?"

"Yes, sir. It really is beyond belief what these people are capable of."

"What effect does it have on the officers who have to deal with it? It can't be easy clocking off after dealing with depravity and degradation all day?"

"We have counsellors available if we need them. Most tend to maybe have a pint or two and talk about anything else other than work before heading home. It is one of those departments which one just doesn't like to talk too much about. It is essential and highly rewarding. You tell yourself you are doing your damnedest to spare some young kiddie here or from abroad from having to go through similar ordeals. But, no sir, the work does not make good bar talk."

"I can imagine. Indeed I can. So can you believe someone who lived his professional life in this wretched world then going home and viewing images and web sites for pleasure? Can you believe that of my client? Can you imagine Detective Superintendent Headleigh sneaking up into his loft and turning on a computer when he was alone in the house and getting his kicks from child pornography?"

"Nor sir, I cannot believe it for one minute."

"So, inspector, what was all this pornography – paedophilia – doing on the computer in your superior's loft? That is what puzzles me."

Inspector Grant paused and looked around the courtroom. "Well sir. I could surmise, but there are enquiries continuing. Police inquiries and I am not...I am not sure I should be offering conjecture in this court."

The paper's advocate rose to interject. "Yes, inspector, there are police inquiries. Indeed there are. I would respectfully request your Lordship to inform all witnesses that they reveal nothing which could be prejudicial to the criminal investigation."

"Thank you, Mr Smith. I am fully aware of that. I would remind you that both parties agreed to this hearing in full knowledge that it was always likely to precede possible criminal hearings. But, yes, we all need to be careful. You chose your words well Inspector Grant. Pray continue cautiously Mr Carel-Hobbs."

"Thank you, My Lord. Now inspector, you are permitted reasonable conjecture in this court. I am sure my learned friend and I will keep the jury advised of what is fact and what is opinion. All we ask is your honestly given opinion – as a professional and as a man. So, in your opinion, inspector, what was this material doing on the computer in Detective Superintendent Headleigh's loft? How on earth did it get there?"

"Well, sir, I am sure I am not alone in wondering that, too. In my opinion I can only assume it was planted there."

"You mean planted by a third party? Placed on the computer to embarrass my client?"

"Yes sir."

"Now who would want to do that?" Carel-Hobbs turned to the jury to ask this question, though clearly it was intended for the witness. He continued to face the 12 men and women and continued. "Who would want to embarrass a senior Essex police officer? A senior Essex detective responsible for putting in prison some of the nastiest pieces of work imaginable. Who, I wonder?" Minor theatre in the great Carel-Hobbs scheme of things. He turned back to regard the inspector and awaited his reply.

"Well, sir, that is the problem. There are simply too many candidates. I did look through some old files in my own time. I ran off a list of 300-plus people convicted of serious crimes in cases involving Henry in the past ten years. I gave the list to Assistant Chief Constable Hill from Dorset. He did ask me if it was possible to narrow it down. So I did. I gave him two lists – those still inside prison and those now released."

"A crime with more than 300 potential perpetrators. You get many cases like that inspector?"

"Not many. Nothing of this kind. I did once investigate a fatal stabbing outside a football ground. There were 7,000 potential killers and

7,000 potential witnesses. We never found who did it." Carel-Hobbs could have done without the extra information, thank you. Clearly Inspector Grant was relaxed and it was time to wind up this line of questioning.

"Thank you, Inspector Grant. Please wait for my learned friend's questions."

Benjamin Smith rose and tugged at his gown. "Inspector Grant – another loyal officer; very commendable. CID usually, but uniform for the CPU. A detective at heart, I assume. Would you say that it is the normal case for detectives to put personal feelings before plain facts when investigating serious crimes, sir?"

"Well, no, it is not the normal case. But if you know the person involved it is highly understandable."

"Is it now? I would have thought it more unusual than understandable. I would think that the police as a general rule would forbid detectives from working on cases where they had a personal interest or involvement. Would I be correct?"

"Yes sir. That is the normal rule. I am not involved in the investigation. I said I made a list as a friendly gesture. The officers from Dorset – Assistant Chief Constable Hill and Inspector Casely – are conducting the inquiry. I tried to help them by giving them the list."

"Let us say, for example, that a detective is acquainted with a man who runs a haulage firm. This haulier is accused of murder and the murder weapon is discovered in his car with his fingerprints all over it. The haulier pleads innocence. 'It must have been planted,' he protests. Would you expect the police to charge him? Or to wade through all his clients for the past ten years or so to try and discover if he was telling the truth?"

"Well…"

"And normally, sir, in your considerable experience as a fine detective, the facts are what count, not personal feelings?"

"Yes, but…"

"Thank you, Inspector Grant. No further questions, My Lord."

Not bad at all, thought Harvey. Bryan Richardson may have thought the same if he hadn't been fiddling with his expensive gold watch in a bid to stay awake. Carel-Hobbs was very alert. An obvious ploy from his learned rival, but really it was bad form to interrupt witnesses. Juries recognised that; most of them were employees who knew that irritating feeling of not being allowed to finish your sentences. Carel-Hobbs used the ploy himself now and then – against his better judgement, and not too often. Not good when the witness is a police officer, Benjamin old chap.

The judge discharged the jury for the day and spent two hours with the legal camps. They had previously agreed that the police evidence against Headleigh was open for the court to discuss, but Inspector Grant's testimony had persuaded Mr Justice Grant that the matter needed reiterating. Disrobed, they could have been three city high-flyers discussing a corporate raid. Less formal than in court, the two barristers still respected the judge's authority.

"You just have to ensure that fact and opinion are distinguished," said the judge. "The only problematic witness could be the chap from Dorset who's conducting the inquiry. He's one of yours, Benjamin?"

"Yes sir, I would say a slightly reluctant witness but he has agreed to give evidence."

"I have a note from the Chief Constable, too – it appears he is not entirely happy about appearing, Quentin?"

"So I am informed sir. But he is the highest officer in the county and I think the court needs to hear his opinion of my client. I promise to be gentle with him."

Day Three

Carel-Hobbs was as good as his word. He was polite and gentle with James McNish. But he made sure he got his money's worth out of the Chief Constable of Essex. DS Lewis and Inspector Grant had been called as they worked closely with Henry Headleigh – they said (or wrote) what was much to be expected of subordinate officers.

McNish did not seem a figure of fun as he stood in the box. He did not seem to be a genial superior. Frosty was a more suitable name, thought Carel-Hobbs. It was understandable; McNish could be an extremely amusing fellow when the occasion suited. He enjoyed a drink at the bar with his officers; he appreciated the finer things in life, usually rounded off with a hearty meal.

These days he was miserable McNish. He felt himself a reluctant passenger in a series of events taking place on HIS patch. He was tit- ularly in command, responsible for policing Essex. Yet day after day for months now he had struggled to deal as effectively as was his hall- mark with the routine of his office. He felt bogged down and pres- sured by outsiders. The Home Office, Assistant Chief Constable Frederick Hill, and now a string of lawyers and legal officials availing themselves of classified documents from his headquarters.

The spectre of Henry Headleigh hung over him – even in the bloody bathroom for goodness sake! Good cop gone bad? Brilliant detective. Such a shame. A real tragedy.

He plucked an imaginary hair off his spotless uniform as Carel- Hobbs welcomed him to the witness box. He was composed and spoke with a reassuring voice. The acoustics in the courtroom seemed to agree with his vocal level. He couldn't shake off Frosty, though. He spent two hours that morning answering questions as briefly as possi- ble. Carel-Hobbs would have none of it. He wanted a full background on McNish and Essex Police.

How did he manage to land the top job? What was his daily routine? How often did he meet his senior officers? What were the county's priorities for fighting crime? The barrister was armed with facts and figures and biographies of key personalities, but he wanted the jury to hear it for themselves from the horse's mouth.

Headleigh listened intently. Of course, he had heard McNish speak publicly on policing in general and policing in Essex on many stages before, yet Carel-Hobbs gradually made it all seem so informal. Frosty was not about to defrost, but he became warmer.

"Barrel of laughs, isn't he your old boss?" Keith Whiteside said to

Headleigh in between huge gulps of best bitter at lunchtime.

"I've seen him in fouler moods," smiled Headleigh.

"Mind you, that bloody vulture over there doesn't exactly look the life and soul." Whiteside had nodded towards a lone figure standing at the bar about 30 feet from them. Terry James was looking at his pint rather then drinking it. He was alone and appeared deep in thought. "Ten minutes with that bugger, Henry. Just ten minutes and I am sure I'd have some answers for us. Society's gone bloody soft if you ask me. One more for the road?"

If the morning session had been uncomfortable for McNish, the afternoon proved a real pain in the backside. Carel-Hobbs wanted him to tell the court what he thought of Detective Superintendent Henry Headleigh as an officer? As a detective? Didn't Detective Superintendent Headleigh have a record second to none? What would you rate as Detective Superintendent Headleigh's greatess successes for Essex Police; I mean on behalf of the citizens of Essex?

It was about an hour into the afternoon when Michael Feuerstein slipped Headleigh a note. 'You hear he's now calling you Det Supt not Mr anymore?'

Headleigh hadn't noticed. He was so familiar with the cases Carel-Hobbs was dragging out of the chief that he had drifted off with his thoughts. He shook himself back into the real world and smiled as he discovered that, yes, McNish was referring to Detective Superintendent Headleigh.

"Can you think of a finer officer who has served Essex Police in your time as chief constable?"

"Well I have a first-rate deputy who sadly has suffered with a chronic illness, and I have extremely capable assistants…"

"Let me narrow it down for you, Chief Constable McNish," said Carel-Hobbs helpfully. "Can you think of a finer detective?"

McNish was getting tired, physically tired and mentally drained. He had refused a seat. If that bloody lawyer stood all day so would he. "Detective Superintendent Headleigh is a very capable detective…"

Is, not was. The chief was slipping. Does he want me back? Thought Headleigh.

"I have many good detectives working for me, and I would not like to compare."

"I do understand Chief Constable. I would not dream of asking you to name names or to undermine the detectives struggling to live up to the reputation of Henry Headleigh. Clearly he is a figure to be emulated. Let me put it this way, if a close relative or friend had the great misfortune to become the victim of a serious crime against the person; who would you prefer to lead the police investigation? Detective Superintendent Headleigh or..."

"My Lord, Mr Carel-Hobbs is trying to put words into the chief constable's mouth. This really is unacceptable," said Smith.

"My Lord, I am merely attempting to confirm my client's credentials. It is essential that the jury is made fully aware of the high esteem in which he is held by Essex Police."

What Carel-Hobbs did not say was that information had been leaked his way of a major row within the murder squad in Essex just a fortnight ago. McNish had read the riot act after two men had wriggled off the hook due to sloppy police work. "The Chief Constable may answer the question," said Mr Justice Grant.

"Detective Superintendent Headleigh is...probably, yes...probably the best detective I have known....yes...so...I suppose I would want Henry to..."

"Thank you, Chief Constable McNish. You have been most helpful today. No further questions, My Lord." Carel-Hobbs would not really classify that as an interruption. He was actually doing the chief a favour, sparing him greater embarrassment.

"Time is pressing. Mr Smith. Would you like to cross examine now or wait until Monday?"

"I have no questions for the Chief Constable, My Lord. I thank him for his attendance today."

"You may step down Chief Constable McNish. The court will resume on Monday."

Bryan Richardson was not used to being told to keep his voice down. He leaned across the table in the pub and positively hissed at his barrister: "No questions? No bleedin' questions? What the fuck am I paying you for?"

"Kindly watch your language please, Mr Richardson. Let me be the judge of what should and should not be asked in court."

"May I be so bold as to ask why you didn't question him?" said Gary Chalmers, jumping politely to his chairman's aid.

"I saw no point, that is why. The Chief Constable had given the plaintiff a glowing referral. Christ! He was even calling him HENRY by the end. And let us not forget, we are dealing with the present not the past. The man has an excellent track record; we know that. I consider it pointless to even attempt to dismantle that. Have no fear; our day will come when we get to the charges of child pornography. Have no fear. Now I must get home to my wife for the weekend. Enjoy yours, gentlemen."

Enjoy your wife or your weekend? Terry James wasn't sure. He'd better be going, too. Peace to make with the girlfriend if not exactly his lawful wedded wife.

CHAPTER FIFTEEN

TERRY JAMES arrived home later than expected that Friday evening. Annette was sat in an armchair, not on the sofa. She had her arms folded and was watching television, which she rarely did. Not a good sign.

"And what time do you call this? As soon as the court's over for the day; that's what you said? It's almost 7.30! Long day at court was it?"

"Listen Annette, I'm really sorry but the tube was a nightmare…"

"Oh yes, always is on a Friday, isn't it? So you just thought you'd wait for the crowd to thin out – and why not wait in a pub, eh? I can smell it all over you."

"I just had to catch Craig Butler – we had some work matter to go over."

"You mean office gossip to catch up on. Don't try and fool me."

"Come on, sugar. You know I've had this case hanging over me for ages now."

"Of course, I bloody know. Don't you think it's been hanging over me, too? You've more time for that bloody lot than me these days." The artist pointed at a pile of law books and magazines sitting untidily on James's desk.

"Let's go out for a bit, eh love? You choose – meal, movie?"

"Yeah! I think I'll go out for a bit. I think I'll go to Hazel's for a bit. I think maybe you can give me a call when this bloody thing is over and done with. Then let's see if the Terry James I know and love is back in the land of the living. Or should I say the Terry James I used to know and love. Or thought I did."

✝

Day Four

Quentin Carel-Hobbs was bristling with energy and excitement. Court would have to be delayed, sorry sir, but it will take perhaps 30 minutes to set up the equipment. When Carel-Hobbs was certain everything was ready and tested, the jury was called in and soon followed by the judge.

"Mr Carel-Hobbs, proceed please."

"Thank you, My Lord, I call Professor James Arnold."

Arnold was not what one would envisage as a typical university professor. He was 38, stocky, bespectacled a la John Lennon, and wore his hair longish, just touching the lapel of his thick blue woollen jacket. He informed the court that he oversaw the Information Technology Department at Warwick University; photography was his speciality – professionally and a passionate hobby. He humbly admitted he was considered an expert in digital imagery. Yes, West Midlands Police had enjoyed his professional expertise from time to time.

"Now, if I may draw the court's attention to the screen I have had erected over here," said Carel-Hobbs. "The screen is linked via cable to this computer." The screen was 42in by 60in – a reasonable size for all bar those right at the back to have a decent view.

"The first image you see is a page from The Daily Mirror last June. Now if I click here…yes, there we go. This is a page from the Evening Gazette published a few days later. You will notice that the page features the same photograph as seen on The Daily Mirror page.

"The text accompanying it is credited to the owner of the Evening Gazette and is outrageously defamatory of my client, Detective Superintendent Headleigh."

Benjamin Smith interjected. "On a technicality, My Lord, I think my learned friend should make it plain to the jury that his client is no longer a police officer and has not been for several months."

Carel-Hobbs nodded to his rival. "I am sure my learned friend would not wish to rob a man of his legacy, My Lord. And my client has a legacy to be proud of. As an example, General Woolfson retired many years ago but he is still referred to as general – and hear, hear, I say. He served the British Army honourably and valiantly for decades."

"Please continue, Mr Carel-Hobbs," said the judge, completely ignoring the defence barrister's quibble.

"Thank you, My Lord. As I was saying, the words used by the owner of the Evening Gazette are an appalling slur on my client. They accuse him of being a paedophile. The headline attempts to mock Detective Superintendent Headleigh by employing the worst of tabloid humour: TWO PAEDOS IN A POD. They are accusing a senior police officer of being a depraved pervert and they attempt to find humour in it.

"We shall return to the text later. For now I would like Professor Arnold to tell the court what he discovered while examining the original photograph which was handed to him by the police at my request in September. Professor Arnold, quite simply, it's a fake, isn't it?"

"Aha, sir! Well yes, in your terms it is a fake; in my terminology it is a mock-up."

"For the benefit of those of us without your expertise professor, could you please explain the difference?"

"I'd be pleased to. Of course it's a fake, I didn't mean to sound pompous. But we use the term mock-up when more than one photograph has been used to make a composite photograph."

"Like putting the Prime Minister's head on the body of a donkey, you mean?" Laughter in the court. Carel-Hobbs had considered citing a member of the Royal Family but as the PM was such an easy target these days why not pander to the populace?

"Exactly. It's not difficult to do, especially with digital technology these days. A child could do it with, say, an hour's instruction. You can blend in tones – skin tones, background tones; that sort of thing. You can add trees or landscapes and make them all look like the original part of the photograph."

"But how can you tell when a photograph is a mock-up?"

"Often you can't – unless you have the most sophisticated software. Even that may not work if the original photographs are of similar quality and have been mocked-up by a skilled artist."

"But this is most definitely a fake? Sorry, Professor, of course I mean a mock-up?"

"Yes it is. As you can see, the photograph is poor quality. I would say that was deliberate. The artist possibly had little choice; it would depend on the source material he was given to work with."

"You mean the original photographs?"

"Yes. The poorest quality one would dictate what standard of mock-up could be achieved. Even computers have their limits."

"Please carry on. How can you tell this is definitely a fake?" Carel-Hobbs purposefully didn't correct himself this time. Fake was what he wanted the jury to know, not mock-up, thank you kindly Professor.

"If you blow up the image you will notice there is a significant dif-ference in the dot grain between the man on the left and the one on the right. As you can see the photograph is not the greatest quality, and I would say that is why it was then printed and a Polaroid was taken of the print: to make it virtually impossible to discover it was a fake."

Fake. Very good professor; follow me and let's all call it a fake.

"Let's be clear about this, professor. The artist combined two separate photographs using a computer? He then used his skill to make the background look the same. Then he printed out the fake and took a photograph of it with one of those Polaroid instant cameras?"

"Exactly. You would not see the join, so to speak, without blowing it up. The artist has done a good job, as I say; but it's merely a five-minute job to a skilled user."

"Five minutes? Hmmm…I am sure the court would love to see a demonstration. My Lord, with permission I would like Professor Arnold to provide a five-minute demonstration."

"Yes, certainly. I am sure we would all like to see the marvels of mod-ern technology at play. I can sustain my interest in computers for five minutes."

"Thank you, My Lord. I have prepared one photograph already. Now I need a volunteer." Carel-Hobbs was in his element. Oh the wonder-ful stage was his. What theatre!

"My Lord, I can see no finer profile than your own in this room. May

I be so bold as to ask you to pose for me while I take for posterity a photograph with this £135.99 digital camera I just happened to purchase over the weekend?"

"Heavens above, Mr Carel-Hobbs! For one moment I thought you were wishing to use my courtroom for some advertising campaign. Get on with it."

"A little to the left, My Lord." There was laughter in the court as Mr Justice Grant posed for the country's leading advocate. Had court 14 ever seen such a sight? Mr Carel-Hobbs clicked away four or five times and then profusely thanked the judge.

The laughter did not reach the defence benches. Benjamin Smith QC frowned and looked at John Franzeb. The solicitor shrugged his shoulders and looked behind at Arthur Jacobs. The Gazette editorial lawyer was staring at the large screen. Bryan Richardson was whispering like fury to his editor. Andrew Harvey grasped Terry James's lapel, but the crime reporter shrugged and held his arms open wide.

"We won't time you Professor Arnold, and I am certain his Lordship was jesting when he said his interest was sustainable for just five minutes. There you go, that's the one I prepared earlier, as all the best chefs say."

Bryan Richardson could gladly have punched the effete buffoon's lights out. Smith QC noticed the jury men and women were giving the effete buffoon their rapt attention.

The professor sat down and smiled as he worked. Meanwhile, Carel-Hobbs handed out photocopies of the Gazette article to the judge and members of the jury. He bowed reverentially as he passed copies to the defence bench. Richardson snarled and wanted to rip his bleedin' cocky head off.

Approximately three minutes and 40 seconds into his test, Professor Arnold beckoned Carel-Hobbs to the computer. The barrister clapped his hands and beamed a radiant smile, firstly at the computer and then around the courtroom. He slapped the techno-wizard on the back and asked him to return to the witness box.

"My Lord and members of the jury, if you would look at the screen please." Carel-Hobbs clicked the computer mouse. Deadly silence, then a few titters, and then the loudest, most ribald laughter possibly ever heard in the High Court. Even Mr Justice Grant could not prevent himself from chuckling. There was his noble face in glorious technicolour; his face, adorning the body of a very delectable young lady indeed. The court gradually regained its decency.

"You have amused us all with your demonstration, Mr Carel-Hobbs. I am not averse to a little levity in my court, but pray get to your point."

"Certainly your Lordship. I thank you for your participation. The point is that the photograph of yourself is from this digital camera – a medium range model within most budgets. The photograph of the young lady is from yesterday's Daily Mirror.

"If I may draw the court's attention to the screen. I am blowing up a section of the combined image and the jury will note that the photo of the young lady is considerably fuzzier than the photo of his Lordship; there is significantly more grain in the photo.

"If we turn to the photo of my client and this wanted man, the jury will note a similar pattern. The image of my client shows similar characteristics to that of the young lady. In terms of grain, of course.

"I will let you see each blow up again for a few seconds so you can grasp the differences." There was absolute silence in the courtroom as both images were displayed for several seconds.

The journalists stared at the screen with a wide-eyed intensity. They were aware of the tricks of the trade, photo-manipulation a speciality but be careful. Warnings had been issued to papers after photographs of an estranged Royal couple had been doctored to make them appear closer to each other at a charity function than they actually had been.

"Right. Now that suggests the image of my client is taken from a newspaper. I can tell you that it *IS* taken from a newspaper. This newspaper." Carel-Hobbs held aloft an inside page from a newspaper. The image also appeared on the screen.

"This is page 15 of The East Anglian Daily Times of March 12th last year. The caption reads 'Detective Superintendent Henry Headleigh with his wife Jane at a charity ball which raised £2,650 for the

Colchester branch of the NSPCC'. The NSPCC is, I am sure most of you know, a children's charity. A children's charity and a very worthy cause; one which the Headleigh family has supported for many years.

"The computer artist used a photograph of my client from a newspaper and made this fake. This fake was part of an attempt to compound this wicked slur on my client's reputation. Thank you for your expertise, Professor Arnold."

"Mr Smith?"

"My Lord, no questions for the time being. But I would respectfully like to request that the court make Professor Arnold available for questioning at a later date."

No-one on the defence team asked their barrister why he had decided against asking questions. There was confusion over lunch. Confusion and fear. A fake! John Franzeb joined the morose crowd half an hour later.

"I've made two calls. The police say they never suspected it could have been a fake, just a lousy photo, so they didn't bother examining it that closely. A photography expert we sometimes use says he is willing to examine it for us. But he knows Professor Arnold and said if he says it is a fake, then it will be a fake."

The defence team had not held out much hope, but the confirmation increased the gloom. Thankfully, Richardson had stormed off to dine with Gary Chalmers. The chairman was rarely lost for words, but this lunchtime he could not even find foul ones to sum up his mood. Richardson was in such a foul mood that he skipped the afternoon session at court. The jury were discharged for the day as Mr Justice Grant heard legal submissions.

He retired to his chambers shortly after 4pm, but not before drawing Carel-Hobbs to one side. "Any chance of a copy of that photograph, Quentin? I'd enjoy surprising Lady Grant over dinner."

Days Five-Seven

Some would consider Keith Whiteside's nine hours in the witness box an ordeal; quite an ordeal as his past was dissected by two of the finest legal brains Britain had to offer. His testimony spread over three days owing to interruptions as the judge argued with the barristers, particularly Benjamin Smith who was decidedly unhappy at playing on the back foot.

It was all water off a duck's back to Whiteside – Detective Chief Inspector Whiteside of Great Manchester Police and damned proud of it. You may call me Mr Whiteside if that makes you happier Mr Smith. That exchange made Headleigh grin. Yes, he could have worked with Whiteside, cautiously though.

Terry James was very wary of Whiteside, more wary than Headleigh. Whiteside had just happened to bump into James during the summer in the grounds of Eton College of all places.

The reporter and Annette had gone to a festival of classical music. James and Annette were lying on their rug listening to Handel's Water Music. In truth, James was dozing when the large figure tripped over his feet, spilling beer onto the rug and his jeans. A tiny amount landed on Annette's skirt. Profuse apologies followed during which the beer-spiller demanded that they send him any cleaning bill and handed them his card.

"Here, I'm working in the south for several weeks. I can be contacted here," and he scribbled the name, address and phone number of Feuerstein, Savage and Amrein on the back of his card.

"Sorry again; clumsiness is one of my better traits actually. Ha-ha. Enjoy the music. Please do send the bill."

James did not send the bill, but the incident worried him even though he assured himself it was just a scare tactic. It had worked: that big bastard did scare him.

Carel-Hobbs introduced the burly northerner to the witness box. He was wearing a new dark grey – or should that be light black? – suit which he had sensibly broken in during the first few days of the trial. It was a more modern cut than he was used to. Pricey, too. He still looked like a copper.

Gentle questioning at first by Carel-Hobbs endeared Whiteside to the jury. The barrister gradually stepped up the heat with a pre-emptive strike.

"You made a few enemies within the Manchester force, though, didn't you, Detective Chief Inspector? Let's say some of your methods were unconventional. Is that fair?"

"I suppose so. I make no bones about that, sir. My job was to catch villains, and believe me we have some bad ones back home. I got results – that was my job. I hurt a few villains, I admit. But I also stopped some getting badly hurt. And I mean BADLY."

"Explain, please."

"Well one time, I had to drag a youngish detective constable off a suspected rapist. This bloke was wanted for a series of sexual attacks in the Cheatham Hill area. We found him late one night and were struggling to get the cuffs on him. The constable started laying into him. I told him to back off and things seemed to have calmed down. I went to open the car and the constable started again, really smacking this guy. I had to pull him away again. Over a pint before bed the constable apologised to me but said his wife had been raped two years previously. Mucky work, very mucky and you'd need to be a saint not to step over the line now and then. I just made sure I didn't step too far."

"You yourself were once investigated. Tell the court about that please?"

Whiteside calmly informed the court of his dealings with Assistant Chief Constable Frederick Hill – the very same Dorset officer who was conducting the inquiry into Henry Headleigh. He co-operated fully and no evidence was found to warrant pressing charges.

The morning session closed with Carel-Hobbs stressing to the jury that the witness was a highly-respected detective who had been commended for bravery on several occasions. He did not suffer fools or villains lightly. Just in case the jury had forgotten his comments, Carel-Hobbs opened the afternoon session by repeating them.

Then he was most intrigued by the work done by the witness and his fellow former detectives. Please let the court hear how you operate, Detective Chief Inspector Whiteside.

"We only work for official bodies, so don't ring us if you want someone to check out your husband or wife's wanderings. It gets us out of
doing the gardening, and is a nice supplement to the pension. Pays for
the odd holiday; that sort of thing.

"Solicitors provide most of the work. Background checks – a lot of
that work. This is my second libel case. I should say, there is a tacit
understanding that if we come across any sign of criminal activity the
solicitors are obliged to pass it on to the police."

"Ah! Very good. And have you stumbled across any sign of criminal
activity while working on my client's case?"

"No, sir; none at all. Apart from the files provided by ACC Hill's
inquiry, obviously."

"Now let us make this absolutely clear: you have been working for
Feuerstein, Savage and Amrein in attempting to help Detective
Superintendent Headleigh clear his name. If you had discovered any
new evidence of guilt you would have passed it onto the police?"

"Yes, sir."

"Fine now we are clear on that; and may I say it is a commendable
attitude. I am sure we wish all private investigators had similarly high
standards.

"During the course of your investigation, you examined all the files
provided by Essex Police and conducted many interviews of your own.
What were you able to find that the police apparently have not?"

"I interviewed Detective Superintendent Headleigh initially in the
presence of his solicitor Michael Feurstein and then by myself. I have
done hundreds – possibly thousands – of interviews with crime suspects, sir. It very quickly became clear that either Detective
Superintendent Headleigh was the greatest liar I have ever come
across…or he was innocent of the charges."

"How long did the interview last? You believed he was telling the
truth from the outset?"

"Not long at all – maybe a couple of hours over a friendly drink. That
is a much better way to get information and to get to the truth, I find,
than in an official police interview room. His whole body language

reeked of innocence. There are manuals on interview technique – page after page of classic case studies and the like. I could let ACC Hill borrow mine if he has mislaid his."

Don't get cocky, Keith. Don't get cocky and don't appear bitter. Whiteside got the message from the steely gaze Carel-Hobbs gave him. There was power in the eyes if not the miserable frame. The barrister waited a couple of seconds longer than usual before continuing.

"His innocence was confirmed in your opinion shortly afterwards."

"The story in The Daily Mirror, you mean, yes. It was all too convenient; like finding a dead body on a bed and a gun on the dressing table. It just doesn't happen that way, believe me."

"What happened next?"

"I confronted Detective Superintendent Headleigh with the paper first thing in the morning, so he would not have had chance to see it himself; unless he had driven out to pick up an early edition. He was shocked and angry.

"I later collected a considerable volume of files from Essex Police and spent the rest of the day examining them back at my hotel."

"And they prompted you to make several phone calls; to Mrs Headleigh, among others?"

"Yes, sir, that is correct."

"My Lord, I now beg the court's permission to provide another visual exhibit. It may take a few minutes to set up."

"I hope it will not prove as racy as the last one, Mr Carel-Hobbs. We shall adjourn for the day as tempus fugit. Please make sure your exhibition is ready on time."

CHAPTER SIXTEEN

Day Six

CAREL-HOBBS was glad of the previous day's adjournment. In fact he had timed it accordingly. This day's exhibition would not be as light as the previous one – nor as racy, as the judge had surprisingly put it.

The barrister wanted the jury to view the pictures on the screen bright and early so they could sink in throughout the day. He wanted the message to last. He wanted them to know why the newspaper needed to be punished. He wanted them to know why his client was so incensed. He wanted the jury to fully comprehend the scale of the allegations. After that it was up to Henry Headleigh to convince them of the absurdity of the claims. Carel-Hobbs had faith.

"My Lord, I should begin by saying that the images on this computer feature many despicable and depraved acts. In short, they show young children being sexually abused by the dregs of society. They will shock the jury. They will disgust them. However, I feel it is essential that they be aired in court so that all can understand fully the nature of the charges against my client and the vehemence with which he is determined to clear his name."

"I see, Mr Carel-Hobbs. I thank you for warning me in private. I have sought guidance on this matter. Yes, they must be viewed in court."

Mr Justice Grant turned to address the jury, "Ladies and gentlemen of the jury, you will recall that you were informed of the nature of this case when you were selected for duty. You were warned to expect to hear details of the most sordid acts and crimes against children.

Prepare yourself for what you are about to witness. The legal advisers for the plaintiff and the defence have agreed with me in chambers that just a selection of material will be shown in open court.

"However, all the files will be available on a computer in the jury room for you to view at the end of today's proceedings and for the remainder of the trial. No matter how distasteful you find the content, I recommend you do try to examine the evidence.

"I will also recommend you avail yourself of the expert guidance and counselling the court provides both during the trial and afterwards. There is no shame in admitting that the images disturb you. Please bear that in mind.

"Mr Carel-Hobbs."

"Thank you, My Lord. Let me also add my voice to My Lord's sentiments. These images you are about to see ladies and gentlemen of the jury were found on a computer in the loft at the home of my client. There is no disputing that. They WERE found in Detective Superintendent Headleigh's home. How they got there is another matter."

Immediately he had finished speaking, one of his assistants clicked the computer mouse and a fuzzy photograph appeared on the large screen. It had been blown up as much as possible without affecting the image quality. The content was clear for all to see. An overweight man wore a leather mask, leather gloves and what appeared to be leather boots. He was holding a whip in his left hand. He was sodomising a boy who could have been ten years old at most. In the background the court could just make out three figures: another masked man was standing between two boys of similar age. They were naked and tied or chained to a wall. They were clearly in a state of distress, panic, fear, revulsion.

Carel-Hobbs moved slowly into the shadows just in front of the judge's box. He had a good view of the jury but they could not see his face. He studied their reactions as his assistant slowly brought up more images. The legal team had timed the video display to last 30 minutes. They had discussed a longer, slower showing but decided 30 minutes should sufficiently put across their message. After three photos had been displayed, Carel-Hobbs noticed the male grandparent had taken the hand of the female sat beside him and was gently stroking her arm. He realised the effect the display would have. The jury would be upset – some more than others – and they would be sickened. They would be also angry; very, very angry. They would be out for blood and demand that someone pay. That was only natural.

He was surprised that all 12 members of the jury were staring open-eyed at the screen, with no attempt to mask their eyes. Strange, though, that they all tried to mask their mouths, as if to prevent themselves from crying or screaming out, perhaps. All four women and two of the men held handkerchiefs to their faces, to cover their mouths, not to dry their eyes. One of the men sat back in his chair with his right hand over his mouth and his left hand clutching it just below the wrist in support. The male grandparent alternated between hiding his mouth and stroking his neighbour's arm. Was he comforting her or trying to steel himself? The others sat with their knees hunched up, with their clasped hands on them. Their chins rested on their hands and they kept their heads bowed.

Carel-Hobbs turned to discern the cause of shuffling in the public gallery. Some people appeared to be leaving. He studied the faces on both benches and noticed Benjamin Smith, too, was glancing now and then at the jury. Of course they had all seen the images before, some of them many, many times. Headleigh shook his head now and then; Keith Whiteside seemed distracted and disinterested.

The images were eventually replaced by web pages, again featuring paedophilia and inviting the viewer into their sick world to feast on the hottest, youngest boys and girls on the World Wide Web. The display ended, the lights came back on full and two jurors excused themselves.

"You sick bastard! You sick, sick bastard! You want hanging!" There was scuffle as officials grabbed the offender from the public gallery. Something was thrown in the direction of the plaintiff's bench. It was fortunately just some screwed up paper and missed Headleigh by a good few feet. The judge coughed and banged on his gavel to restore order. He ordered an adjournment while the display was dismantled. The adjournment lasted longer than anticipated while the judge enquired whether the jury felt able to continue. Lunch was taken early for those who felt like eating, and it was afternoon when Keith Whiteside took to the witness box for the first time that day.

"Detective Chief Inspector, we have all now seen the pornography discovered in Detective Superintendent Headleigh's loft. You are of the firm opinion that it was obviously planted by a third party. What convinced you that was the case?"

"The dates he was alleged to have been looking at child pornography on the Internet conflicted with some entries in his diary, sir."

"In what way did they conflict?"

"The Internet log files revealed that someone had been viewing certain web pages between 9.57pm on March 23rd and 1.20am the following morning – more than three hours."

"And that someone could not have been the plaintiff?"

"No, sir. He was 200 miles away in Bristol."

Carel-Hobbs allowed a pause as he made an extravagant circle around the court floor, his gown flowing elegantly behind him. Whiteside gritted his teeth. The hand, Quentin! The bleedin' hand! Take if off your hip!

"Two hundred miles away in Bristol! Detective Superintendent Headleigh was 200 miles away in Bristol! You are sure of this?"

"Absolutely. I checked the date against Detective Superintendent Headleigh's office diary. The diary is a bit of a shambles as I gather his staff used it for writing notes and details of appointments in it for him. But there was an entry for March 23rd-24th. It read 'overnight Avon with Jane'.

"So I rang Mrs Headleigh. She was still very distressed by the revelations in the papers but agreed to speak to me for a few minutes. She informed me that she had accompanied her husband to a conference hosted by Avon Police in Bristol. She told me that she had visited Bath during the day and returned to Bristol for a dinner in the evening. They had stayed up having drinks with police officers and their spouses till almost midnight and then retired to their hotel room. They left the hotel after breakfast the following day and were back in Essex mid-afternoon. I checked the facts with the Assistant Chief Constable hosting the conference and also contacted the hotel which confirmed the Headleighs had stayed there."

"So Detective Superintendent Headleigh was 200 miles away in Bristol. Two hundred miles away at a police conference. And at 9.57pm, can you pinpoint what he would have been doing at that precise point?"

"Dinner finished at around 8.50, some officers left to go home. Those who were staying at the hotel moved to the bar area. Without disturbing Mrs Headleigh further, I managed to trace two senior officers who were in the party. They confirmed that the Headleighs were in the bar from around 9pm until almost midnight."

"Two hundred miles away in Bristol!" By now Whiteside was certain everyone in the courtroom knew the distance from Brentwood to Bristol. Should he have said approximately 200 miles? Get on with it, Quentin.

"Was Mrs Headleigh aware that you were batting for her husband's side when you questioned her?"

"Yes, sir, I told her I was employed by Feuerstein, Savage and Amrein. But I did not tell her why I wanted to know details of the trip to Bristol. I merely told her I was compiling a timetable of all Mr Headleigh's movements since Christmas and wondered if she could confirm that date as the diary was obscure."

"Was she aware that someone had been using their computer to access pornography that night?"

"No, she wasn't. Not from me at any rate."

"So if it wasn't Detective Superintendent Headleigh, who was on the Internet on his computer browsing through this foul material, Detective Chief Inspector? Who?"

"That is the puzzle, sir. And one I am afraid I have not been able to solve. I am convinced the material was planted to embarrass Detective Superintendent Headleigh. My money would say a criminal with a grudge against him. But as we know there is no shortage of them."

"But it definitely could not have been the plaintiff? Definitely?"

"No way, sir. It was definitely not Henry."

Wonderful, excellent timing. 'Henry' will be good now and then; just not all the time, Keith.

"Did you spot any further discrepancies while checking the diary? Any more conflicts between dates?"

"I noticed some, sir, though it is not quite as simple to disprove those. There is one log file which shows someone connected to a certain child pornography web site at 10.11pm on the night of April 17th. Detective Superintendent Headleigh was checking on an investigation in Clacton that day.

"My enquiries have revealed that he left Clacton sometime after 9.15 but before 9.30, according to local officers. That would have entailed him driving home with all the traffic lights in his favour and probably exceeding a few speed limits, which is not recommended with all the cameras in Essex…"

"And dashed upstairs into his loft and started looking at these web sites? All without Mrs Headleigh noticing anything strange?"

"Yes, sir. Mrs Headleigh was home that evening."

"During unofficial police questioning shortly after the computer had been taken from their home, Mrs Headleigh told an officer that as far as she was aware her husband had not been in the loft since the previous Christmas. Is that correct?"

"I only know the same as you do, sir – what is on the police files."

"What else did your examination of these files reveal?"

"As I said, sir, there are other instances where it would have been just about possible for Detective Superintendent Headleigh to have logged onto the Internet at the times suggested on the files. But he would have needed Michael Schumacher as his chauffeur I would say.

"I would point out that the log files show someone kept long and late hours online; some stretch to 3am. You would expect a man doing a highly-charged job and keeping those sort of hours to show some signs of stress or fatigue, especially a middle-aged man. There are no reports of anything like that."

"Now, sir, this bit is puzzling us all here. You are absolutely of the opinion that someone else was doing this and trying to put the blame on Detective Superintendent Headleigh. I appreciate you cannot tell us who or why; but how? How on earth did this person or persons manage to have such access to the Headleigh home?"

"I am not saying they used the computer in the loft, sir. I am saying they transferred the information onto that computer – the computer used solely by the Headleighs' children over the years."

"Please explain in more detail what you mean by transferred?"

"They would have collected all the information on a different computer – in their own home or workplace – and then copied it to a compact disc. Just like the police in Essex copied all their files to disc for me.

"From the dates on the files I would say the culprit went into the loft sometime in May, possibly early June, and transferred the files to that computer in the loft. I would think the job would take around 15 to 20 minutes."

"Someone broke into the home and did this?"

"Possibly a break-in, though there were no visible signs of a forced entry. It would also require knowledge of the computer in the loft. Many of the children's friends and schoolmates had been in that loft over several years. People talk, people overhear, so how information like that leaked out is not surprising. I admit I cannot say with any degree of certainty how access was gained, unfortunately.

"The house benefits from a modern alarm system which showed no signs of being tampered with. The Headleighs did keep one small window in the bathroom ajar, and a slim man could have gained access via that, but he would have required a ladder. I find that unlikely.

"If I had to put money on it, I would probably have to say it was an invited house guest – a personal friend, a worker, meter-reader – or someone pretending to be such. I am sorry I cannot shed any substantial light on that point, sir."

"That's all right, Detective Chief Inspector Whiteside. We all appreciate your candour. Let's leave conjecture aside and stick to facts. To recap what you are telling the court today: The material was gathered elsewhere and then planted on the computer in the loft at a later date?"

"Yes, sir."

"And it could not have been Detective Superintendent Headleigh gathering the information as he was 200 miles away in Bristol?"

"Yes, sir, he would have been a long way from home on that particular night."

Carel-Hobbs thanked Whiteside. Then, before sitting down, he informed the jury that the Internet log files were on the computer available for their use. They should open the folder titled 'log files' as that contained the dates and scans from the office diary. The adjacent folder marked with a warning symbol contained the images which they had seen earlier in the day.

Day Seven

The defence team had been busy overnight and first thing that morning; busy checking the facts of Whiteside's testimony and busy keeping out of Bryan Richardson's way. The owner felt the sway of the trial and it made him sea-sick.

Andrew Harvey was not feeling at his best, either. He took the brunt of Richardson's wrath and collared Terry James, pleading with him to go back to his source and dig out any information, any extra information at all that could get their case back on track.

Benjamin Smith had been busy amending his plan of attack on Whiteside. Smith began his cross-examination with a deeper, less gentle probing into the former detective chief inspector's past. Whiteside stood firm. He had been on the rack so many times before that his responses, if anything, seemed a shade too well-rehearsed.

He was convinced he had won the jury over. He was convinced he had convinced them he was a solid copper; one they would welcome patrolling their streets; one who got results. Now hands up if you really care that a few bad, bad boys got a little damaged along the way? Benjamin Smith, if he was pushed, would have admitted that Whiteside was his kind of copper.

By the afternoon, Smith had become more aggressive. Whiteside's evidence needed dismantling. "You were most insistent yesterday, Mr Whiteside, that the pornography must have been planted on Mr Headleigh's computer by a third party. Yet you admit that there was no sign of any forced entry. Did you ever consider exploring any other avenues of inquiry?"

"Such as, sir?" Whiteside replied with a quizzical twist of the head.

"Did you not consider that perhaps someone gained entry to the house with Mr Headleigh's permission? With, let's say, a key provided by Mr Headleigh?"

"Are you saying that he allowed paedophiles to use his home when he was not there?"

"I am asking, Mr Whiteside, if it is possible that a person could have gained entry to the house using a key provided by him. Isn't that a reasonable possibility?"

"Not really, sir; an incredible possibility but not a reasonable one." Whiteside may have been the copper you'd want manning your beat, but Smith was not accustomed to impertinence. He glowered at the witness.

"Oh really! Incredible is it that someone would give a fellow conspirator, a fellow paedophile a key to his home?"

"Naturally I checked with neighbours, sir, and none reported seeing anything suspicious at the house. I checked with the people who lived either side of the Headleighs and I spoke with residents directly opposite; the ones with the clearest view of the house.

"No-one had seen anyone enter the house except Mr and Mrs Headleigh. It's quite a select estate and we all know how keen those kind of people are on neighbourhood watch. So, yes sir, I do find it incredible that someone was toing and froing without being seen or heard."

"But I put it to you Mr Whiteside that a stealthy person COULD have managed it. I am sure a criminal or someone with expertise – someone like yourself perhaps – COULD have entered that house discreetly."

"Possible, yes. Anything is possible. But unlikely I would have to say."

"Unlikely? Ah yes, we all know about unlikely happenings, don't we? Unlikely happenings keep the courts and the police busy day after day. I am glad we now agree that it could have happened. So we now agree that someone could have sneaked into the house and used the computer, right?"

"Without leaving fingerprints, sir?" Whiteside looked at the barrister with a slight frown; was it a puzzled frown? Or the kind of frown one reserves for a child who is struggling with a simple question?

"Now, now Mr Whiteside, he or she could have been wearing gloves?"

"I see. With all due respect, have you ever tried operating a mouse while wearing gloves, sir?" Smith could feel the heat rise up from his shoulders to his face as giggling flitted around the courtroom. Whiteside spoke just as the laughter was subsiding, a masterful tactic.

"I am sorry, sir. I did not wish to show disrespect for your authority. But your suggestion indicates the actions of someone who was expecting the computer to be examined forensically.

"Yes, I agree it is possible that some clever person could have sneaked in using a key; and, yes, they could have used the thin, latex-type gloves. But for up to four hours, sir? No way. I have a vivid imagination, as many coppers do, but I simply cannot envisage a seedy paedophile sneaking unnoticed into a smart house in Brentwood, climbing into the loft and then surfing the Internet for four hours – all while wearing latex gloves.

"The dirty work was done elsewhere and then planted on the computer in the loft, possibly by someone wearing latex gloves for a short while." More laughter.

Smith was struggling for words. He knew it was a thin line of questioning, but he hadn't anticipated such ridicule. Right at that moment he would have loved nothing better than to stick a surgically-gloved hand right up Keith Whiteside's rectum. Smith pretended to be leafing through his notes.

"Well," he mumbled. "We shall just have to disagree on that."

CHAPTER SEVENTEEN

HENRY HEADLEIGH dined with Keith Whiteside and Michael Feuerstein on the Thursday night. Headleigh was by now a recognisable personality. His photograph had featured daily in the newspapers.

Whiteside, too, was in the spotlight after his 'bombshell, shock, trial sensation' disclosure of the trip to Bristol. Neither man was accustomed to being pointed at or subjected to knowing eyes. The group managed to secure an alcove table at the rear of the restaurant in the Park Lane Hotel. Quentin Carel-Hobbs joined them for an aperitif before departing for a dinner date at his Inn. Whiteside was toasted for the excellence of his testimony.

"Your turn in the morning, Henry old chap," said the happy and relieved former detective chief inspector.

"Don't worry about that Benny boy. I suggest you don a pair of rubber gloves when he starts to question you" Merriment around the table. Close, Keith. If only you realised how close, thought Headleigh.

Headleigh was a good eater. That evening his appetite took a vacation. His guests understood and left him lost in his thoughts while they tucked into three courses.

"A bit rich for a humble lad like me, but not bad," said Whiteside, patting his stomach. "At least the portions were decent – well, decent for down here."

"Missing the northern grease?" said Headleigh with the faintest of smiles.

"Now, Henry my lad, I want to see you tuck into a hearty breakfast in the morning."

"The condemned man, you mean?"

"Now don't be morose. We don't want you fainting in that bloody box."

"I'd better be going, gentlemen," said Feuerstein. "Important day tomorrow, Henry. So get yourself to bed early. I know what you police chaps are like; don't want you two staying at the bar all night and chatting about all the good times."

Day Eight

Headleigh breakfasted under the watchful eye of Whiteside. They shared the same hotel but thankfully not the same room. Headleigh had heeded his lawyer's advice and retired before 11pm. His face remained frozen that morning. It was frozen at breakfast and remained that way despite the best bedside manner Carel-Hobbs could muster.

"Too rigid, Henry, if you don't mind me saying so. It just doesn't feel right, and the jury will notice that – subconsciously, at least." Headleigh nodded as he picked at the food on his plate. The barrister was right, of course.

"I don't want you doing cartwheels in the witness box this afternoon, but maybe just relax a bit. Let the shoulders down a little. OK?"

"I'll try."

It was not as though Carel-Hobbs had hit his client with any thorny questions that morning; background on his life and family. They were about 45 minutes into his police record when the court adjourned for lunch.

"I have been doing some research, Detective Superintendent Headleigh. Very interesting. Were you aware that since the war there is just one Essex officer with a success-rate equal to your own?"

"No, I wasn't, sir."

"The great Isaac Walters; Detective Chief Inspector Walters by the time he retired." Carel-Hobbs saw Headleigh visibly relax. "You worked closely with Detective Chief Inspector Walters, I believe?"

Headleigh spent an hour answering questions on his time under the wing of the renowned Walters, his own rapid promotion and success after success. He told the jury how he used to make notes nightly after working with Walters. He had files and folders which he had kept for years, detailing the inner workings of the great detective. Carel-Hobbs brought him back to the present with a bump.

"And then suddenly, right out of the blue, you are accused of being a paedophile. You are accused just as your team investigating these evil people is finding its feet. Detective Superintendent Headleigh, have you ever viewed pornographic material of any nature for pleasure?"

"Most definitely not, sir." Return of the rigid Headleigh. Strong voice, authoritarian demeanour. Carel-Hobbs wanted emotion; not tears, but some emotion, please Henry.

"You worked in this field, you saw these images, and you interviewed child abusers. You know what these fiends are capable of. You are a father of three grown-up children. Cast your mind back to say when they would have been ten or 11 years old, how would you feel if they had been subjected to this dreadful abuse?"

Headleigh was silent for two or three seconds, and he gripped the rail of the witness box with both hands. "That is something I do not like to contemplate. I...I...cannot imagine anyone doing those sort of things to my children; it fills me with horror."

"How do you think you would react?"

"My children are grown. I like to think I gave them a happy child-hood. I wish all children could grow up in a climate of happiness rather than one of wickedness. I really can't say how I personally would react, sir. The work I did...well I would like to think I could deal with an issue professionally...but ... my own children? I really don't know."

"You love your children very much, don't you, Detective Superintendent Headleigh?"

"More than anything on this planet, sir."

"You have loved them, nourished them and reared them to be decent, law-abiding citizens. You have seen the images planted on your com-puter. I ask you again, what would you do if one of your children was treated in such a way?"

"I...if you mean would I take the law into my own hands ...I...Perhaps. Yes, perhaps, I would."

"Tell me about last November? Is it true that you delayed intervening in an incident at a house in Essex so that the father of a child abuse victim could have a little time with the suspect?"

"I do recall an arrest about 12 months ago at which I was present. I am certain I remained in my car during the arrest."

"Ah! Yes! You remained in your car and the arresting officers remained in theirs for three minutes after the father had entered the house. Does that ring a bell?"

Headleigh looked down at his feet. Excellent, Henry. "No need to answer the question, Detective Superintendent. You are not on trial for delaying helping a paedophile in distress. You are here because you have been accused of BEING a paedophile.

"Anyone who knows you realises the accusation is absurd, scandalous in the extreme and based on false evidence; planted evidence. Let us now talk about that evidence. Can you enlighten us as to how it managed to find its way onto the computer in your loft?"

Headleigh couldn't. He cited an equally baffling case he had worked about a decade ago. A gun used to commit a murder had been found in the glove compartment of a car owned by the victim's wife. The wife – and her car – had been 60 miles away at the time of the murder. She was never a serious suspect; and how the gun got into the glove compartment remains a mystery to this day.

"And we know you could not have been surfing the Internet, as it is alleged, on the night of March 23rd as you were approximately 200 miles away in Bristol."

"That is correct, sir."

"What about April 17th – the night it is claimed you dashed home from Clacton and ran like the wind upstairs to enjoy this alleged hobby? It is claimed you were on the Internet at 10.11pm. Is that possible?"

"No, sir. I have found a receipt for petrol I purchased at a garage

20 miles away. The receipt is timed 9.58."

"The receipt is in the folder provided this morning, My Lord." Carel-Hobbs nodded to the judge.

"So that would have left 13 minutes to return to your car, drive 20 miles home, park, dash inside, up the stairs to the loft and turn on your computer. Impossible rather than unlikely I would say. No further questions, My Lord."

Headleigh was surprised by the abrupt ending. "Effect, Henry," Carel-Hobbs told him after Mr Justice Grant had adjourned for the weekend.

"You did much better this afternoon, Henry. Well done. And we left the jury with a nice, solid fact to digest this evening. A solid fact backed up by evidence. Right now they are probably discussing how fast one would have to drive to cover 20 miles in 13 minutes. Enjoy the weekend but prepare for a tougher grilling from Benjamin Smith on Monday. We're just like the police really, good cop-bad cop."

☩

Bryan Richardson hosted a crisis summit at his home on Sunday. He did not like inviting minions to Le Chateau D'Or, but it was preferable to driving to the office. Benjamin Smith attended, too. Of course, it would be added to his charges – he would not dream of spending a Sunday away from home without good cause or cost. The collective musings from his brains trust did not pacify the newspaper proprietor.

"We're losing it; fuckin' losin' it," he screamed time and time again, much to Smith's distaste. They all knew they were losing it.

Andrew Harvey seemed the worst affected. He'd lost a little weight, which made the bags under his eyes appear more prominent. He looked like Jimmy Cagney. He had slept poorly since Keith Whiteside's Bristol revelation. He hadn't bothered to shave that morning, not even for a rare visit to Le Chateau D'Or.

Phil Calvin felt embarrassed, and prayed that the owner was aware that the publication of the story had nothing to do with him. Every man for himself now; I'm a reporter, women and children to the back of the queue.

Terry James, Arthur Jacobs and John Franzeb fiddled with anything they could lay their hands on – as long as they didn't have to make eye contact with Richardson.

Gary Chalmers was there, supportive of his raving lunatic of a boss as ever. He was silent, too. Eventually, the barrister interrupted the Richardson rant.

"We're losing it, Mr Richardson, because I was not provided with all the facts, or so it appears. Did our own private investigations not reveal details of this trip to Bristol, for example?" Smith did not like himself for putting the solicitor on the spot. Tough. Every man for himself now; I'm a Queen's Counsel, women and children to the back of the queue.

Franzeb blushed. "No, Benjamin. It seems he didn't have access to the diary."

"Didn't HAVE access or didn't ask for access?" grunted Harvey. Every man for himself.

Jacobs stiffened his back. Even on a Sunday he was wearing a pin-stripe. He coughed. "Recriminations will not get us anywhere, gentlemen." He coughed again. "We could always seek an out of court settlement, Bryan?"

"What? What? You mean pay the fuckin' pervert? Don't be fuckin' daft. He started this fight but we're gonna fuckin' finish it." Actually, we started the fight. But James kept his thoughts to himself.

"I need something to confront Headleigh with on Monday, chaps. Any bright ideas?"

"I'm paying you enough; don't You have any bright ideas?"

"Mr Richardson, I am only as good as my briefing permits. I cannot conjure facts from thin air. I intend to attack the absurdity of the mysterious break-in, but I can guess the nature of the replies.

"And then there is the matter of our witnesses. As we have discussed previously, I think we can dispense with the technical expert as the plaintiff's camp readily admit the existence of the material. Assistant

Chief Constable Hill will find himself in a predicament, too. I believe John spoke with him yesterday?"

"Yes, he said preliminary checks showed that everything Whiteside said was true. He also had Headleigh's petrol receipt checked. The time is as he said. Sorry."

"Tell us again about the credit card, Benjamin? Why do you believe the defence never brought that up?"

"Because I would guess that dear old Quentin Carel-Hobbs, bless his cotton socks, is saving the pleasure for me. The police files say that no card has ever been found. There was just one sheet of paper in a drawer of the table which held the computer. One single sheet of an account statement. An account used solely to pay for Internet facilities to the grand tune of £35.46. The account was opened in February and used five times up until the middle of April. Fictitious name, address is a small flat in a run-down part of Basildon. No neighbours recognised Headleigh from the photograph the police showed them. That, dear Arthur, is the reason why Quentin Carel-Hobbs is simply dying for me to ask our Dorset investigator about it."

"You've lost me," said News Editor Calvin. "Why is Carel-Hobbs waiting for you?"

"It is another piece of evidence that the police have been unable to clear up. So Carel-Hobbs will no doubt attempt to torment Hill on the issue. It fits in neatly with their plant theory. It is also an extra string to their bow when they have exhausted their witnesses, which they did on Friday in case anyone needs reminding."

"Ahem. Well…"

"Yes, John? Something you wish to tell us?"

"I have more bad news, I'm afraid, Benjamin. I was checking the diary again last night. The account was opened in Basildon town centre between 10.30 and 11 in the morning. According to the diary, Headleigh held meetings all day in Chelmsford. I haven't made Hill aware of that yet, but I guess his people will."

"Christ! This just gets worse." Smith leaned back in his armchair. It was very comfortable but he longed for his own in his sanctuary, miles away from these amateurs. He slightly pitied Franzeb for allowing himself to be bullied by these hacks. If the firm required his services in the future, he would insist on a shrewd operator like that big northern so-and-so in their camp.

"What about you Terry Fuckin' James? Bit quiet this morning, aren't we Mr Crime Reporter Supreme? Why hasn't your oh-so-valuable contact come up with the goods?"

"He's a contact not fuckin' Superman!"

Harvey and Calvin were startled. Richardson didn't bat an eyelid.

"Everything he has given me has been spot on, at least in detail even if the timing was a little out. Spot on. He told me there was child porn at Headleigh's home – and there was. OK, so Kent was off track, and he doesn't know what happened down there. But you can't blame me for that Mirror photograph. It wasn't my..."

"OK Terry, calm down," said Harvey. James quickly calmed down; but he had already been consigned to the dustbin of British crime reporting.

✝

Day Nine

Benjamin Smith's heart wasn't in it. Quentin Carel-Hobbs could gather that from his opening forays. To be fair, it was a professional cross-examination, sufficiently precise in its forensic detail to merit entry to the bar at junior level. But it was not the Benjamin Smith known and admired by many, and even loved by a few.

The defence barrister skipped over the first 50 years of Headleigh's life. Fifty years of hard work, at school, college and then with the police force. Fifty years of decent, honest toil. He did not want the members of the jury to dwell on that. Concentrate on the murky mystery of this dastardly chap's life over six months at the start of this year when he plumbed the very depths of depravity – alone in his loft.

Benjamin Smith never mentioned once the fine city of Bristol in

Avon, which lay approximately 200 miles from Brentwood in Essex. Smith did briefly come to life when he attempted to probe into the story of the plant. Did he seriously expect the jury to believe that? Yes he did because he was in Bristol…

And who was behind this alleged plant? The Invisible Man was it? I am no wiser today than I was last June, Headleigh told the court. He hoped the police had sufficient resources to investigate the crime fully.

Smith sat down, drained by just three hours of fruitless questioning. He had been known to go after his quarry for days on end without showing the slightest sign of fatigue. Amateurs! Bloody amateurs. He silently cursed the owner of the Evening Gazette as he awaited the arrival of Assistant Chief Constable Frederick Hill of Dorset Police in the witness box. This was his witness, a witness for the defence, yet Smith was terrified of asking questions. Terrified because he knew the policeman would answer them truthfully. It was a dreadful feeling for a barrister.

The preliminaries were short, almost to the point of insult. Smith cut to the chase. "I understand you have been investigating the alleged plant at the home of Mr Headleigh since June. Is that correct, Assistant Chief Constable?"

"It has been one of our lines of inquiry, sir."

"Could you tell the court what success your team has had following this line of inquiry?"

"None at the moment, sir, but…"

"None? Since June you have been unable to find out ANY information on this alleged plant?"

"No, sir. We were concentrating on other matters as all the hard evidence point to the accused; I mean to the plaintiff."

"Near on six months and not a shred of evidence to back up the claims of the plaintiff that this pornography was planted on his computer. Doesn't that make the story appear a trifle thin, Assistant Chief Constable?"

"Well, sir, we only heard about the discrepancies the other day; about the trip to Bristol and …"

"Nevertheless, six months and no evidence...dear me..." All or nothing, thought Smith. "...and then there is the credit card statement. There was a fictitious account set up used to fund these pornographic web sites. A statement for this account was found in Mr Headleigh's drawer, isn't that so?"

"Yes, sir."

"So all the evidence, all the hard evidence that police rely on to catch wrong-doers, points to Mr Headleigh being involved with paedophiles: the material on his computer in his loft; a credit card in his drawer; and his fingerprints on the computer. Is that correct?"

"Yes, sir."

"No further questions, My Lord." Smith turned his back to the witness and shuffled back to his bench. He appeared jaded and hardly the imposing figure that commanded up to a grand a day for his services.

Carel-Hobbs rose to his feet, flicked his gown behind him and smiled at the witness. He never looked jaded, not even in his worst nightmares. "I'll try not to keep you long Assistant Chief Constable. The court appreciates you have important police work to attend to. We are all aware of the details of the material found on the computer, so I would like to concentrate on your inquiry – without prejudicing possible criminal action, of course.

"Six months...six months? How many police man hours would you say – at an educated guess – have been spent on your investigation?"

"I...I...really wouldn't know for certain, sir. Myself and a colleague from Dorset have been on the case full time, plus we have had some assistance on admin matters from Essex Police."

"Fine, fine. So two officers working full time for, say 25 weeks; that would be a thousand hours at least?"

"That sounds about right, sir, though we often work longer hours than a regular 40-hour week."

"Of course, you do, and the British public is eternally grateful. But I have to ask you how many of those hours – those full-time hours by yourself and your Dorset colleague – would you say were spent investigating Detective Superintendent Headleigh's absolute insistence that the material was planted? A rough guess, if you please?" Some blush, others turn white. ACC Hill's face slowly turned paler, but it was his body that gave the game away. He shuffled on the spot and his hands seemed to be unsure where to rest.

"We have been very busy with the hard evidence, sir. As you are aware there were hundreds of images and several web links to check out. Those led to other web sites which in turn provided further links. It is a tangled web which stretches around the globe."

"Am I correct in thinking that not many man-hours have been devoted into checking Detective Superintendent Headleigh's claims?"

"That is so, sir, unfortunately. I would add that we only became aware of the conflicts between the dates on the Internet logs and Mr Headleigh's whereabouts following the evidence of Mr Whiteside the other day. My colleague has been checking out the dates."

"Ah! Good! And what has your colleague discovered so far?"

"That Mr Headleigh was indeed in Bristol at the time he said he was."

"And therefore he could not have been skulking in his loft surfing the Internet for seedy pornography?"

"No, sir, he could not."

"Christ!" mumbled a voice from the defence benches.

"Silence in court," roared Mr Justice Grant. "I will not have blasphemy nor interruptions of any kind in this courtroom. And all show due respect to the witnesses appearing here. Please continue, Mr Carel-Hobbs."

"Thank you, My Lord. Has your colleague as yet had time to check the time that Detective Superintendent Headleigh bought petrol on his return home from Clacton?"

"Yes, sir. It was 9.58pm."

"So it would have been physically impossible for Detective Superintendent Headleigh to drive the 20 miles home in time to log onto the Internet at the time your files say someone did?"

"Yes, sir." Carel-Hobbs walked back towards his bench. He appeared to have finished his questioning. Suddenly, he twisted around; a twirl of breathtaking athleticism and elegance. It must have been 450 degrees; the gown billowed about the barrister. Keith Whiteside almost burst out laughing. Carel-Hobbs raised his hand and allowed the sleeve of his gown to reach his suit cuff.

"One final question Assistant Chief Constable: the credit card. I must be slipping. It totally escaped my mind when I was questioning Detective Chief Inspector Whiteside the other day. The account was opened in Basildon by an unknown person. You are of course aware that Detective Superintendent Headleigh was at that very time in a meeting with three child care officials in Chelmsford?"

"Yes I am sir; it was brought to my attention last night."

"And you have checked it out?"

"Yes, sir. My assistant has spoken to two of the officials and they have confirmed they were in a meeting with Henry that morning..."

"Good. Thank you." No-one in the court for one moment believed Carel-Hobbs was slipping; certainly not Benjamin Smith, and certainly not Bryan Richardson who huffed out of his seat and stormed off to find a place where a newspaper proprietor could have a bloody good rant, blasphemous or otherwise.

CHAPTER EIGHTEEN

Day Ten

ANDREW HARVEY was surprisingly composed in the witness box. He was surprised himself. He hadn't had a decent night's sleep in a fortnight until last night. He had cleared his conscience and slept like a baby. He had felt like lying in but knew he had to obey the alarm clock. He would stand by Terry James and his decision to publish, but he would tell the truth, the whole truth so help him God; and Bryan Richardson could go stick a caber up his backside.

The bags remained under his eyes, but he had shaven, felt physically refreshed and mentally alert. He spent the morning regaling the court with stories of epic British journalism he had either composed or overseen. Quack medical companies forced to close; corrupt council officials and politicians exposed; and, yes, a few off-field activities of footballers and assorted celebrities. The Evening Gazette had a good rapport with all the police forces in their circulation area. They were always willing and available to help the police catch criminals. They responded promptly to police appeals for help. But, yes, it fell within his remit to expose wrongdoings among police officers.

After lunch, the editor sang the praises of his crime ace. He had known Terry James for many years. He had a fully-deserved reputation as the finest crime reporter in the land, earned by long, long hours – many of them unpaid. He had a bank of first-class sources. He trusted Terry James implicitly.

Bryan Richardson wanted to throw up. He was in court under

sufferance; his chief executive Gary Chalmers had persuaded him it was the correct thing to do. Harvey droned on. Terry James had never been wrong on a story. Like all reporters he liked to be first with the news, but he understood completely the need for accuracy. It was an editor's responsibility to back reporters they trusted.

"And this was at the back of your mind on that Friday in June when James approached you concerning the child pornography story? A trusted reporter came to you with a big story – one that you could not ignore?" said Benjamin Smith.

"Exactly. Of course, I was aware of the legal implications…but, as I have said, Terry's sources were the best."

"So you felt you had a duty to publish the accusations? Particularly as they concerned such a senior police officer in such a sensitive position?"

"True, very true. One of our main functions is to report on major public officials – the good news and the bad when it is necessary."

"It was your duty, and you published in good faith, based on accurate information. Is that correct?"

"Yes, sir. I would never have published if I had not believed the story. I would never publish any story I did not believe in. In fact, we omitted certain sensitive information in order not to hinder possible police operations."

"Very good – a quite responsible attitude, if I may say so. As we know the story was accurate: pornography was found on the plaintiff's computer and there is an investigation. The story was accurate and published in good faith – is that it in a nutshell?"

"Yes, sir."

"Thank you, Mr Harvey. No further questions, My Lord."

Carel-Hobbs smiled that Carel-Hobbs 'you-can-trust-me' smile and promised not to detain Harvey for long.

"Knowing what you do now, Mr Harvey – what you have heard these past few days in this court – would you have gone ahead and published the story that Friday last June?"

"Well I would have suggested to Terry that he check out some facts."

"So you would NOT have published the story?"

"I decided to publish the story based on the evidence available…"

"Forgive me, Mr Harvey; not evidence, speculation. The allegedly informed word of your crime reporter, but not evidence. You took the word of your reporter on its own without any evidence to back it up, isn't that so?"

"Yes, that is what an editor often has to do…take the word of his staff. I would have thought that was obvious. But, as I said, Terry had never let the paper down by writing incorrect or inaccurate reports."

Carel-Hobbs kept smiling. He knew what was obvious and what was not and did not need a trumped-up editor to tell him, thank you. His thoughts remained inside his head.

"Until now, that is. Terry James had not written inaccurate reports until now. There is a first time for everything, Mr Harvey. I ask you again: would you publish that same story today? Knowing what you now know, would you sanction publication in today's edition of the Evening Gazette?"

Harvey licked his lips and swallowed hard. His mouth all of a sudden felt incredibly dry. He shifted to balance his body first on his right foot, and then on his left. He repeated the movement twice more.

"I take your obvious discomfort as a 'No'. No you would most certainly not publish those scandalous allegations. No decent editor would. But please answer the question for the jury – would you publish in today's Evening Gazette with the benefit of hindsight? Now that you know Detective Superintendent Headleigh was in Bristol, for example, when he was allegedly in his loft seedily sifting through pornographic images; would you publish?"

"Well…I suppose I would want some check calls made to verify certain facts."

"You suppose you would want some check calls made? Well, Mr Harvey, you have had several months to make those check calls. Any success to report?"

Harvey shuffled his feet again, scratched his neck even though his shirt collar was loose enough. He tried to look away; to look away from Carel-Hobbs, away from the jury, away from the judge and most of all away from Bryan Richardson and the Gazette benches. His eyes could find no friendly faces. Christ! This snotty barrister was the friendliest face in the room. Carel-Hobbs let Harvey wriggle for around 20 seconds.

"No further questions, My Lord," he said without smiling.

Day Eleven

Déjà vu. Terry James's career was placed under the microscope. The court heard how he had started as a junior reporter, covering local fetes, attending meetings of school governors and the like; all essential grounding he told them. He had never been one of those boys who wanted to join the police force, nor to drive a fire engine as much as he could recall.

Words had always fascinated him. He had read morning, noon and night. He began writing short stories while still at junior school. His stories were longer than the essays expected of pre-teen pupils and generally involved dashing heroes performing miracles of outrageous audacity. His first detective story was based not so loosely on Sherlock Holmes as he had just started reading the Conan Doyle masterpieces. He finished the entire body of work on the great gentleman sleuth before his 13th birthday.

He began to be assigned crime stories to cover on local papers who would not afford a specialist crime reporter. He was ecstatic when he landed the role on the Evening Gazette. It was a dream come true and a match made in heaven. They followed each other's star. He had many sources. They were invaluable in his line of work.

"Now I am sure the court realises a journalist has to protect his sources, but I have to ask you if you are prepared to reveal the name of your source for the information on Mr Headleigh?"

"No, sir, that would be against a fundamental principle of journalism in this country. All I can say is that he had provided much information in the past and all had been accurate." James spoke confidently. He was confident by nature; not arrogant, just confident that he was right. He looked a little too sharp that day for Harvey's liking. He rarely wore a suit in the office, preferring casual jackets and trousers. His hair appeared tidier, too; a neat trim.

"You had no reason to doubt he was telling the truth?"

"None whatsoever."

"The story was written in good faith – to alert the public that a senior police officer was storing pornographic images – pornographic images of minors – on his personal computer..."

"My Lord, I must object," said Carel-Hobbs, rising swiftly yet still elegantly to his feet. "There is no evidence that Detective Superintendent Headleigh was storing these images. There is no disputing that the material was found on a computer in his loft. We have successfully proven that the plaintiff could not have been viewing those images or collecting them for storage as – he was 200 miles away."

"I am sure we can all recall your questioning, Mr Carel-Hobbs. Perhaps Mr Smith would rephrase his question?"

The defence barrister nodded solemnly at the judge. "Mr James, you wrote the story in good faith based on solid information from a respected and reliable contact. You wrote it in good faith to alert the public?"

"That is correct, sir."

"No further questions, My Lord."

Carel-Hobbs was back on his feet and slowly approaching the witness box. "I am sure you did write the story in good faith, Mr James. I will not doubt your integrity on that count. Is it fair to say that the story was rushed out onto the streets so that you could claim exclusivity? You wanted to steal a march on your rivals?"

"It's fair to say that, sir. Yes."

"So the normal checks you would make on a highly controversial story were not made?"

"There was no time, sir."

"Your editor says that he would not have published the story, having heard the testimony given in this court. Would you agree with him?"

James, unlike his editor, did not wriggle or shuffle or hesitate. "Yes, I would." All over bar the shouting. Game, set and match to Carel-Hobbs.

Henry Headleigh's barrister had commenced his closing address carefully that afternoon by reminding the jury of the plaintiff's excellent record – not just as a servant of the police, mind you; he was an excellent father, too, with three wonderful, bright children as living proof. He would wind up in the morning. Maybe an hour at most to put across the points he wanted the jury to remember very clearly.

The owner of the Gazette went missing again. The rest of the defence team went their separate ways after a solitary post-trial drink. They had little to talk about; well, little that they wanted to talk about.

Day Twelve

An excellent police officer and a wonderful, caring and loving father, Carel-Hobbs reminded the jury first thing on a miserable Thursday. Members of the jury and the public showed signs of a thorough soaking in the storm that continued unabated outside the High Court. Carel-Hobbs looked as immaculate as ever.

"Detective Superintendent Headleigh made many enemies, however, in the course of performing his duty bravely and honestly. We have to assume that it was one of these enemies who planted the paedophilic material on the computer in the loft.

"An enemy who wanted revenge over the plaintiff. An enemy who dreamt up the worst stain he could leave on a man's reputation. Imagine the reception a police officer with paedophilic tendencies would receive as a guest in one of Her Majesty's Prisons. Murderers, robbers, thieves, men of extreme violence are generally made to feel at home inside these establishments. But not sex offenders, especially sex offenders who have committed appalling acts against children.

"So that is the mark this evil enemy planned to make on Detective Superintendent Headleigh.

"Think, ladies and gentlemen of the jury, think whether you would rather have a train robber as a neighbour or a paedophile? Think, if you can, of a more scandalous accusation to hurl at a man? And why was this attempt to besmirch the plaintiff's reputation placed into the public domain so hurriedly?

"Now this is a shocking betrayal of the British Press: it was dashed off to print because experienced, senior journalists wanted to shout EXCLUSIVE! Don't let them fool you by claiming they were doing a public service by outing a paedophile.

"The editor and the reporter have both admitted they should have checked out the facts. They did not. They let down themselves, their paper and journalists at large. Because they wanted to climb to the rooftops and shout EXCLUSIVE! Evening Gazette EXCLUSIVE!"

Carel-Hobbs was in solid form – not too theatrical as he felt the case did not demand it, though he did make a rather decent attempt at mimicking a street paper seller. He paraded himself before the jury demurely, sometimes with his hands clasped behind his back, other times in front of him as if to emphasise a point.

"They had the opportunity to apologise to Detective Superintendent Headleigh. Did they take it? No, ladies and gentlemen, they did not.

"In fact, the owner of the paper, who unfortunately decided against defending his actions in this court, compounded the defamatory comments in the most obscene terms. And he used a borrowed photograph to amplify his point. That photograph, as we have heard, is a fake.

"The photograph is a fake, the story is a fake; a most wretched fake. It has destroyed the plaintiff's professional and family life. Fifty-one years of honest toil ruined in a scandalous way, for the sake of an EXCLUSIVE! Evening Gazette EXCLUSIVE!

"I am confident the jury will reach the only possible verdict and call on the guilty parties to make suitable recompense for the damage done. Thank you."

Benjamin Smith had defended many lost causes. He had defended many clients who he knew to be guilty. That had rarely troubled his conscience; every man or woman was entitled to the best defence available – if they could afford the best, naturally. Now he was tasked with persuading a jury that an innocent man was in fact a paedophile. If the money hadn't been so damned good he would have preferred to treat sewage for a living some days. Once again he concentrated on the mystery man who allegedly planted this material.

"Beyond belief, I tell you. You all have homes, can you imagine someone gaining access for at least 20 minutes and you not being aware you had an unwanted visitor? Can you imagine that?"

That was rather pathetic, Benjamin, of course they probably could. But Carel-Hobbs continued to look solemn. Smith did a fair job of defending the British Press without mentioning the word exclusive. Had Carel-Hobbs shouted EXCLUSIVE loud and often enough?

"It is not a right of journalists to pry into the private affairs of others. But it is their solemn duty to expose the criminal activities of individuals, particularly individuals in the public eye; individuals who claim to be something they are not.

"I am sure, ladies and gentlemen, that you will reach the correct verdict: that the Evening Gazette acted honourably and published their story in good faith. Thank you."

Day Thirteen

Mr Justice Grant summed up the evidence in two hours. He realised it was very one-sided but tried his hardest to give equal weight to both arguments. His problem was that the defence had just one argument – the computer belonged to Henry Headleigh and had been discovered in his loft. He closed by reminding the jury that the onus was not on the plaintiff to prove he was innocent of the accusations. The burden of proof was on the newspaper. They had to prove to the court that the stories they printed were true in fact.

The jury reached their verdict within three hours. Ten of them had been convinced of Headleigh's innocence very early in the trial. Surprisingly, the two that needed convincing were young males who didn't have children and didn't want any, thank you very much.

They belonged to the 'no smoke without fire' new school but not enough to condemn Headleigh. Ideally, they would have abstained but saw no cause to delay matters.

"For the plaintiff, My Lord," the foreman announced. No loud cheering rang out, but there was a smattering of applause. Headleigh was the sole member of his family in court.

Mr Justice Grant thanked the jury for their deliberations and verdict. He informed them that they would now be guided on the penalties to be imposed on the newspaper and its representatives. He apologised for keeping them over the weekend but they needed to discuss with court officials the appropriate measures for assessing levels of damages. The courts had tried to reduce the levels of damages in recent years. Newspapers had lobbied friends on high and the law sided with them. No longer could people expect a massive windfall over the most trivial of slurs. The costs associated with resort to the legal process persuaded many to let the mud stick. What was the point?

The jury in Headleigh v Evening Gazette were made aware of this. They were also made aware – thanks to documents provided by Feuerstein, Savage and Amrein – that this case went way beyond the bounds of trivia.

This was not some pop star accused of being too emotional to perform; some footballer playing away from home; not some political official taking a back-hander to grease a few palms.

These unfounded allegations had cost Henry Headleigh his job: the jury should consider how much a senior policeman could expect to earn over ten years or so if he had wished to continue past his retirement date.

They had cost the plaintiff his marriage: at best his assets would be split 50-50. And then there was his reputation and his friends. What price they? The toll on his mental state of health was immeasurable. But experts suggested he would be haunted by the memory of his ordeal till his dying day.

The paper should also be punished for publishing such defamatory remarks in its bid to improve circulation.

Day Fourteen

The public gallery was less crowded. Even a few court reporters had decided to move onto fresh trials. The legal teams were in attendance. Gary Chalmers had persuaded Bryan Richardson to hold his inquest into the affair after today's final hearing in court.

Henry Headleigh had celebrated his triumph quietly. Keith Whiteside did join him for lunch and a few pints on the Sunday. They had read article after article in the papers over the weekend. The Saturday papers had concentrated on the trial itself. The Sundays had been more introspective; columnists poured forth thousands of words on the Press and the laws of libel. Some attacked the owner of the Gazette with unbounded glee. His own article had provoked a torrent of condemnation.

£1.7m? Was that what the foreman of the jury had just said? There was no visible reaction from Richardson. Chief Executive Chalmers whistled, Harvey gulped, Jacobs coughed, and James rearranged his tie. Benjamin Smith decided to wait before suggesting an appeal.

£1.7m? Yes, all had heard correctly. One million and seven-hundred thousand pounds. Headleigh's face betrayed no emotion but he looked at the jury and nodded. It was not clear whether it was a sign of assent or gratitude; for their services or the amount of the award. One million and seven-hundred thousand pounds. A tidy sum, he smiled inwardly. Worth it; yes, it was worth it… almost.

Michael Feurstein slapped Headleigh on the back. Quentin Carel-Hobbs placed a bony hand on his shoulder and whispered: "Not bad at all."

Mr Justice Grant discharged the jury after expressing his gratitude for their deliberations and reminding them of the available counselling.

Headleigh's team held a modest but joyful luncheon party in a private room at Ruffles in Covent Garden. "A book, Henry. You should consider writing a book – be a best-seller," said Carel-Hobbs.

"You could perhaps ask Terry James to ghost-write it?" laughed Feuerstein.

The mood inside the Evening Gazette boardroom was depressing. The journalists were very wary of the owner in his quiet moods. They knew only too well his rants and rages. This was a different side to him. He had brushed his barrister aside when he collared him outside the courtroom. No, he wasn't bothered about a fuckin' appeal.

It was the embarrassment that ate away at his insides; the sheer humiliation of losing cut deep for a man used to getting his own way. The total bill for the trial would approach £3m. It would eat into the paper's accounts but was not a sum to cause the chairman sleepless nights. Humiliation on a grand public scale, however, would. Part of him realised much of it was his own making. But someone else would have to pay.

The Gazette was running a front page apology that day. It had been composed by John Franzeb. The paper unreservedly apologised for the distress caused to Henry Headleigh. At the foot of the text there were a few paragraphs claiming that the Gazette would continue to keep a watch over public officials. It carried all the weight of an empty plastic carrier bag.

Never again must such sloppy reporting get onto the pages of the Evening Gazette, Richardson told the journalists. Never again. He dismissed all except Andrew Harvey. He needed a few moments in private.

"I want Terry Fuckin' James out of the building within the hour." Harvey did not try to protest. "We'll renegotiate your contract at the end of the week. Hopefully, this will have blown over by then."

When Harvey had been dismissed from the room, Chalmers passed the owner a sheet of paper. Four possible candidates for the role of editor had been discreetly sounded out over the weekend. Two had made positive noises. "Let's try him first," said Richardson, pointing at a name on the paper with not much enthusiasm. "Shambles. Fuckin' shambles."

＋

Four days later

Keith Whiteside's paid work was finished. But, once a copper always a copper; he hated loose ends. He had been waiting for Terry James.

"A penny for them?" he said as the reporter turned the corner of the walkway leading to his flat.

"What?" James looked up and was shocked to see the imposing figure before him.

"A penny for your thoughts, Mr former crime reporter. I could possibly pay more for the name of your contact?"

"Get out of my way, please."

"You never know when you might need a little extra cash, laddie; good employment is hard to find. Take my card, just in case you have mislaid the other one. Any time you feel like a chat."

James brushed past him and hurriedly made the last hundred yards home.

CHAPTER NINETEEN

Six weeks later

DETECTIVE INSPECTOR Colin Grant was called to the scene of a grisly murder on the outskirts of Basildon. All murders are depressing, even for hardened officers. Some are more depressing than others owing to the sheer savagery employed in the act. This one had been savage and messy.

The Scene of Crime officer lifted a blanket so that the inspector could view the battered and broken body of a white male. He would have stood roughly six feet tall. There was no way of telling his age until they got the corpse back to the lab. The face had been bludgeoned beyond recognition, blood covered the victim's yellow shirt – the result of multiple knife wounds, it seemed. The white-suited officer lifted up the victim's left hand. That, too, was heavily bruised and marked. A heavy gold ring adorned the middle finger, but it was the tattoo which caught Grant's eye.

"Baggie Brooks, well, well," said the inspector.

"Know him, then, sir?"

"Yes, I know him. Wouldn't wish this kind of end on anyone, but if I was pushed to, then, yes, I may wish it on Scott 'Baggie' Brooks. Any keys? Car or house?"

"In that bag over there, sir, with a wallet. The wallet's been cleaned out."

Detective Inspector Grant returned to his car with his partner, DS Andy Wellock. "Ring in and get us a last known on Baggie Brooks, would you, Andy?" Grant was glad to be out of uniform and out of the sick world of child porn and back solving good, old murders – even brutal ones. You met a better class of villain. There were a few of them these days on his new patch with Basildon CID.

Brooks was in his mid-40s and a well-known drug dealer in the Basildon area. Once upon a time he had run a profitable little empire which covered most of Essex; until he got greedy and was caught red-handed, supervising a delivery down by Tilbury docks. He'd been sent down for ten years and his empire split up as gang members fought among themselves for supremacy.

Baggie Brooks had ruined many a young life, turned many a kid to crime to pay for their habit. Yes, if anyone deserved a messy end, then Baggie did.

Grant and Wellock received a last known address back from the station and drove to a council estate a couple of miles from the centre of Basildon. There was no reply to their knocks so they tested the keys and let themselves into the two-up, two-down house.

There was some unopened mail on a table in the hall, two bills addressed to Mr S Brooks. The house could have done with a lick of paint but otherwise was surprisingly tidy for a drug dealer. A few magazines were scattered here and there, the kitchen contained unwashed cups and plates, but DI Grant had seen a lot worse.

"Up here, sir. Something you should see," called DS Wellock from upstairs.

Grant passed the bedroom and joined Wellock in the second room, which seemed to serve as a study. Wellock handed a set of photographs to his boss. There were seven of them, glossy 10x8in black and white photographs. Grant was shocked at what he saw; they were all of Henry Headleigh, taken, it seemed, outside his former home in Brentwood.

"There's more here, boss." Wellock had opened a plain brown folder and started handing more photos to his boss: Jane Headleigh, the Headleigh children and more of Henry, all at their home. The sergeant produced more scraps of paper, newspaper cuttings, one featuring a photograph of him and Jane at one of her charity functions and the rest articles concerning Headleigh's career. One, in particular, attracted Grant's attention. It was a front page of the Essex Chronicle and reported a major drug bust. Police led by Detective Chief Inspector Henry Headleigh had arrested a major gangland figure and smashed a multi-million pound racket.

"Do me a favour, Andy, turn on that computer over there." Grant examined the cuttings and the photographs as the computer sparked into life. He walked over to it and this time was not surprised at what he saw. There had been no attempt to hide the folder: HH was one of a dozen or so folders on the desktop. Grant clicked it open and clicked again. The image that sprang into view made DS Wellock step back.

"Fuck! That's sick! Sir? Sir…are you thinking what I'm thinking?"

Grant was thinking, all right. He was thinking that if anyone deserved a messy end, then Scott 'Baggie' Brooks did.

✝

Five months later

Terry James strolled happily along the seafront of Puerto del Carmen, the main tourist trap on Lanzarote and his favoured Canary Island. He had landed the previous evening, checked into his hotel and done a recce of the bars that stretched for two miles along this bright and noisy promenade.

It was busy as usual, but thankfully the summer hordes of sun, sea and sex-seekers were still two months away. He had had a nightcap at Charlie's and checked out the layout of the slightly upmarket bar, café, cocktail joint. It appeared that Charlie, if he existed, could not make up his mind what his hostelry was supposed to be. James preferred a gold-fashioned British pub himself, but beggars couldn't be choosers.

He tried to keep his mind alert and focus on his surroundings rather than dream of how he planned to spend his new riches, though he had thought of little else since losing his job.

"Well, well, well, there you are Henry. I must say the climate has done wonders for you; almost didn't recognise your mug. You look, ohhhh, at least ten years younger. Found a suitable filly yet? Plenty of choice here from what I have seen."

Henry Headleigh half raised from his comfortable wicker chair and offered the former journalist a warm sun-tanned smile and his leathery hand.

"Mustn't grumble. Now, how are you, old friend? You do look like you need some sun on that pale frame of yours. Best I can offer for now is a drink. I forget, what's your poison?"

James arranged the cushion on his chair and sat down opposite the retired police chief and browsed through a baffling cocktail menu. "It sounds horribly tacky and probably looks even worse but I'll risk a Flamin' Macarena, thanks."

Headleigh beckoned over a waiter, and the two men stared at each without speaking until the Flamin' Macarena arrived, complete with all the trimmings and a pair of sparklers. "One for me, one for you," smiled James as he watched the fireworks fizzle out. "Dear me, is it safe to drink this concoction? I'm on holiday so here we go – cheers."

"Cheers, Terry. Nice to see you again."

James jokingly grimaced as he sipped from the extravagant glass. At least none of the crowd from his local was present to witness this act of ale treachery. He lit up a cigarette and offered one to his companion.

"No, thank you. I just limit myself to the occasional cigar; a more acquired and expensive taste these days."

"Ah yes. I hope you are being thrifty with OUR money."

"Of course, dear boy. Thrifty could be my middle name." Headleigh adopted a posh accent and laughed. "I have something here for you. Don't open it now. Let's finish our drinks like two civilised chaps, then we can have a stroll and discuss business."

James accepted the bulky brown package from his drinking chum. It felt reassuringly heavy. James had managed to get through the previous five months on dreams. Big dreams, usually focused on exotic locations. He had scheduled a year out enjoying his share of the libel victory before starting up his own freelance business; the location had yet to be decided but he had a leaning towards foreign fields. Somewhere warm and sunny. Maybe the Canary Islands needed a seasoned British hack like him.

They watched the world pass by as they savoured the moment and their drinks. Nothing quite like a promenade mid-evening; tourists were strolling along happily, decked out in the brightest colours especially reserved or purchased for sunspots like Puerto del Carmen. The hardy ones still sported their beachwear, though the evening was turning colder. The cafes and restaurants were doing a brisk trade. Families were rounding off their day; couples were feasting before heading for the clubs and several more hours of escapism.

Headleigh and James exchanged some polite chit-chat. No, James hadn't sought new employment. Yes, the weather was shite as usual back home.

"That was pleasant." Headleigh smacked his lips together. "Now, how about we take a little walk and have a proper chat. Then I know a wonderful little restaurant. Always eat where the locals eat, I say."

Headleigh paid the waiter and included a healthy tip. The pair crossed the busy road and decided the beach was nicely quiet for their business conference. James could hardly wait to check the contents of his package. Bad manners be buggered. "It's all there, naturally. Fifty grand in euros – but please count it."

"Oh, I trust you, Henry. I just wanted to see what 50k looked like. It looks and smells just dandy."

"If you're happy, then I'm happy," smiled the older man. "Now, we need to discuss the transfer of the balance sometime soon."

James's share of the £1.7m libel award had been agreed at £700,000. He hadn't quibbled with Headleigh, who had a liking for round figures.

"So, you're certain no-one suspects a thing?" asked Headleigh.

"Positive. That junkie sorted things out. Poor fella. Dare I ask who did him in?"

"Now, now, ask silly questions…"

"Yeah, OK. Necessary, I suppose. That bloody Whiteside put the willies up me, I don't mind admitting."

"Yes, he was very conscientious. It was a good job he was on my side and not yours," laughed Headleigh. "How's the British Press? Gazette managing without you?"

"I've seen a few of my old Press crowd, just tea and sympathy kind of thing. They've all drifted away now after expressing their deep, deep sadness for my plight. Christine Harrison took my old job. She was ever so sorry for me. Hope the witch burns. Harvey's doing some consultancy work – got a nice, fat pay-off. No sign of any coppers around, if that's what you mean. Not a dicky bird."

"Good. Just needed to check, not that I expected anything. I, too, am now consigned to the dustbin of detection. And, no-one knows you are here, right?"

"Right. A few pals down the boozer think I am in Florida. You?"

"Well the chief constable and his missus did pay me a fleeting visit in Alicante in January. I guess they felt obliged to drop in as they were in the area. I could tell they were desperate to beat a retreat as soon as they arrived. Still, a decent gesture from a decent enough bloke. Very indecent of him to put me in charge of hounding bloody paedos, though."

"So, we're both satisfied no hellhounds are on our trail. What about the money?"

"Suitably settled in various accounts here and there. Growing at a decent rate, I am pleased to report; more than enough to keep both of us happy. Just the minutiae now, old chap. I can't let 700 grand disappear overnight. I mean my accountant may feel obliged to inform the police. You had any better ideas?"

A few months back, James had suggested a break-in at Headleigh's Spanish villa until the former detective questioned why he would have had £700,000 in cash lying around his home. Good point, James had conceded and they had agreed to meet at a later date and work out a transfer. Headleigh had given James a secret cell phone number to call when he was convinced they were both in the clear; a number reserved for the reporter and Headleigh's children. James had rung two weeks previously and been surprised to discover his partner in crime had left Spain. How easy it would have been for the copper to disappear with all their ill-gotten gains?

"Well, I have been thinking and agree it would arouse suspicion if you simply handed over the lot in one hit. Even instalments would look funny, unless you want to pass me off as your new, expensive fancy woman?" the reporter chuckled. Headleigh merely smiled.

After a few seconds of silence, James turned his face towards Headleigh. "Ever been to Las Vegas?"

"Las Vegas? Why on earth would I want to go there? From what I have read and seen on TV it seems one of the tackiest places on this planet."

"I won't argue THAT point with you. But it's an ideal place to lose a lot of money. Or to win a lot of money. You lose, I win. The casinos are extremely discreet; their fortunes depend on discretion. Hear me out. Trust me, this is perfect."

Headleigh adopted the demeanour of a patient parent as James unfolded his ruse. He sounded convincing and had clearly done some homework. Headleigh was to lose 700k to James at a private poker table. Of course, the house would want a cut. But James was happy for that to come out of his share.

"Everyone should try Vegas just once at least," claimed James. "Entertainment capital of the world. Nowhere quite like it; thrives on sin and power and money and lust. Have to watch out for the women, though. They'll be hanging around a high-roller like you like flies round shit." Headleigh pondered James's suggestion for a few moments. The reporter did amuse him.

"It does sound ridiculously plausible, I suppose. Hmmmm. I suggest we wait until the divorce is finalised and then maybe give it a whirl. That can be my excuse for going to such a god-awful place and blowing such a ludicrous amount – drowning my sorrows."

"So, the divorce is going through, then. I always expected you two to patch things up. Sorry."

"No need to be sorry, my friend. Good riddance to the miserable old cow, I say."

"When will it be final? Is she hitting you hard?"

"Should be over within six weeks at most, according to my solicitor. A blessed relief, I can tell you. You aren't in a desperate hurry for money are you? The 50 grand should keep you going for now?"

"No, I am fine, thank you. I must admit my paltry pay-off from the paper is running out but this will keep me going for a few weeks. No problem. You mind telling me how much she is getting?"

"Not as much as she would like, the greedy bugger. You see, she burned her bridges by deserting me in my hour of need. You did a fine job of convincing her I was a pervert. Thankfully, the jury was less easily won over.

"The lawyers, hers and mine, have persuaded her that though she may have a legal right to a share of the damages, it would get very messy in court and she would lose anyway. So she has taken the house and gets her grubby hands on a large chunk of my pension. I could be a pauper."

"I'm really sorry, Henry."

"Oh, no need. No need. Really, there isn't, old boy. I am happier without her inane domestic nonsense and charity outings. I stomached them for many years. She can't complain."

"The kids OK? See much of them?"

Headleigh turned to face the sea. There was a slight breeze wafting inland. It was refreshing and Headleigh could taste the salt. His right foot dug a small hole in the sand, as he appeared lost in thought.

"The twins finish college this summer," he told James. "Sarah is at Trinity and Theresa Edinburgh. I assume they still plan to go onto post-graduate courses. Jonathan was doing well selling mansions in Berkshire last I heard." Headleigh's face looked pained.

"Not see much of them, then?" James sensed Headleigh's distress.

"No, not at all; not since the trial ended. In fact, I haven't actually SEEN them since last summer. Just one or two uneasy phone chats –

short phone chats. It seems they are not convinced of their father's innocence. Mud sticks. I pray daily that they will come round eventually." A tear gently worked its way down the cheek of the case-hardened former police officer before he hurriedly wiped it away and stiffened his back.

James could find no words to say. Headleigh regained his composure and broke the terrible silence. The noise from the holiday-makers across the road seemed a thousand miles away.

"You see, Terry, old chap. I never expected this when you got me into this scheme. The job I knew was on the line. Sure, they would have been obliged to reinstate me once the trial was successfully concluded. But I was more than happy to take early retirement; what, with my windfall to ease my fading years. And Jane? Well I truly am indebted to you for ridding me of her. But the children...."

Tears welled up in Headleigh's eyes again as he turned to face the reporter. James swallowed hard – twice.

"I never expected them to forsake me so easily. I never imagined the effect it would have on them. I trusted their intelligence and natural bonding to pull them through. What kind of father does that make me?

"I expected them to support me because I was their father. All my life I have supported them. Financially and morally. Of course, the job meant I wasn't able to spend as much time with them as many fathers have the luxury of doing. But I supported them as best I could.

"They repay me by casting me from their lives as if I was a toy that had outlived its interest. I was angry at first. Then I put myself in their shoes. And I found myself sympathising with them. Understanding them, and AGREEING with them.

"I have seen too many perverts, real sick cases who I would be happy to see dead. Now I found my own children viewing me in that same light. How do you think I felt, Terry? Can you imagine how I still feel? Abandoned, perhaps forever, by my own children who I reared for more than 20 years." Headleigh paused to blow his nose and wipe his face. James tried to speak.

"I'm so sorry, Henry. I really am so..."

Headleigh interrupted his regrets. "For that I can never forgive you. You won me a fortune but broke my heart." Headleigh blew his nose again and pointed over James's shoulder.

"You remember George, don't you? Of course, you do."

James turned round and saw a tall figure emerge from the shadows of the promenade wall. The figure became clear as it walked towards the two men by the shore.

"Hello, Terry. What a pleasant surprise bumping into you here of all places," said Detective Sergeant George Lewis.

Confusion and shock consumed Terry James.

Of course he knew George! Of course he bloody did. George Lewis was his contact. George Lewis was the mystery man at the centre of the allegations. George Lewis had told James about a late night drunken conversation with a very depressed superintendent who was thoroughly pissed off at being put in command of a paedophile unit. Pissed off in the extreme at being told he was wonderful at his job – too good at his job to warrant further promotion. Here, go chase some kiddie fiddlers.

Of course he knew George Lewis! James and Lewis concocted the whole ruse. George Lewis had come up with the Kent angle to keep the cops on the hop. He had approached the two freelances. A pound to a penny said he had sorted Scott 'Baggie' Brooks, too.

Of course he knew George Lewis! George Lewis was to receive 50 grand from the pot, wasn't he? Headleigh was sorting that side, wasn't he?

"Goodbye, Terry. I'll leave you and George to finalise the details." The crouched figure of Henry Headleigh slowly walked towards the promenade steps. He stopped once, not to look back but to blow his nose before disappearing among the revellers.

✝

Four days later, three short paragraphs appeared at the foot of an inside column in the Evening Gazette.

Terry James, a former reporter with the Evening Gazette, drowned in a swimming accident in Puerto del Carmen, Lanzarote.
The body of James, 42, was discovered in a cave on the holiday island by a group of snorkellers.
He is believed to have decided to go for a late night swim after drinking heavily.

╈

✝

Author's Notes

Libel is the publication of a statement which exposes a person to:
*Hatred, ridicule or contempt or which causes him to be
shunned or avoided or which has a tendency to injure him in his
office, trade or profession in the estimation of right-thinking people.*
**The onus is on the plaintiff to prove that the published remarks
refer to them and are indeed defamatory.**

In practice, a person also needs to prove he or she has a reputation
capable of being harmed. A mass murderer cannot sue if he has been
accused of petty theft – innocent or not.

Pure abuse is not defamatory per se. Nor can the dead sue, so basically you can say anything you like about a person as soon as his body
is cold.

A classic example of this came in the wake of the mysterious death
by drowning near Tenerife of Robert Maxwell in November 1991. The
millionaire publisher was a frequent user/abuser of the court system,
threatening legal action and economic ruination on anyone who med-
dled in his business affairs.

His death prompted tributes from greats across the globe, and sent
journalists delving deeper and with less fear. It was soon revealed he
was a master thief and among his many victims were the pensioners
of one of his companies, Mirror Group Newspapers. A £400 million
hole was discovered in the pension fund – money which had been used
illegally to finance operations elsewhere in his empire.

London used to be viewed as the libel capital of the world as juries
dished out quite punitive (for publishers) damages. In recent years
High Court judges have provided juries with more detailed guidelines
on what they should consider appropriate recompense and punish-
ment.

Jeffrey Archer received half a million from The Daily Star in 1987 –
because they claimed he had slept with a prostitute. Seventeen years

later (December 2004) politician George Galloway was awarded £150,000 by a judge after The Daily Telegraph virtually accused him of treason, claiming he was in the pay of Saddam Hussein. Playing away from home or treason? I will leave you the reader to decide which is the greater 'crime'.

Tory high-flier Jonathan Aitken was jailed for perjury and perverting the course of justice in 1999 following the collapse of his libel case against The Guardian and World in Action.

"If it has fallen to my destiny to start a fight to cut out the cancer of bent and twisted journalism in our country with the simple sword of truth and the trusty shield of British fair play, so be it," pronounced Aitken as he launched his libel battle over claims that he had abused his Government position and accepted favours from Saudi Arabian businessmen.

Celebrities have long been going to court to defend their reputations. Oscar Wilde withdrew a libel claim against the Marquis of Queensberry who had accused him of homosexuality but he later lost a criminal case and was jailed for two years.

Liberace took the Daily Mirror for £8,000 in 1959 over claims made three years earlier by columnist Cassandra. Mind you, Cassandra did go to town:

"I spoke to sad but kindly men on this newspaper who have met every celebrity coming from America for the past 30 years. They say that this deadly, winking, sniggering, snuggling, chromium-plated, scent-impregnated, luminous, quivering, giggling, fruit-flavored, mincing, ice-covered heap of mother love has had the biggest reception and impact on London since Charlie Chaplin arrived at the same station, Waterloo, on September 12, 1921...He reeks with emetic language that can only make grown men long for a quiet corner, an aspidistra, a handkerchief, and the old heave-ho. Without doubt, he is the biggest sentimental vomit of all time. Slobbering over his mother, winking at his brother, and counting the cash at every second, this superb piece of calculating candy-floss..."

Great stuff, Cassandra, but humour is no defence.

Elton John won damages of one million from The Sun over allegations involving rent boys. He also took the Sunday Mirror to court after they wrote that he was struggling against bulimia. In a landmark case, the Court Of Appeal reduced the damages from £350,000 to £75,000. I calculate that that is court-speak for saying accusing someone of treason is twice as bad as saying they don't swallow all their food – not taking into account inflation. Or bulimia is half as bad as treason?

How some stories get into the Press is beyond me. I mean who told The Daily Mirror that actress Daryl Hannah had skipped rehearsals so she could attend her dog's birthday? Valuable court time was thankfully shortened when the Mirror coughed up undisclosed damages.

✝

I was a newcomer on The Daily Star at the time of the original Archer case in 1986-87. Whenever the editor, Lloyd Turner, appeared in the production rooms, compositors would commence whistling the theme tune to The Archers (a BBC Radio soap). Turner took it without flinching. Yet when Turner died following a heart attack in 1996, his widow said: "I shall always wonder whether the stress of the libel case precipitated his premature death."

The case was a strange affair. The News of The World had published photographs of one of Archer's friends handing over £2,000 to a prostitute, Monica Coghlan.

Archer was then deputy chairman of the Conservative party. He denied knowing Coghlan and claimed the money was paid to avoid potential embarrassment to the party.

The Star went one step further, claming he had spent the night with the prostitute.

The judge, Mr Justice Caulfield, asked why a man married to the 'fragrant' Mary Archer would pay for "cold, unloving, rubber-insulated sex" with a prostitute.

Archer won £500,000 damages. He resigned his post with the party and was later ennobled. Several years later an associate revealed he had been asked to provide a false alibi for Archer. He was also charged with making fake diary entries.

Jailing Lord Archer of Weston-super-Mare for four years in July

2001 for perverting the course of justice and perjury, Justice Francis Potts said: "It has been an extremely distasteful case...These charges represent as serious an offence of perjury as I have had experience of and have been able to find in the books."

Archer was released in 2003 after serving two years and two days.

The prosititute died shortly before the 2001 trial. Coghlan was involved in a car crash caused by an escaping robber. On hearing of his impending trial she had said: "I want him to suffer like I have suffered. I want him to squirm. But most of all I want him to tell the truth. I have never denied what I was: I was a prostitute. But I wasn't a liar. He is."

After the trial, a House Of Lords spokesman said the liar could remain a lord. "There is no precedent for a life peerage being removed. I think treason would be the only exception."

Dog's birthday bashes, sexual indiscretions, corruption in high places and let's not forget good, old treason – the trusty sword of truth indeed.

Tom J Sandy

January 2005

✝

✝

The record award is still £1.5million pounds granted to Lord Aldington who had been accused of war crimes by Nikolai Tolstoy.
Tolstoy claimed Aldington was responsible for the forced repatriation of 70,000 people to Yugoslavia after World War Two – almost certainly to their deaths.

✝

The longest libel case – indeed the longest in British legal history – is the McLibel case which ran for 314 court days between 1994-97. McDonald's sued two London activists over a pamphlet entitled What's Wrong With McDonald's? Chief Justice Bell's conclusions ran to 800 pages. McDonald's were awarded £60,000.

For links to more libel information visit:
www.tomjsandy.co.uk

✝

Many thanks to:

Karla Mahar and Andy James for editorial assistance.
Numerous legal brains and police officers who helped unwittingly.
Twenty years of schooling at the top, bottom and middle ends of British journalism.

Also by Tom J Sandy

SCATE (Speed Cameras Are The Enemy)

Published by Eye 5

www.tomjsandy.co.uk

+

Tom J Sandy

Tom J Sandy was born in Bury, Lancashire and educated at the University of North Humberside, Hull.

He lives in Essex, with his two children.

He is the author of SCATE (Speed Cameras Are The Enemy) and Perverting The Course Of Justice.

He is currently finishing a third book.

✝

✝

'Many motorists will empathise with the
themes in the novel' - TOP GEAR

ISBN: 0-9546897-3-9
PAGES: 177
FORMAT: Λ5 (148x210mm)
PUBLISHED: Nov 19th 2004

✝

✝